A Violation

CHARLOTTE LAMB was born in Dagenham, Essex, and left school at sixteen to be a bank clerk. She now writes twelve books a year, still works office hours and writes 10,000 words a day.

It was at her husband's suggestion that she started writing when she was housebound with small children. Her first book was written in three days. Now she is one of Mills and Boon's top authors and has written over sixty romantic novels. Her style is famous and her books are compulsive reading. *A Violation* is her first novel to be published by Fontana.

Charlotte Lamb lives with her husband and five children on the Isle of Man,

CHARLOTTE LAMB

A Violation

Fontana Paperbacks

First published by Fontana Paperbacks 1983

Copyright © Charlotte Lamb 1983

Made and printed in Great Britain by
William Collins Sons & Co. Ltd, Glasgow

To Frances Whitehead

CHAPTER ONE

Clare sometimes felt she worked at the Tower of Babel, especially during those round-table discussions of campaigns which the agency had just undertaken, when everyone talked at once at the tops of their voices and nobody listened to anything anybody else said. Larry had gathered together a highly creative bunch – writers, artists, ideasmen; all clever and articulate, with egos as big as houses, each of them convinced he was the world's answer to everything. It was incredible that anything ever emerged from these frenetic shouting matches, but somehow it always did. From the tumult and hullabaloo a single voice finally emerged, usually Larry's.

'What we want is to be simple and direct,' the head of the Graphics department was snarling. Ian was on the defensive, angrily aware that his suggestions for the Purewash campaign had met with universal scorn.

'You're losing your grip,' Phil Dalby said, waving a strip of graphics at him. 'Just look at this bilge . . .'

Everyone looked at the beaming, cute kids and the radiant mother with her pile of snowy washing, and made disgusted noises.

'This stuff's so pedestrian, it's practically stationary! Years out of date . . .'

'What we need is zip and dazzle,' one of the junior copy-writers said.

'Sounds like a breakfast commercial,' said a voice at the door, cutting through the ensuing din, without effort.

Everyone stopped yelling and looked round, hurriedly dragging smiles into their faces. Larry had arrived, although that was a misuse of the English language since Larry Hillier did not simply arrive anywhere; he exploded into places and situations like a living bomb and drastically re-structured everything he met. Watching him as he walked across the room Clare felt like someone at the

7

circus, watching the smiling lion-tamer with his hidden whip lowered at his side. The lions crouched on their chairs, alert and dangerous, pretending to purr, and the lion-tamer watched them with amused, attentive eyes knowing perfectly well that he only had to look away for a second to have them leaping for his throat.

A restless, energetic man in his late thirties, tall, thin and olive-skinned, Larry Hillier met life with his teeth bared, daring it to challenge him. He thrived on difficult situations, he enjoyed making his captive lions jump through hoops. Clare could never be certain how she felt about Larry. She only knew that every time she saw him, she felt as though she had been given an electric shock, she felt her eyes open wide, her whole metabolism quicken.

'Problems?' he enquired now, taking the chair at the head of the table.

'Have you seen Ian's...' began Phil. Ian interrupted excitedly.

'You can't sell washing powder with sex, that's Phil's answer to everything. Our target...'

'If you ever stopped talking long enough to listen,' Phil growled and Ian went an interesting shade of mulberry, gulping in his throat like a bullfrog.

'Why don't we have some coffee?' Clare murmured, as everyone started shouting at once.

'Good idea,' Larry told her above the hubbub. He was leaning back in his chair looking as cool as someone at Wimbledon, his gaze flashing from one face to another as he waited for his moment to intervene. Tie off, collar open, his jacket discarded, he was deceptively casual.

The agency was expanding at a rate which made her feel excited, dazzled and alarmed. It filled her with the panic people feel when they sense that their lives have suddenly been taken out of their control. It had all happened too fast; they hadn't expected it. Until two years ago the agency had been a small, quiet backwater which handled a number of minor accounts. Larry Hillier had taken over the reins of management when his father, Joe Hillier, died of a heart attack. Larry had been working over in the States on a big

8

New York agency. He had flown home and within a few months had turned the firm upside down, retiring most of the older staff and headhunting to form a brilliant new team. They shed most of their small clients and acquired some far more lucrative accounts. Their profits began to soar; clients flocked in once word of Larry's dazzling success rate spread. Everyone who worked for the agency had either left or had had to revise their attitudes and sharpen up their minds. Larry demanded high calibre work, and would accept nothing less, setting an example by meeting the shock waves of change without flinching, his own store of energy apparently boundless. He made Clare feel at times that she was on a bolting horse; afraid to yank on the reins to halt it in case she was thrown, nervously exhilarated despite her inner alarm. That was the effect Larry had on people – he excited and disturbed them. You had to be tough to cope with him, but the end result was a more colourful world.

Clare went out to get the coffee which was being made by her secretary. 'I was just coming in with it,' Jeanie said reproachfully, her mouth a prim, pink bow. She was a very good secretary, unflappable and efficient, but she always gave Clare the distinct impression that she was critical of everything around her. That might have been the effect of her features rather than her thoughts: she had round, staring brown eyes and a short, obstinate censorious nose, which, together, gave her a permanently smug expression.

'I wanted to get out of the room,' Clare said with a placating smile. She couldn't afford to have Jeanie in one of her offended moods. 'It was getting very fraught in there.'

'I heard,' Jeanie said. 'I don't know why they get so worked up, like a lot of kids.' She started loading mugs on to a battered old tin tray which still bore lingering traces of red enamel. 'Take themselves too seriously, if you ask me, that's their trouble.'

'That's their trouble,' Clare agreed, staring out of the window at the sky, which had become the luminous violet of stained glass; an omen of approaching storm if the airless heat was anything to go by. Clare could feel her silk blouse sticking to her spine; it peeled off her skin as she lifted a hand to push back a lock of brown hair from her sweating forehead. 'Hot, isn't it?' she said but Jeanie wasn't listening.

'I'll take it in,' she was saying as she stalked towards the door with the tray.

The phone rang and Clare picked it up. 'Clare Forrester speaking.'

'Look, I'm too tired to go out tonight,' Tom said in an aggressive voice. 'It's been one hell of a day. Why don't we settle for a couple of steaks and a quiet evening at your flat?'

Clare felt like throwing something; the last thing she wanted to do was cook steaks, she had been looking forward to eating out tonight. 'Well...' she began and Tom breathed heavily at the other end of the phone.

'Clare, I'm absolutely dead. I haven't got the energy to go dragging out to dinner.'

The door was open and Clare was conscious of Larry looming up, impatiently tapping his watch as she glanced his way. 'Okay,' she agreed reluctantly and Tom said: 'Fine, see you when I get there,' hanging up before she had a chance to ask when he thought that might be.

'I don't know what you see in that guy,' Larry said scathingly. 'You could do better for yourself than that.'

'Do I curtsey?' Clare said, halting on her way to the door as she found his lean figure blocking her path.

'What?' His brows met and his eyes, under them, were sharp.

'That was supposed to be flattering, wasn't it?' She watched Larry's mouth curl in a sudden, wicked smile and became apprehensive – he had a mischievous streak which bothered Clare; it made her uncertain what he was about to do and that was not an easy sensation. Larry in an unpredictable mood was even more alarming than usual.

'You're wasted on Tom Prescott,' he said in a soft, lowered voice, looking down at her in a way which made her colour rise. She was angry with herself for being so self-conscious under that wandering gaze, far too aware of the fact that he was openly assessing her figure. When he put out a hand she practically jumped with alarm. Larry's long, index finger trailed from the base of her throat to her top button.

'Your button's undone,' he said, amused by her frozen expression, and coolly did it up for her without any sign of haste. 'We don't want the sight of your delectable cleavage to put unbusinesslike ideas into Ian's head, do we? You know he's got a down on using sex as the bait these days, ever since his wife ran off with an insurance agent.'

'Oh, is that it?' Clare managed to say, wishing he would not stand so close.

'That's it,' Larry nodded. 'He'll get over it and we'll just have to nurse him along until his work gets back that old sparkle.' He smiled at her, the tanned skin around his eyes wrinkling, and she involuntarily smiled back. Larry turned and walked back into the meeting, which was boiling over into a free-for-all again as Ian and Phil flung insults at each other, Ian's hair standing up in harassed ruffles where he had run his fingers through it, the rest of the team happily joining in at the top of their voices, apparently to prolong the fun. Jeanie was plonking mugs of coffee in front of each, her lips pursed disapprovingly, especially when someone pinched her as she moved away. Her muffled little squeak and glare of outrage sent a wave of laughter running through them all. Jeanie stalked out, nose in the air, and Larry sat down, grinning.

'Okay, let's have injury time, shall we? Drink your coffee and shut up. Let your brains work instead of your mouths.'

Clare drank her coffee and became aware of a headache pressing behind her forehead. When the argument began again she listened, the pain in her head getting worse, her eyes seemed to get smaller and smaller, trying to exclude the light, but nobody appeared to notice. She began to feel invisible as they all talked at her and around her, completely engrossed in getting their own way, putting their own point of view and trampling on the views of everyone else.

The meeting broke up without any decision and Clare

shot off with Larry to meet a client who was in an irate mood, burning with indignation because his very expensive television campaign was not showing instant results in terms of sales. Larry soothed and smiled and poured oil on his troubled waters until he departed convinced that everything was going to be just fine.

By the time Clare made her way home through hectic rush-hour London traffic, she felt like a zombie. Letting herself into her flat, she went into the kitchen and sank into a chair for a minute or two, aching with exhaustion. It took an effort of will to force herself to get up and check that she had the ingredients for dinner in the fridge. She had bought two steaks on the way home, pretty sure that she had vegetables to go with them, and was relieved to see she was right.

Closing the fridge door she looked at her watch and groaned aloud. Nearly seven, Tom would be here any minute and she hadn't had a bath or changed, let alone started the supper. She made herself a cup of instant black coffee to wake herself up, taking it down the hall to the bathroom and putting it on the windowsill while she ran the bath and dumped in some rose-fragrant bath oil. She went into the bedroom and laid out on the bed a peacock blue kaftan which always made her feel relaxed and feminine, the sweeping folds of it soft against her skin. In front of the mirror she rapidly pinned up her hair, wishing she did not feel she was always running on tiptoe and never getting anywhere.

If anyone had asked her what she really wanted to do that evening, she would have said, honestly, that she wanted to go to sleep; shut out the deafening clamour of the world she lived in and sink into a soothing emptiness, the warm dark womb-like silence of a bed, where she need not talk or think or nerve herself to face up to anything.

Going back into the bathroom she turned off the taps and stepped into the warm, silky water, picking up her cup of coffee as she did so. She lay back, her head pillowed on the primrose yellow bath, water lapping along her calves and thighs. Sipping coffee, she stared at the pink stubs of toes poking up at the far end of the bath like a line of small rocks. Steam had misted the mirror, which reflected nothing, the windows sweated and her skin seemed to be drinking thirstily, her pores open and oozing the dust and smoke of the city.

Tom would be arriving any minute, she would have to get out of this sensual haven, dress and be in the kitchen, ready to get the meal; but for now, for this one blissful minute, she could shut down her head, slam the door on thought of any kind, and just exist, a stranded pinky-white whale in an ocean of tactile comfort.

She had finished her coffee. She leaned over and placed the empty cup on the floor and began soaping herself with half-closed eyes, her fingers cupping the soft flesh of her breasts, her shoulderblades, the long smooth line of her legs. In bathrooms she had discovered herself, soon after her first period, realising for the first time then that she had a body, she wasn't just Clare, a mind struggling with new impressions all the time. Behind locked doors she watched her breasts growing, like a gardener with a secret garden; the tiny biscuit-coloured nipples rising like currants on top of a round little cake, a waist appearing, a new roundedness about her belly and flanks where she had once been as flat as a board from neck to knee. She had smudged the steam off the mirror and stared at herself naked until her flesh had mottled.

Stepping reluctantly out of the bath she towelled, pulled out the plug and padded into the bedroom while the water gurgled away down the drain. Waves of steam came with her into the warm, summer air in the bedroom. When she had dressed, she sat down in front of the dressing table and brushed out her hair. Shoulder long, it curled damply, a rich, warm golden brown. Her eyebrows were slightly too thick, she never had time to pluck them, and they arched in apparent surprise over hazel eyes which couldn't make up their mind what colour they were, changing with her moods, from green to blue or a dully muddy colour which was neither. Her skin had acquired a pale tan, she did not bother with make-up other than a trace of green glitter brushed over her lids and a soft pink smoothed into her lips.

The window was open, the curtains hardly stirring the breeze, and she could hear the sound of traffic in the street. It reminded her that Tom's car would soon be braking outside.

When she heard a key turning in the front door lock, she hurried out, expecting to see Tom, but it was her flatmate, Pamela, rushing in from work. She waved a greeting. 'Hi, can't stop, I'm going to a party,' and dived into the other bedroom.

Clare started to get the dinner; put the steaks to marinate, prepared a green salad, placed the bottle of red wine in the sitting room so that it would be the right temperature. Tom was fussy about such things; he liked to think of himself as a wine buff.

A delicate cloud of very good French perfume warned her of Pamela's approach; she turned and smiled. 'You were quick.' Pamela looked as sexy as ever in her skintight jeans and low-necked t-shirt. She managed to make the most casual clothes look as if they came straight from an exclusive Paris boutique. A top photographic model, she had heaven knew how many men on a string; she played the field and avoided getting bored by becoming elusive whenever anyone tried to stake a claim on her.

'It isn't a dressing-up kind of party,' Pamela said, picking a piece of lettuce out of the bowl and nibbling at it. 'Why don't you come?'

'Tom's coming round.'

'So what?' Pamela looked at Clare with challenge in her golden eyes, the eyes of a lion, Clare thought, hard black pupils rayed with green, which emphasised the predatory felinity of her stare. 'I don't know what you see in him anyway.'

'Not you, too!'

Pamela looked interested. 'Who else has some sense?'

'Larry,' Clare said drily and Pamela's eyes gleamed.

'Now he's a different proposition, a very sexy guy. I fancy him.'

'I'm sure it's mutual,' Clare said and only heard the coldness in her own voice a second after she had spoken.

Pamela gave her a mocking little smile which made her look away in confusion, furious with herself. She knew what Pamela was thinking and it wasn't true; she did not fancy Larry. She had more brains than that; Larry Hillier was not a safe man to get involved with.

'What time does your party start?' she asked, glancing at her watch to cover her embarrassment.

'When I get there,' Pamela said with arrogant amusement, laughing at her own self-assurance but meaning it all the same. 'Andy's picking me up, he said seven-thirty but he's always late.' She picked at another piece of lettuce and Clare said impatiently: 'Have you eaten?'

'I had lunch,' Pamela said wistfully. She was always on a diet, always hungry, her waist and hips tiny although she constantly moaned that she was getting huge. To fight off the encroaching inches she tried to eat just one meal a day, and Clare sometimes wondered if it was malnutrition which made her so ferociously sex-mad, maybe she was sublimating her real desires, gobbling up men instead of chips.

A car hooted outside the block of flats and Pamela said: 'That must be Andy. 'Bye,' and a moment later was gone, the front door slamming behind her. Clare watched out of the window as Pamela climbed into the car, her blonde hair shimmering in the evening sunlight. Clare envied her as Pamela laughed at the young man behind the wheel. Just watching, made Clare feel more tired than ever. What was Pamela's secret? How did she combine an exhausting, highly professional job with a hectic social life, and still manage to look as if she was on top of the world? As the car shot away, Clare heard Pamela laughing, a gay amused sound which matched the glow of her face. Pamela was going to enjoy her evening. If you set out to enjoy yourself you always do, Clare thought, turning away with a sigh. If she had Pamela's energy, maybe she would be looking forward to an evening with Tom instead of feeling like death.

Tom arrived ten minutes later, just as Clare was getting irritable.

He was in shirt-sleeves, his tie off, his collar open and his skin flushed and perspiring.

'Hallo, darling.'

He kissed her but his eye was on the steaks as he lifted away. 'How long will supper be? I'm starving. God, I'm dead on my feet, it's been a hectic day. I've been driving from site to site since early this morning. Nothing gets done if I don't keep my eye on them, heaven knows what they get up to once my back is turned.' He took half a tomato out of a bowl of them, popped it into his mouth. 'I could kill a steak,' he said, walking out of the door again. 'Get me a drink, would you, Clare? I'm going to flop out and watch TV; there's some golf on one channel.'

Clare felt a scream pressing against the top of the inside of her head. She stood in the small kitchen with her mouth opening and shutting like a goldfish which has leapt out of its bowl and has been stranded in air it cannot breath.

She heard the television come on, the sound whining for a second until Tom turned it down. 'Where's that drink?' he shouted.

Clare went to the cupboard, moving like a robot. She got out the half-empty bottle of whisky, took down a tumbler, poured whisky into it and walked into the sitting room with the drink.

Tom was sprawled in a chair, his head back, arms folded behind his dark brown head, legs trailing like a limp doll's across the carpet. He didn't look at her, his eyes fixed on the set, but a hand came up and she put the tumbler of whisky into it.

'Look at that,' he said. 'The man's incredible, what a shot!'

Clare walked back to the kitchen and began to cook the steaks, the smell of burning flesh making her nostrils quiver. She hadn't realised she was hungry. She was too tired even to think about food, but she had had a business lunch and been too busy talking to eat anything. Her stomach protested as she turned the meat red side up.

'Clare!' Tom sounded petulant, a fretful child. 'You forgot the soda, you know I like soda in my whisky.'

She took the soda into the sitting room and watched him fix his drink. 'Thanks, angel,' he said without looking at her.

Five minutes later she served the meal at the table in the dining room. Tom sat with his whisky in one hand, apparently unaware of what she was doing as she moved about, but when she said flatly: 'Supper's ready,' he got up, keeping his gaze on the television, went over and switched it off before he came to the table.

During the meal he talked about his job; complaining, telling her how exhausted he was, how uncooperative he found everyone who worked with him. Clare picked at her steak and let the words wash over her head. Her appetite had gone again, she felt queasy, her throat hardening in rings of petrified bone as if she might be going to throw up at any minute.

Tom didn't notice her reluctance to eat, he was forking food into his mouth at speed between outbursts. He was ambitious. He wanted to rise in the firm he now worked for; he was confident of his own ability, scathing about that of everyone else around him. He had trained as an architect with a quiet local firm in his home town, Wolverhampton, but he wasn't prepared to settle for being a large frog in a small pond. He had come up to London to join a giant national firm who built roads, schools and hospitals. He hadn't yet discovered any ceiling to his life; he meant to climb as high as the ladder would take him. Clare admired his determination, his energy and power. He was a large man, his face aggressive. It was an expression that was natural to it; he had the build for belligerence. Even when he smiled, he managed to look as though he might be going to punch somebody. His hair was cut so short it looked like rained-on stubble. He was firm-fleshed, hard-boned, solid, yet often under the hunched angularity a small boy peered out through his eyes in sullen reproach.

It was the small boy Clare loved, he moved something inside her. She would have loved him even more if he could only be satisfied with what she felt, and did not keep demanding more, his bowl held out under her reluctant nose, his eyes pleading, accusing. Tom expected more of her than she was prepared to give, more than she felt she ought to give. She couldn't help thinking him selfish, always trying to grab more of her, refusing to let her be herself, keep herself intact inside her head.

When Tom had finished eating, she cleared the table and went out into the kitchen to make coffee while he finished the bottle of wine, most of which he had drunk during the meal. Clare had only played with her glass, sipping occasionally. She scraped the plates into the waste bin, dumped them into the sink and ran hot water on them while the coffee was percolating. Tom wouldn't drink instant coffee except at his own flat, when he was making it.

When she took the coffee tray into the sitting room, she found him on the couch, the lights turned out except one lamp on a low table. It shed a dim light, just enough for her to see by as she joined him.

'Where's Pamela tonight?' he asked, accepting his cup of coffee without a word, either of praise or gratitude.

'At a party.'

Tom grunted, expressing distaste. 'I don't know why you share a flat with her, she's not your type.'

'She's not yours, you mean,' Clare said before she could stop herself and, at his look of surprise, wondered with jagged alarm just how right she was. Had Tom ever fancied Pamela? Most men seemed to. She had to fight them off, not that she ever bothered, she liked variety.

'What's the matter with you?' Tom asked, then gave her a very different look, one she recognised, a mixture of self-satisfaction and teasing. He put his coffee cup down and took hers out of her hand.

'I know what you need,' he said and she wondered how he had the nerve to make that statement. She wondered if he had ever looked at her at all, ever asked himself what she was like inside her head, that private place which cannot be invaded, can only be entered with permission. Clare had opened the door of it to Tom when they first met, eager to fling herself and all she was at his feet, greedy to welcome him into the sanctuary of her personal world, because he was the first human being she had ever wanted in there. What had happened between them so that the first ecstatic delight in the every existence of this man in the same world

18

as herself should have drained away like water into sand, leaving her dry and parched and lonely?

He started to kiss her, pressing her down against the cushions on the couch, the springs creaking.

His mouth was much bigger than hers; she had a small mouth, pink, shy, reluctant to open. She felt he was eating her: she was being devoured by something warm and soft and moist in slow sucking movements. If she went limp and stopped resisting, she would slip down his throat like an oyster. Stiffening, she clung to her shell with every sucker she had, but Tom didn't seem to notice her lack of passion. He was fumbling with the stiff, pearly buttons at the neck of the kaftan.

'What did you wear this for?' he asked, grumbling.

She did not want to argue with him, she was too tired. Tom flew into a rage whenever she tried to refuse to make love. The first time they slept together had been on their first date and Clare had explained to him that she had a firm rule about sleeping with someone right away. Tom had piled words on her like pillows to suffocate her into submission and she had eventually given way. He was right, after all, rules were made to be broken, she wanted to make love with him, why should she insist on waiting? It wasn't as though she was a virgin or had any moral qualms. She had drawn up her sexual charter when she was seventeen, deciding then that she didn't want to be promiscuous, sleep around with every guy who bought her a hamburger. Tom had said he approved of that, she had the right attitude, towards other men, but he was different. He knew it was going to be serious between them, didn't she feel that way? And she had, she had felt like someone who had discovered a new world, she had been almost raging with happiness, aching with it, dying of it.

Tom had his hand under the kaftan, he was kissing her neck. She tried to go limp, like someone practising meditation, relaxing first her arms and then her legs, only to find that her arms had gone rigid again the minute she took her mind off them. Her spine felt as though it was made of concrete. Her head thudded and her stomach was churning.

'Tom,' she said and he burrowed into the warm cleft between her breasts, his mouth moist.

'Tom,' she repeated, sitting up and pushing his head away. 'Would you mind if we don't make love tonight? I've got an appalling headache. I think I'm going down with 'flu or something.'

'You didn't say anything before,' he said, staring at her with his mouth turning down at the edges sulkily, the little boy out in the open now from where he usually hid.

'I'm sorry,' she said, but she wasn't sorry and she couldn't make it sound convincing because inside she was burning up with resentment over the fact that he had barely seemed to notice her until now. He had talked at her in a long litany of complaint about everyone at his firm but he hadn't stopped to ask her what sort of day she had had. It hadn't occurred to him to ask if she needed any help with cooking supper although he knew she worked long hours too, that her job was as demanding as his own.

'Why didn't you tell me when I arrived?' he asked and she burst out, then, the words erupted like sickness from her.

'You didn't give me a chance. You came in and sat down in front of the television and there hasn't been a chance to say anything to you until now, you were too busy talking about yourself, as usual.'

He looked at her self-righteously, affronted. Under the firm skin on his face she saw tiny threads of blue under the pink, buried veins. Tom played rugger in winter, tennis in summer, he liked to keep fit. She went along to applaud on Saturday afternoons because he liked her to be there and he grinned at her as he came off to shower. She was the audience for his triumph. Tom was a winner, he played to wipe out his opponents and usually did. Heated exercise in the open air was coarsening his skin, though.

'What's the matter with you?' he asked. 'Is it the time of the month?' He smirked, Clare felt, as he said that, pleased with himself for demonstrating his sophistication, enjoying putting her in her place. She was a woman, her moods had no sane basis, they were cycled according to the moon, a man didn't have to take them seriously.

'I'm tired,' she flared up, flushing angrily. 'I've been working full out all day, too, not that it entered your head to ask, so I'm telling you. I had a hell of a day and when I got back here I had to get your supper and wait on you hand and foot while you lounged in a chair and watched TV. You didn't even say thank you when I brought you that drink, you just complained because I'd forgotten the soda.'

'There's no need to shout,' he said. 'It makes you look ugly when you shout, women who shriek like that make me ill. You look like a fishwife.' He got up before she could control her voice enough to speak again. 'I don't think I want to make love to you now, anyway,' he said. 'You've turned me right off.'

'That makes two of us then,' Clare said hoarsely. 'I was turned off from the word go. You're so mechanical, I see all the moves coming. You should have stuck to train sets, at least they don't mind running on rails.'

'Stop yelling,' Tom said, going brick red. 'Do you want the neighbours to hear?'

'Stuff the neighbours,' Clare said. 'You come here and expect me to behave like some geisha girl . . .'

'Don't be ridiculous!'

'Serving you food and wine – I suppose you'd have liked me to do it on my knees.'

'If you don't want to cook for me, don't. I thought you enjoyed it,' he said. 'You always used to say you liked having a meal at home, it made you feel more like a woman.'

'Maybe I wasn't dog-tired then.'

'I didn't know you were so tired, did I? If you don't tell me, how am I supposed to guess?'

'You could try looking at me,' Clare said. 'You even turned out the lights before you started mauling me on the couch.'

'Mauling!' For a minute she thought he was going to hit her, his face raw with fury.

'Once I'd fed you and you'd had a few drinks, you got other ideas. One thing leads to another, doesn't it? You finish your coffee and on to the next course.'

'Christ Almighty,' he said.

'When you play rugger, what do you all get up to in the showers?'

His mouth opened and colour poured up to his hairline. 'What the hell are you getting at?'

'You seem to think sex is part of every social occasion,' Clare said. 'I just wondered . . .'

'I'm no bloody fairy!'

'No, you just expect sex on demand because I'm a woman. It doesn't matter to you what I want, how I feel. You're a selfish bastard.'

'I want to make love to you because I love you,' he said in a voice full of hostility. 'What's so selfish about that? Sex is a part of loving, so you keep telling me.'

'Loving's got nothing to do with what you wanted just now. You wanted to screw because you couldn't think of anything else to do. You and Pamela have a lot in common, she goes to bed at the drop of a hat and hardly even notices who with, either.'

'Maybe you're right,' Tom said thickly. 'Maybe I should be dating her, not you. Thanks for the tip.'

She watched him turn on his heel and stamp out, hating her, the back of his neck dark red. She thought of following him, trying to soften him, say she was sorry, she'd lost her temper, she hadn't meant what she said, but the trouble was she had meant it, at least, some of it. She felt he didn't see her as a person; only as a woman, a sexual fallout shelter, where he could safely burrow out of the rain of disaster which was the world outside. Take me in, he was saying as he reached for her, and one part of her wanted to unlock the tight gate of her body and admit him lovingly, while tonight the other part had refused because he was using her, abusing her love.

He had held up in front of his face the ritualistic, ceremonial mask, which proclaimed him male, one of the master race, and, depersonalised inside the mask of femininity he clamped on her, she had backed away. Why did it never occur to him to offer to cook a meal for her? Why did he get angry because she wasn't in the mood to make love? Why did he talk on about his job but never ask about hers? Why was he allowed to spend an evening out drinking with his friends while she was laughed at if she told him she wanted to spend an evening with girls from work? Tom laughed because he could not believe any woman would rather spend an evening with other women than with her lover. He did not believe in friendship between women, only between men. He had simple unalterable ideas. Women were jealous of each other, catty about each other, stole boyfriends from each other, they could never be genuine friends, she had to be lying if she said she was going out with them. It made him suspicious. Was she seeing someone on the side? What was she up to?

Where had he got his ideas about women? Clare heard the front door slam. He had gone. She cleared away the coffee things, turned out all the lights and made her way to the bedroom.

She knew who had made Tom the way he was – his mother. He had driven Clare to his home in Wolverhampton several times. She had still been at the stage of being dazed with the surprise of love, unable to believe the sheer height and breadth and depth of her emotion. Loving seemed so easy, a natural fountain of feeling shooting up through her and cascading in the air everywhere she went.

Even so she had noticed that Tom was over-mothered, mother-smothered, fed adoration like spoonfuls of sugar between meals. He almost drew her attention to it, wanting her to see how he was loved.

Tom had learnt his attitudes to women on his mother's lap. He had been given everything he wanted before he had even known he wanted it, learning that women were domestic creatures meant to make men happy. In the first excitement of loving Clare, Tom had revised those attitudes. He had really looked at her then, he hadn't taken her for granted, but now he rarely thought about her at all, she was just a peg with a name on which he hung his need for comfort and spoiling.

She undressed in the bedroom and didn't bother to put on a nightie. It was far too hot, the summer night was so close she felt it pressing down all round her like a tomb.

She put out the light and drew a single thin sheet over her perspiring body. Tom had become a habit for her, as she had for him. Sometimes he had to go away alone on business for his firm and then she missed him. She was lonely without him. She had often been lonely before she met him. Her social life was usually busy but loneliness dogged her through the parties and dates with men she didn't particularly like.

Loneliness could become a habit. It always reminded her of walking through the park, watching old men shuffling from litterbin to litterbin, rifling the contents, looking over their shoulders from time to time like anxious dogs. Their faces had lines of loneliness. You always recognised them. It showed in their eyes too, and in the way they talked to themselves; snatches of mumbled words you heard as you walked past. She looked the other way in case one of them spoke to her. If you caught their eye, they stared, half hostile, half briefly hopeful of some contact, but she was afraid to smile in case they followed her. She would be embarrassed, she knew, if one of them spoke to her. They were exiles, outside the usual world of jobs and homes and families, on some desultory odyssey of their own from which they would never return to normal life, but she couldn't help thinking about their past. They must have belonged to someone, somewhere, sometime – how had they drifted away to this?

She had thought when she met Tom that she would never be lonely again, her future was determined at last, she was going to be happy, after all.

Now she felt that she and Tom were facing each other across a great split in the earth they stood on, earth which had once seemed so stable and secure. She had not even noticed when the division started, when the first hairline crack appeared, but she had been forced to realise that inch by inch they were moving apart. The changes at work had helped to drive a wedge between them. Everything around her was in muddled, confused uproar. She was under a pressure she had never faced before, she wasn't certain she could cope with now and she had wanted Tom to be there, to support her, hold her up and reassure her, but Tom had not been interested in anything but his own problems. She had been trying not to drown, fighting to keep her head out of the water, and Tom had not even been looking.

Turning on to her side in a foetal position, spine curved, knees up, she decided not to think any more. She would put it all out of her mind; she would sleep. She was so tired that she thought of sleep covetously, with a lustful greed, her mind drenched with weariness. She must sleep, she had to have it.

When she did drift out of the waking world, it was only to dream in a hot, restless, agitated fashion, processing incident and fears in a rapid stream which made no sense.

Drugged with sleep, she did not hear the door open. Stealthily on rubber soles the man came over to the bed. Unzipping his jeans he dragged them down while he stared at her.

Clare was dreaming of a hotel; she knew it was a hotel although she had never been there before. It was vast, she seemed to run down endless corridors. People ignored her, talked to each other as she ran past as though she was not there. She had to find Tom, she didn't know why, she only knew he was here and she had to find him or . . . or what? She did not know, the urgency came without reason. She turned a corner and was in a dark passage; narrow, blind. She heard breathing somewhere in the shadows.

'Tom?' she whispered.

Out of the darkness leapt a shape, hands closed over her bare breasts, squeezing them brutally.

Clare woke, screaming. Something soft and yet hard clamped over her mouth, forced her head back. Her neck stretched, she couldn't swallow. Dazed, she strained to see. Her arms flailed, her body heaved.

'Who . . .' she tried to say and the hand was rammed further into her open mouth, her cheekbones crushed as though in a vice.

Instinct brought her knee up; it sank into a warm belly. She heard a grunt, a wheeze of air, then the fist raised, coming towards her. She jerked her head aside but the punch landed. Pain exploded behind her eyes, tears gushed, a hot wetness ran down her face. Disbelief, incredulity came and went again as her mind grappled with the fact that it was not a nightmare; it was happening, it was real.

That was when she began to panic, when she began to fight, half crazy with fear.

A thumb ground under her chin, thrust up into the soft underside of her jaw; a fist was slammed into her midriff. She had never been struck like that before. Her father had once or twice smacked her quite hard but no man had ever punched her, meaning to hurt. She gave a muffled whine of anguish, doubling up, but her mind was in a state of petrified confusion. She couldn't believe it was happening, she didn't understand what was going on, torn out of warm, trusting sleep to find herself facing nightmare, wide awake.

All she could see of his face was blackness but through the faint lightness in the room she saw his teeth shine white through the mouth of a woollen helmet as he smashed his fist into her with such violence that she lost consciousness.

Coming back to awareness again she almost vomited with disgust and fear, her body felt sticky and hot, like glass smeared with fingerprints, yet she was cold, her teeth kept chattering, moans came hoarsely from her. Blood was trickling down her face, her nose felt swollen and throbbed, she thought it was broken, and one of her teeth hung loose. She felt it with her tongue, tasted salty sweet sticky blood in her mouth.

Please God, somebody come, why doesn't anyone stop this? she thought, writhing under the jarring, jamming invasion of her body. The fact that she couldn't see his face made it so appalling that her mind reeled with a primitive horror and she began to fight again, with a desperation, a terrified energy, because she had suddenly thought: is he going to kill me afterwards?

She scratched and bit and clawed like an animal with another, stronger, more powerful animal to face. His snarls were guttural, coming right from the back of his throat, and wordless. That was the most frightening part of it all, he hadn't said a word; she had not heard his voice or seen his face, yet she knew deep inside herself that he hated her, wanted to kill her. Clare had never imagined facing such a feeling, she had never seen anyone look at her as though they enjoyed the thought of killing her. But now she felt his enjoyment of her whimpers of pain, her panic-stricken struggles; she sensed his pleasure in causing the rictus of her mouth, her whistling intake of breath which hurt. Silently she was screaming: help me, please, somebody help, come quickly, don't let this happen to me. It could not happen to her, out of the dark, suddenly, without warning, it wasn't fair. Like a child she wanted to protest: I haven't done anything, why is it happening to me?

He grasped both her hands at the wrists, yanked them back over her head, rammed them against the wooden bedhead and held them there, until the blood stopped flowing and her hands were ice-cold. With his free hand he hit her over and over again until she went limp and could fight no more, sobbing, barely conscious.

She had lost track of time. He used her body and she could do nothing. She kept her eyes shut and wanted it to be over, that was all. Even if he was going to kill her, she no longer cared; she just wanted to escape from this.

When a key was inserted into the front door, they both heard it and froze; Clare in sudden, sick hope, the man with his head raised tensely, listening.

Pamela, thought Clare, it's Pamela, she has to be warned, she mustn't come into the flat, but before she had a chance to make a sound he had looked down at her, and his eyes were murderous. They told her what he was going to do before he moved.

CHAPTER TWO

Pamela let herself into the flat. The hall was dark, no light showed beneath Clare's door, Pamela couldn't hear a sound. She closed the front door softly and went into the kitchen, switched on the light and walked over to put on the kettle. She felt like some tea, she wasn't sleepy; her mind was whirring like an electric fan, round and round, buzzing with irritation. Who the hell did he think he was?

She stripped off her jacket and flung it over a chair, picking up the teapot a second later without having any clear idea what she meant to do with it. Her mind was too busy and angry and she stood there, her palms clasped around the smooth round-bellied brown pot and stared at the window where the night pressed, a darkness into which she could not see from a lighted room. She was like an actor on a floodlit stage faced by a cavernous black auditorium. How dare he talk to her, look at her like that? Who was he, anyway? What right did he think he had, what a nerve, she should have slapped his face.

The kettle hummed industriously; she looked at it and was reminded of him. There it sat, polished and metallic, doing its job with a smug self-satisfaction which made her feel like flinging it across the room.

Tonight wasn't the first time she had noticed him. He had been around for some while although Pamela had never spoken to him before. She had not known his name or his job or anything about him, he had been part of the wallpaper at a few parties, that was all. He was so ugly she wouldn't have so much as looked at him twice, normally, but he had forced himself on her attention by the way he looked at her. Pamela wasn't accustomed to being looked at like that, she wasn't even certain how to define the way he looked. He didn't stare, nor was his expression admiring or lustful or envious – he just looked at her from time to time and smiled very slightly. At first his smile had merely registered as something unusual, then it had begun to get on her nerves, she had begun to watch for it, resent it. What was he smiling at? she had asked herself, and had found herself watching him when he wasn't looking her way, watching him talking to other people, particularly other girls because she wanted to know if he always looked at women with that strange, quirky little smile. He didn't.

When he was with other girls, there was nothing in his manner but a pleasant, smiling attention. Pamela noticed that people liked him. You knew that because of the way their faces changed when they saw him, both sexes looked pleased and welcoming as he came into a room. He spoke softly, there was nothing distinguishable about his voice, you wouldn't pick it out among a crowd of chattering strangers. He had a suburban London accent, very ordinary. It went with his face: thin and bony, his skin always having a city pallor, as though he rarely saw the sun, his hair straight and black and neatly brushed. He wore boring clothes, old ones which were well-worn, clean but shabby. He was poor, Pamela could see that just from his clothes, which made it all the more surprising that he was always greeted with such warmth by everyone. The people at those parties were either wealthy or moved in a wealthy world: businessmen, models, show-business luminaries. Someone so badly dressed, so quiet and unimpressive, was an odd man out at such gatherings. Pamela couldn't help wondering why he was there, who he knew, who he was.

When she was curious about someone, she usually found a friend to introduce her – Pamela could look after herself, she knew the ropes in that world; she had been part of it for a couple of years now. If she saw someone she fancied, she coolly made his acquaintance, she rarely failed to score. Her beauty and her reputation as one of today's top models made her almost irresistible. Few men could bring themselves to turn down that unspoken invitation which her smouldering golden eyes issued.

Her arrival at a party was always noticed, too. She swayed in, long-legged, blonde, her rounded body flinging a flaunted sexuality at every man she passed so that eyes

29

followed her, those of the men admiring or covetous, those of the women narrowed and resentful.

When she had got to the party tonight, she had seen him on the other side of the room talking to a small girl in red, a very pretty girl, Pamela had noted, if you liked the dimpled, cute-type face – and he appeared to. He was smiling at her and looking into her eyes as if he did.

'Darling, those jeans! They look terrific on you. Did they spray them on, however will you get them off?'

'Oh, hi, Jenny.' Pamela could not summon any enthusiasm for the other girl. She had heard the barely hidden note of malice in Jenny Weldon's voice.

'Did you hear about Anthea?'

'No,' Pamela said, her eyes on the couple on the other side of the room.

'Haven't you? Well . . .'

'Jenny, who *is* that?' Pamela interrupted.

'What? Who?' Jenny looked irritated but turned and stared across the room, following Pamela's gaze.

'I've seen him around but his face doesn't seem to fit. Who is he? The one in the old cord jacket?'

'Oh, that's Joe,' Jenny said, as though that explained everything. 'I was going to tell you about Anthea.'

'Joe who? What does he do?'

Jenny's very red lips pouted, she hesitated before choosing her attitude but finally decided on a patronising smile. 'Don't you know Joe? Everyone does. Surely you've run into him before? Why, he's always around.'

'I think I'll get myself a drink,' Pamela said, turning away without waiting to hear Jenny's next remark.

'Well! Really! How bloody rude. Did you see that?' Jenny said to someone as Pamela walked away.

Getting herself a martini, Pamela drifted unobtrusively around the room, talking to a few people here and there. She did not look in any one direction but gradually she came closer to the tall, thin man in a brown cord jacket gone threadbare at the cuffs and elbows. The little group standing next to him and the girl in red held several old acquaintances. Pamela chatted to them, sipping her drink.

One man told a long golfing story to which she listened with all apparent amusement. Stepping back, laughing, she bumped into the man called Joe and her drink went flying.

'Oh, dear,' Pamela said, helpless, wide-eyed.

He retrieved her empty glass, produced a handkerchief and offered it to her to wipe her jeans, which were splashed with martini.

'Sorry to be so clumsy,' Pamela said, giving him her special smile, the one which had them giving at the knees.

Not this man, though. He looked at her drily, reflectively, very much immune and every hair on the back of her neck bristled in a sort of shocked surprise. She looked at him like a cat looking at a mouse which doesn't run away or cower in a corner but stares back unmoved. What was the matter with him, didn't he like women? For a second the thought flashed through her head – was he gay? Then she looked into his blue eyes and the idea was gone again. With disbelief it dawned on her then – he didn't like her. Women often didn't, she expected that, shrugged at it, but a man? It was a first. When she made up her mind to charm a man, he was charmed and he stayed charmed until Pamela was tired of the game.

She smiled at him again, watching his face. 'You're Joe, aren't you?'

'That's right,' he agreed and she waited for him to express surprise that she should know his name. They had never been introduced, she was sure he was aware of that. He ought to be flattered, intrigued, by the fact that she knew him, but his face stayed cool.

'I'm Pamela Rawlings.'

He nodded again. From his blank expression the name meant nothing to him, but she knew he must have heard it, he must have seen her; her face was always on magazine covers, billboards, television advertisements. People didn't always know her name but they knew her face. They stared as she walked past in the street, in supermarkets, in restaurants.

'What do you do, Joe?' she asked, refusing to give up in the face of his bland, icecream indifference.

31

'I'm a doctor,' he said and her eyes widened.

'What sort of doctor?'

'I'm a physician at St Aidan's.' He gave out information about himself in icy little drops. It should have irritated her but she found herself needing to hear more, catching the tiny scraps thirstily, feeling them sink into her, become absorbed.

The girl in red had moved off, retreating before Pamela's invasion as other girls often did. Pamela had him to herself. He was propping up the wall with one hand, his thin body at ease as he surveyed her with calm observation.

'How fascinating,' she said over-emphatically. 'Are you a specialist?'

'No,' he said. 'This is my first year on the wards. I only qualified last year.'

'Really?' Her glance assessed his age and she frowned.

'I'm thirty-three,' he told her, realising what she was thinking. 'I came round to medicine rather late in life.'

'What did you do before you took up medicine?' Men always liked to talk about themselves, you could see them expanding as they launched into self-explanation, like those paper flowers you drop into water and which unfurl jerkily until they are spread out for you to see, bright and full-petalled. She watched him, but although he answered he measured out the words in the same grave way, giving her only what he decided she should receive.

'I was working in the City.'

'Business?' He nodded and she waited, but got no more than that. 'What made you swap horses?' she asked.

'I decided to become a doctor.'

Pamela forced a little soft laughter and ran one finger down the side of his face. He didn't flinch away or flush, he stood there, watching her, his cool skin leaving an imprint on her own so that as her hand dropped awkwardly away she still felt the touch of his flesh, her fingertip tingling.

'Well, obviously, but why?' she asked, hiding her surge of fury. Her laughter, her fluttered lashes, her deliberate touch had made no more impression on him than it had on the wall.

That was when he leaned towards her and spoke softly, so softly she had to strain to hear him, and, listening, could not believe her own ears.

'Don't waste your time, Miss Rawlings. I don't bed hop and I don't bother with girls who do – try your luck elsewhere. I wouldn't want you to end up in bed alone tonight. You might get withdrawal symptoms.'

Her mouth opened but she couldn't speak. She was reddening, her face was burning. He had spoken quietly but she was terrified someone else might have overheard and she was trembling with shock and rage.

He straightened and moved away. She stood there, staring at the empty glass in her hand as though she had just noticed it and was considering whether to get another drink. She left it a minute and then walked vaguely away, putting the glass down as she went towards the door. The room was crowded, she had to squeeze through laughing groups of people several times. Twice she was spoken to and answered, smiled. She couldn't have told you what she said, what had been said to her. She was moving like a robot.

She caught a taxi on the corner of the street, gave the address of her flat and then changed her mind and told the driver to cruise around the West End. He looked at her suspiciously and she said: 'I've got a headache, I need some air before I go home.' He drove her through the lit streets for a while, eyeing her in his driving mirror in a way she resented, then he took her back to Chelsea and she paid him and watched him drive away before she turned into the block of flats. She was afraid Clare and Tom would be there, still up, but to her relief the flat was silent and dark.

While she made her tea she thought of nothing but what had happened, what Joe had said. She ran the moments endlessly through her head, ironing them into her brain in indelible, scorching images. Her family somehow came into her mind. Pamela never thought of her parents voluntarily and when a memory of them did surface, she thrust it back down into the dark lake of the unconscious in the angry haste of someone who is afraid. She did not want to remember. Her life had begun when she came to London over eight years ago. Remembering her family was thinking herself back into a world she almost felt she had read about rather than lived in – small, narrow, parochial, dull. She had hated that world and been desperate to escape it, to be free to make her own rules and live by them without anyone having the right to interfere. So who did he think he was? She despised that sort of thinking. Did he talk to other men like that? Did he feel he had some Godgiven right to be scornful of one of his friends if he played the field? Did he hell – he envied them, laughed admiringly, wished he had the guts to do just as he liked. If the room hadn't been crammed with people she'd have slapped his face except that such melodramatic gestures were so dumb and stupid they made her sick. She was boiling over with words she hadn't said to him. She wished she knew his phone number. She would ring and tell him now, tell him precisely what she thought of an attitude which should have gone out with the dodo.

She poured herself some tea and carried the cup out of the kitchen. She wouldn't get to sleep for hours; she was too wide awake. She would listen to some music, if she kept the volume low she wouldn't wake Clare.

The sitting room door was closed. She opened it, switched on the light with her free hand, and took one step before looking at the room.

'God,' she said, stiffening. Her hand jerked involuntarily, the tea splashed over the rim of the cup, scalding her wrist. She almost dropped the cup. Her eyes flashed round the room and saw everything that had happened to it in a succession of horrific images – the scored, defaced wallpaper, the litter of broken gramophone records on the floor, the books flung higgledy-piggledy on top of them, the obscenities printed in lipstick in great, sprawling letters a foot high. The television had gone, so had the stereo. The drawers in a long, teak sideboard had been pulled out and emptied.

Pamela saw it all in less than a moment, too shocked to think, just standing there staring.

Her brain began to work again with a jagged screech like the sound of a gramophone needle dragged across a record.

'Clare . . . God . . . Clare.' She turned and ran down the hall, in the dark, opened Clare's door, trembling and still holding the cup. 'Clare,' she said in a hoarse, raw gasp as she switched on the light, but that was before she had looked at the bed.

The cup leapt out of her hand, spilling tan liquid in all directions, splashing down the wallpaper and seeping, staining, the pale carpet.

'Christ Almighty, oh, Christ.'

Stumbling, she ran, her breath coming in painful little spurts, like sobs, her ears ringing with a bitter pulse, deafening herself with the turbulence of her own blood. She sank to her knees beside the bed, as much because she could not stand as to feel with a shaking hand for the pulse which would betray life in Clare. She didn't expect to pick it up, she knew Clare was dead. This was how death looked, chalk white, bruised beneath the eyes, blood trickling from a corner of the mouth, the body rigid and ice-cold. It was Clare lying there but Pamela felt the Clare she knew was no longer present in that battered tissue of flesh.

Even as she fumbled, pressing her fingers into the cold neck, other instincts were at work. She was looking over her shoulder, her eyes huge, all pupil, a hard glazed blackness from terror. Was whoever had done this still in the flat? Was he about to come swooping out of the darkness? Another part of her mind was urging her to get to the phone, ring the police, an ambulance, get help.

When she heard a tiny sound, her mind went jittery, she gasped, looking around the room to track it down before realising it came from Clare, who was sighing, breathing audibly.

Her eyes were still shut but her lips were open and through them came the weak, thin mew of a moan again.

Pamela leant over. 'Clare, Clare.'

She got no answer but when she was even closer the breathing became more obvious. Hurriedly, she scrambled to her feet and ran back down the hall to the sitting room to snatch up the telephone. As she began to dial, she realised it was dead. Her eye followed the cord along the wall. He had cut it, of course, of course he would. She thought feverishly; she had to get to a phone. The girl across the lobby had one. Pamela ran back to the front door, left it wide open while she put her thumb on the other girl's door-bell and left it there, leaning on it as if her body was too weak to stand upright.

As Clare's mind groped through damp waves of awareness, she thought at first that she was waking from sleep, then that she had had a nightmare, some black, heavy dream – and almost at once sensed that the nightmare was still going on, was all around her, that she did not want to wake because in doing so she would be waking in the nightmare from which she had escaped into sleep.

'Don't move!' She imagined it as a voice, shrieking imperatives at her. 'Don't move!'

The voice was inside her own skull, echoing with the heavy clangour of a bell in a cathedral at night. She obeyed it, playing dead like a frightened animal. She had no idea what had happened, where she was, even who she was – her mind was disorientated, confused, too numbed to think clearly.

She lay very still while along her nerve paths poured messages, like word from a stricken city to a distant government – help, help, her body cabled to her brain, which with bureaucratic caution refused to act until all the reports had been filed, her senses had finished recording the exact nature of the damage.

The first messages were so simple. She was in pain. She was cold. She was sick with fear.

'Don't move!'

At the same time she was listening to the sounds outside herself: from the room, her ears picking up the far-off rumble of traffic in the streets, the flutter of curtains in a breeze, the faint whine of an insect which was flying around the room, and then from further off distinctly – Pamela's voice.

'Pamela!'

Clare's eyes opened, she staggered, shaking, to her knees on the crumpled bed. The light was on, her eyes were blind in the glare of it. She had to get to Pamela, what was happening to her? Was he out there? She tried to get off the bed and her legs gave way. She fell heavily to her knees again, her head bowing, touching the carpet, her outstretched hands curling into the pile as though she clawed at shifting, unstable sand to stop herself from being carried out on a dark tide. She had to get to Pamela, she had to get up, she must not lose consciousness again.

She heard the running feet, and with a great effort raised her head and looked through a tousled web of hair.

Like an animal, Pamela thought, going down on her knees beside her. She looked at me the way an animal looks when it is afraid; cringing, beaten, trembling. A terrible anger went flowing through her as she put her arms round Clare, who resisted, pulling back, away, her teeth chattering audibly. Pamela had never held a naked woman before, never really looked at one except briefly in sex magazines and then with irritation and indifference, yet always noting the beauty of the smooth soft skin, the curved female body which was a mirror to her own. She had seen other models dress and undress but never looked the way she looked at a man, curious, assessing, aware of that difference in texture, shape and grace. A man was an alien territory she explored in detail; another woman held no mystery for her. But she looked now and grew angrier, seeing the bruised, stained skin, the puffy eyes, the swollen lips, the scratched and defaced body which had been attacked the way their sitting room had been attacked.

'I rang the police, they're on their way, and an ambulance is coming too.'

Clare's hand searched sideways and Pamela looked in that direction. 'What do you want?' Then she understood. 'I'll get it.' She pulled the crumpled sheet down and wrapped it round Clare.

Huddled in it like a pale squaw, Clare crouched on the floor, rocking herself, her arms folded across her body, her head bent.

'Are you okay?' Stupid, Pamela thought, as she asked, what a damn stupid question, but she could not think of anything to say. She was trying to keep her voice matter-of-fact, calm. 'Why don't you lie down?' she asked to cover her irritation with herself. Clare flinched, shaking her head violently. Pamela closed her eyes briefly, even more furious with herself.

'Would you like some tea?' She was making a hash of the whole thing, she hadn't got a clue how to handle this, she despised herself. Some women would be good at this sort of thing but Pamela was not the type to be soothing in a crisis, her instinct made her try to stabilise the situation, bring it back to some pretence of normality. She was listening for some outside hint about how to react, but she had to rely on her own intuition. She asked herself how she would feel if this had happened to her, what would she want from another woman at this moment? And knew that she would want to be alone, to hide herself, she would be sick if she was asked about it, had to talk. But she couldn't leave Clare. She put her arm round her and said: 'Can you get up? Come into the kitchen and have a cup of tea, come out of here.'

Clare was so taut her teeth were jarring. They kept chattering as though she was dying of cold, she felt dirty, sick.

'I want a bath,' she whispered, her mouth ugly, lips rubbery, enormous, feeling as they did when she had been to the dentist and had novocaine, hanging slackly as she spoke, while from the corner of her mouth oozed a thin trickle of moisture flecked with blood.

'The police warned me not to let you.' Pamela had not understood why they said: don't let her have a bath. She hadn't been thinking, only gabbling at them, feverish to get them there. Now she realised both why they had said: don't let her have a bath and why they had known so clearly that Clare would want one.

'I must.'

Pamela kept her arm round her, although she felt Clare constantly pulling away, rejecting her touch, shivering with repulsion at it.

Fretfully, Clare pushed at her hand, like a sick child. 'Let go.' She could not bear it, being touched was painful, her skin winced.

'Come into the kitchen and have that tea.' She had begun to use a voice she remembered from childhood: quiet, firm, unstressed. Inside, Pamela wanted to cry, to break down, get away from it all, but she fell into the pattern which was asserting itself. 'Come along,' she said, and heard her mother's voice with a desire to break into hysterical laughter. How many times had she thought: I'll never be like her! She had grimaced with distaste at the idea of growing into a woman like that. Not me, oh, no! not me, she had told herself, watching her mother day by day, filling her hours with dull, busy tasks, cleaning and cooking and waiting on her husband, feeding her bedridden old father who had lived there for so long Pamela could not remember how many years he had been with them, wiping his thin crumpled mouth as if he was a baby, attending to all his needs in a pathetic reversion of their roles. In her spare time she drove old folk to and from the hospital or did voluntary work of some kind or another. Pamela could not have borne that life, she disliked her father and was repelled by the old man upstairs who whined and was obsessed with himself. Both of them, the middle-aged man and the old, were obsessed with their own narrow world and both saw Pamela's mother in the same light, she was there to look after them. Mrs Rawlings didn't even seem to find that attitude strange; she accepted her fate with a cheerful smile, she welcomed it with open arms. Pamela could not understand it, she fled from home to escape the same fate.

And here she was using that old, familiar phrase. 'What you need is a cup of tea.' She steered Clare into the kitchen and got her to sit down, poured tea and spooned so much sugar into it that Clare grimaced in disgust as she sipped. Wasn't that what you did? Pamela thought, feeling helpless and unsure of herself. Oh, this was a day for first experiences.

She looked at Clare uneasily, Clare was clasping the cup in both hands and visibly shaking. What the hell did you do? Pamela thought, in a surge of anger with herself for her own helpless inability to cope. What did you say?

Pamela had made it an unbreakable rule that she did not get involved with other people's lives. She was responsible for herself and nobody else – people were parasitic, clung to the nearest strong object and wound themselves round and round it for support, so that they could climb up to the sun. It did not matter a damn to them that in the process they strangled their host, sucked all the strength out of her. Pamela had watched it happening to her mother, she had watched as it began to happen to Clare and neither of them had taken any notice of what she said.

Now she was facing a situation where her self-made rule about not getting involved did not apply. She was a confused mass of contradictory feelings. She wanted to put her arms around Clare, hug her, comfort her, do something to ease the drawn white misery of her face. She wanted to cry, and Pamela had not cried for so long she couldn't even remember the last time. She wanted to scream and break things in her rage against what had happened in this flat tonight, the vicious, cruel destruction which had been committed. She felt the hatred of the man who had been here as if he was still there – he had been full of hate, the careful brutality made that clear; pointless, meaningless hatred which wanted to smash and destroy, to deface and humiliate.

Tentatively she put her hand on Clare's head, meaning to stroke her hair, offering comfort – but Clare flinched away and Pamela's hand dropped down.

She was afraid of doing the wrong thing, saying the wrong thing. All the gestures she would have used seemed clumsy – you offered physical comfort to a hurt child, but what did you do when someone looked sick if you came near them?

She had shared the flat with Clare on a basis of strict neutrality – they had worked out a fair division of responsibilities – which chores each did, how much of the rent, the various bills, the cost of staple foods like milk and coffee and eggs, each paid. They lived under the same roof like strangers, rarely seeing much of each other, both of them too busy, engrossed in their own lives. Sometimes days passed without them doing more than mutter 'Hi!' in the morning, or adding a casual: 'Busy?' or saying: 'God, it isn't raining *again*?' as they left together for work by accident. Their relationship was not so much a friendship as a system for living, and it had worked out, but at times, watching Clare with Tom, Pamela could have shaken her. Stand up for yourself, don't let him turn you into a servant, can't you see what he's doing? she wanted to say. She had been angry enough to mention it once or twice but she always regretted it afterwards. It broke her golden rule – never get involved.

The doorbell rang sharply and they both jumped. Pamela saw Clare's eyes roll upwards, the whites blood-flecked. She risked putting an arm round her, hugging her.

'It must be the ambulance, it's okay.' Clare was in shock, she thought, her skin icy and white, her teeth chattering. I should have wrapped her in blankets. Wasn't that what you did for shock? Kept the victim warm?

When she opened the front door, she found herself facing two policemen, both youngish men in uniform, looking as excited as pink blancmange.

'Miss Rawlings, is it? Did you ring the emergency services, Miss?'

The door opposite opened and the curious, staring eyes of the girl from the flat from which Pamela had telephoned stared at them. 'If there's anything I can do . . .' she began.

'Thanks, I'll remember,' Pamela said, brusquely. She had already refused the offer earlier.

The policemen glanced at the girl then, as Pamela moved back, they walked past her into the flat and she shut the door. Something in the way they were looking at her made her add defensively: 'I had to use her phone, he had cut ours off.'

'Wanted to get in on the act, did she?' the taller of the two men asked and, contrarily, Pamela said: 'It's very kind of her.'

The other man had his cap under his arm. He looked

comically young to Pamela, not old enough to wear a police uniform; he looked as if he was dressing up in his father's clothes. He had a round, babyish face and curly fair hair with very bright blue eyes, and he was staring at her eagerly with a coaxing half-smile.

'Are you okay, Miss?'

'I'm perfectly okay,' Pamela said, irritated, and saw his face fall. He looked disconsolate, staring down at his polished shoes.

The taller man was much older, raw-boned, steady-eyed. He regarded his colleague with a look which seemed amused. 'It's his first week with us, Miss,' he said as he walked to the sitting room door and glanced in at the disorder. When he turned round again his face was exactly the same. The destruction had left him untouched. Pamela looked at him and disliked him. How could he look at that and just turn away?

'Anything taken, Miss?' he asked.

'Several things – I'm not sure how many but the TV and the stereo have gone. I haven't really looked to see what else.'

The young man had gone to the door and Pamela heard him whistle. She followed the other one into the kitchen and found him looking at Clare who was staring into her empty cup and ignoring him.

'How do you feel, Miss?' he asked.

Clare was silent.

'She's in shock,' Pamela said, accusingly.

'Said anything?'

Pamela shook her head. 'I didn't ask her, not while she's like that. You can see . . .'

'Yes,' he said, cutting her short without rudeness. 'Would you like to tell us what happened as far as you come into it, Miss?'

'I was at a party tonight. I got back and found . . .'

'What time did you get back, would you say?'

Impatiently she said: 'I don't know, around one, maybe, I wasn't looking at my watch.'

'How long ago would you say it was?'

'Not long – I rang almost immediately after seeing her . . .'

Clare sat and stared into the cup, letting the voices wash over her head. The cup was white earthenware; a crack had run from where the handle was cemented to the rim at the base. Clare kept following it and then going back to the place where it started and following it again. She was not listening to what was being said. She was not thinking. She was intent on the thin crack, fine and dark against the white glaze, as if a hair had clung to the side of the cup.

She was so cold. If only her teeth would stop grating and grinding, it was making her jaw ache, making her face vibrate with a dull, dead tension.

The older policeman was watching her. He looked at Pamela. 'Got any blankets? A quilt?'

'Yes,' she said and went out to find blankets. The man stood back and let her wrap them around Clare.

'Where's that ambulance?' Pamela said, her voice ragged.

The policeman squatted down in front of Clare so that his eyes were just below her own eye level. 'I don't want to upset you, Miss, but it would help if we had a description, you see – you saw him, did you?'

Clare stared into the cup.

He waited a minute and then said: 'If you could just give us some idea who we're looking for . . . take your time, we're in no hurry.'

Clare gave no sign of having heard him.

He waited patiently, then stood up and looked at Pamela. 'Could you talk to her, Miss? He might still be in the area, we need to know what he looks like.'

Pamela tried to take the cup out of Clare's hand and Clare clung to it with surprising determination. 'Would you like some more tea?' Pamela asked. 'Clare, this man – was he young?'

Clare frowned involuntarily. Her lower lip twitched. She stared into the cup and followed the crack slowly, intently; it did not run straight, it curved, it had a shape, it looked like a meandering little stream, it looked like the initial of her own name.

'Only, we can't catch him if we don't know what he looked like,' the policeman said.

The young, fair boy came into the kitchen and said: 'He's done a real job on the other bedroom.'

Pamela hadn't even thought of her own room, she felt sickness clawing at her stomach at the idea of ever sleeping in it again. She didn't even want to see what had been done to it, she felt the taste of yellow bile burning her throat.

'Was he dark, Miss?' The policemen watched Clare. 'Fair? Was he tall or short?'

She wanted them to be quiet, to go away. Every time one of them moved she felt her whole body jerk to terrified attention. Her nerves were screaming as though they were on fire. Although she had not even looked at them she was deeply aware of them, of their sex. You didn't have to see them to know that they were men, they smelt like men, they moved like men; their presence in the room threatened. They spoke in quiet, flat voices and moved slowly but Clare was shaking.

'We have to know, Miss,' the patient voice said.

'She doesn't want to talk about it,' Pamela said in a burst of aggression. 'Why don't you leave her alone? Can't you see the state she's in?'

He ignored her and moved away from Clare. Leaning on the table, he said: 'Suppose I ask you a few questions, Miss, and if I'm right, you nod? Just a little nod, that's all I want.'

He waited to let that sink in, then asked: 'Was he anyone you knew?' Clare didn't move. 'You'd never seen him before?' Her bruised bluish lids were almost covering her eyes, her features were rigid. 'Was he young? In his twenties, say?'

Clare felt his slow, calm patience walling her in, pressing at her. He was not going to stop asking questions until she answered. A deep, hoarse sigh came up out of her stomach.

'I didn't see. I was asleep when . . .' Her voice sounded thin and reedlike, it seemed to come from the very top of her head.

'You must have seen his face, Miss.'

Pamela screwed her hands into fists at her side, glaring at

him. She felt the shudder Clare gave as if she had given it herself.

Clare whispered: 'He was wearing a black thing on his face.'

'A mask?'

'I . . . I think . . . a balaclava helmet.'

'Did you see his eyes?'

Clare's teeth bit down into her lower lip.

'What colour were they?'

'I don't know, I don't know . . . leave me alone . . .'

'Did you get the impression he was a young man?'

She nodded very briefly.

'How young? Teens?' No response. 'Twenties?'

She frowned. 'You think he may be in his twenties, Miss?' he pressed and she half-nodded.

'Tall or short?'

'Tall,' she said wearily.

'Hair? Did you get a look at that?'

Another frown. 'I'm . . . I don't . . . oh, maybe dark . . . not fair, anyway . . . brown or . . .'

'His eyes weren't brown, were they, Miss? Can you remember that? If they were brown, wouldn't you have noticed that?'

'They weren't brown,' she said.

'Blue?'

'Pale,' she said. 'They shone . . .' Her voice broke off and she retched, bending forward in a convulsive spasm. Pamela flung herself down on her knees beside her and held her, huddled in her arms, murmuring broken words neither of them really heard. 'No, don't, Clare, ssh . . . you're okay, you're safe now . . .'

The young policeman looked at his shoes, his face red. The older one watched them, then he crooked a finger in the direction of his colleague, moving to the door. Pamela heard them talking in the hall, in lowered voices, she couldn't pick out what was being said.

The doorbell rang and she felt Clare's whole body jerk. She tightened her grip of her.

From the hall, she heard a breezy voice: 'Hallo, Freddy,

thought you were still on holiday? Had a good time, did you?'

'Great, we had the weather for it,' the older policeman said. 'The kids never came off the beach all fortnight, brown as berries, all three of them.'

'Lucky bastard, I'm not due for mine until September. It'll be raining cats and dogs with my luck. What have you got for us tonight? Rape, is that right?'

All in a night's work, Pamela thought, listening.

'Give us another five minutes,' the older policeman said. 'She's hardly opened her mouth. I need a better description than she's given me so far.'

'In a state, is she?'

'Shock, not making much sense at the moment. I've rung in to ask Doc Pullman to call at the hospital to examine her. We'd better have a full report, she's been pretty badly beaten up.'

'Not talking, though?' There was a note in the other voice which Pamela picked up but could not identify.

'The flat's been done over, looks like a break-in which turned into something else.'

Clare was shivering from head to foot. Her head was pressed against Pamela's shoulder. It was impossible to be sure how much she was hearing.

The group of men loomed into view. Pamela looked at them over Clare's head, her face pale and aggressive. 'I want her taken to hospital now,' she said in a high voice. 'Now, do you understand?'

'I just want to know what clothes...' the policeman began and Pamela cut into the words.

'Screw his clothes. She's going out of her mind, if you don't let her go to the hospital now, right now, I'll put in a complaint...'

Clare lifted her head slowly, as if it were too heavy for her neck. In a slow voice she said: 'Dark clothes... all black... sweater... and gym shoes, he didn't take them off.'

'That's it,' Pamela said. 'That's enough, do you hear? She's had enough and so have I.'

'We're only doing our job, Miss. You want the bastard caught, don't you?'

'At the moment all I want is Clare out of this,' Pamela said. 'Everything else can wait.'

CHAPTER THREE

Clare in a narrow, white iron-framed bed, a heaped pile of hard hospital pillows under her head, her hands lying outside, flat, cold, empty on the white honeycomb weave cover. The linen felt starched and neutral around her and she had not moved since the nurse neatly brushed a hand over the covers once she had watched Clare climb unsteadily into the bed. Floor-length cotton curtains hung around her bed, they were a creamy yellow colour printed with rather ugly violets and green leaves. They had been washed so often that the colours had run and the pattern was no longer sharp and clear. Clare's eye dully followed the pleats and folds in the material up to where the curtains hung from brass rings suspended on a metal rod fixed into the ceiling.

Outside her private refuge she could hear the noises in the ward: bedpans rattling, flat shoes padding on the rubber-tiled floor, a chair scraping as it was moved; a woman in a nearby bed coughed, another breathed thickly, stertorously.

There was a window behind her bed, the glass admitting light but not allowing anyone outside to see into the ward. Clare had been relieved to notice that. She liked having the curtains drawn. The nurse had asked if she wanted them open now and Clare had shaken her head.

'No, keep them that way.'

She liked watching the sunlight shining through the thin cotton, rippling like water on the bed cover. With the curtains drawn she was invisible, safe, she was in a light-filled cave alone, she did not have to feel people looking at her, she was not threatened with any more questions.

They had let her have a bath, at last, after the police doctor had examined her at great length. Clare had been as rigid as a board during his examination and he had been politely impatient with her.

'I know you're nervous, but please let your muscles

relax. I'm not going to hurt you, just let yourself sag. It will be over sooner.'

She had not looked at him. If anyone had asked her now she would not be able to describe him. A blur in a white coat with cold hands and a tired voice – that was all he had been to her and he had inflicted a distress on her which her rational mind knew he had not intended and could not avoid. She had loathed every second of what happened in the clinical, white examination room. She had had to force herself to answer his questions.

'Did he . . .' the questions always seemed to start. She would have given a great deal to shut her mind off before she had to hear those questions, but if she did not answer the doctor merely asked her again until she did. He was right, it would all be over much sooner if she faced up to what she was trying to forget.

'Are you on the pill?' he had asked. She had said she was and heard the doctor say: 'Well, that's good, isn't it?'

'Is it?' Clare had said, then caught up with what he meant and said with a shiver: 'Yes.' At least she wouldn't have to face any consequences like that. Her mind sheered away from the thought, but it persisted. What if she hadn't been on the pill? What if that creature had left his seed inside her, part of him embedded in her flesh? She closed her eyes with a moan of disgust at the image, remembering; her sickened mind filled with images of what he had done to her, she felt her throat burn with nausea, her stomach heave.

She kept her eyes shut, forcing back the memories. She had to stop herself from thinking, it was the only way she could face being alive at all at the moment. She was hibernating in her light-filled cave, the only touch she could stand the feel of sunlight on her cold skin.

Pamela sat in an echoing stone-floored corridor on a very hard chair with a moulded plastic back which dug into her spine. Who designed these things? Someone who didn't intend to sit on them, obviously, or someone with a deformed anatomy.

People walked past without looking at her, talking to each other; some in white coats or nurses' uniforms, some in outdoor clothes, carrying tight little bunches of flowers bought from the stall at the hospital gates, some going on laggard feet to appointments with specialists, their faces apprehensive. Sometimes Pamela watched them, sometimes she stared at the magazine she was holding, but her mind refused to concentrate on the articles, the short stories about young love, the cooking instructions and knitting patterns.

She had not slept at all; she had divided the night between the hospital and the police station, and she seemed to have been sitting around waiting for most of the time. She had sat, fuming, in a waiting room at the police station, staring at the clock on the wall. 'How much longer am I going to be kept hanging around here?' she had demanded from the police-woman who was keeping her company.

'Would you like another cup of tea?' the other had answered evasively, and gone out to get one, returning with two detectives in plain clothes who were carrying their own tea and sat down on the hard chairs with loud sighs. 'Nice to get the weight off the feet,' they told each other and Pamela had eyed them irritably.

'Hallo, Miss Rawlings,' the older of the two had said, smiling as he looked at her and she had bristled as she felt them staring, their faces surprised, interested, admiring, as they took in her blonde hair and the sexy curve of her figure in the tight jeans and low-necked t-shirt. 'Sorry to keep you waiting,' he added and Pamela gave him a cold look, rejecting the smile in his voice.

'Have you caught him yet?'

'Not yet, Miss,' he admitted as if she was being unreasonable.

'Are you going to?' Her voice carried unhidden contempt, but it was water off a duck's back. They both smiled.

'We'll do our best.' They showed no sense of urgency; their voices, faces, the way they moved, were leisurely, unhurried, matter of fact. This was work; their emotions were not involved.

'I should hope so,' Pamela said in a voice raw with a desire to have revenge, and that almost shocked her, too. She had always thought of herself as rational, sophisticated, a modern liberal with an open mind – but her attitudes had undergone a sea change overnight. She was burning with hatred for the man who had raped Clare, she was choking with confused, chaotic emotion.

They asked her a long string of questions about her own movements, how she had first discovered that the flat had been broken into, how she had found Clare.

'You didn't see anyone?'

Pamela shook her head.

'Heard nothing?'

'No, not a thing.' She took a long breath. 'How long had Clare . . . been like that? Did she say?'

'We aren't sure, not long. We've talked to the other tenants in your block. He did several flats. Their owners were away, luckily for them, but an old lady on the top floor saw a van parked round the back of the flats, on the service road, at around midnight. She saw a man carrying a television towards it, so she decided he was a television engineer. He must have shifted all the stuff out and then gone back and attacked your friend.' He used the euphemism smoothly and Pamela felt herself shaking with rage.

'Animal,' she almost hissed, her hands clenched.

'Cigarette, Miss?' one of them asked, leaning forward to offer her an opened packet.

'I don't smoke.'

'Very wise, I wish I could give it up,' he said, lighting one. He blew smoke into the air in a meditative way, watching the pale ring float away. 'Have you noticed anyone hanging around lately? A stranger? Anyone you can't account for, who doesn't live in the immediate area?'

'I haven't noticed anyone.' Her voice had strained impatience. 'I'm very busy, I dash in and out without looking around to see if there are any strangers about.'

'Your friend has boyfriends?'

'One, Tom Prescott.'

'Could we have his address and telephone number?'

Pamela had given it to them, watched them write it down carefully, and broken out in renewed anger: 'Tom's got nothing to do with this, why aren't you looking for the man who did it instead of wasting time talking and drinking tea?'

They stared at her with a clinical detachment which increased her rage. She wanted them to show some emotion, too; to reveal whatever they were thinking, to declare themselves. They were supposed to be on her side, on Clare's side, weren't they? There they sat, two very ordinary men, one in a creased old sports coat, the other in a dark jacket and dull grey trousers, watching her impassively and with an indefinable distance between them and her. They reminded her of plumbers who have come in to stop a leak and tramp cheerfully over ruined carpets and saturated floorboards already beginning to smell of mould, talking about a nice cup of tea and with no intention of rushing the job. They didn't care, that was what she found intolerable. Her own feelings were boiling and bubbling over and she needed to let them out, she needed to talk to someone who would respond. These men did not respond, they listened, oh! they listened, and their eyes watched you as you talked, but their quiet voices held no response other than a calm encouragement. She felt everything she said to them was assessed and filed away but their neutrality offended her.

When they let her go, she came back to the hospital. She couldn't get Clare out of her mind. She felt oddly that last night she had been raped too; what had happened had happened to them both. The police had made her look at her bedroom. They wanted, they said, to know if anything was missing. Pamela had nerved herself to walk into the room with a detective following her, like a bridesmaid accompanying a bride to the altar, a step behind, his face attentive. She had swallowed, shocked and sickened, looking around reluctantly. Her bedroom was so personal, so private; the place where she slept each night, as Clare had been sleeping, vulnerable, helpless. When you fell asleep, it was with a sense of escape to somewhere safe and comforting. How ironic that she knew now she would never again be able to go to sleep in this violated room. She had looked at her bed with its pale lemon sheets sprinkled with pretty white daisies and turned her head away, her nose wrinkling, her mouth wry with disgust.

'You'll have to wash those,' the detective had said. 'They often urinate in beds – kinky minds they've got.'

The whole room had smelt of him: a sour, revolting, seminal smell which made her stomach heave. It was mostly in her own mind, she knew that, her imagination supplying the physical image of the man who had been there, but it had left her with a strong feeling of having been touched, used, humiliated.

She had spoken to the sister on Clare's ward when she got to the hospital and had been promised a chance to see Clare later.

'I'm afraid you'll have to wait for half an hour. She's under sedation. Doctor does his rounds at ten-thirty. I'll ask him when he's here if she can have visitors.'

'How is she?' Pamela had asked.

'Doing quite nicely,' the woman had said before bustling away, her apron slapping against her skirt. Stranded on her chair in the corridor outside the ward, Pamela had been waiting ever since. She would have flown into irritated rage once upon a time and stalked out of the place, but now she found the busy, self-obsessed quietness of the hospital strangely hypnotic, soothing. She felt she was beached on a stretch of isolated sand, watching the yellow-beaked gulls diving into the waves, the thin-legged waders darting along the edge of the water, digging their beaks down in search of food, leaving pale triangular footprints on damp sand – the hospital gave her that same sense of engrossed activity far away from the ordinary world. She could watch and listen without being involved. How many other worlds were there, hidden one inside the other, like Russian dolls, each separate, self-contained, unique yet fitting smoothly one into the other? Her own world of modelling seemed unreal. She thought of it with surprise as though it no longer existed. Somewhere in London girls were lying on fake beaches under hot lights, tossing their hair or arching their bodies for the camera. Clare's office would be in its usual turmoil, with rows exploding between the art editor and the chief copy-writer, quarrels which had all the tension and personal hostility of a world war. At the police station men with flat, matter-of-fact voices would talk about rape and murder and embezzlement as calmly as if they were discussing what to have for lunch. People settled for one world and revolved inside it from day to day, never stopping to think about the mysteries and excitements of all the other worlds which existed around them. It took a violent event to shock you out of that blinkered condition, to make you aware that your way of life was not the only one.

She sat staring at the stone floor, her head bent, inspecting the way the worn squares fitted, absently beginning to count how many there were in each row from wall to wall. People walked past all the time and she did not look up although she noted the difference in their strides, the noise of their shoes, their sex and way of moving.

When a pair of black shoes stopped in front of her she glanced up, blank-faced, and then stiffened.

'What are you doing here?' he asked.

'Waiting,' Pamela said, struggling with a sense of shock.

He looked so different – thinner, younger, in a white coat and suddenly at home against his own background, on his own territory. He knew it too. His manner was even more assured. He had the look of someone caught in the midstream of life, going somewhere, busy, preoccupied when something unusual halts them. He glanced at his watch and she saw the fine black hairs on his arm; she observed them curiously, wondering if his whole body had hairs like that, short, curly, rough.

'What are you waiting for?' he asked. 'Visiting someone?'

She nodded. The question reminded her of Clare and her skin paled abruptly, she looked down, her lashes falling against her cheeks.

'You haven't got any make-up on,' he said, his voice surprised. Then he moved and sat down on the chair next to her. 'What's wrong?'

'I . . .' She started to speak and then the pressure of her own feelings burst like an over-stressed dam and she felt tears gushing out of her. They welled up in her eyes and ran down her face and she covered it with her hands, too distraught to pretend, unable to stop the tears.

People were still walking past, she felt them staring. She had never in her life broken down in a public place, she wouldn't have believed it would ever happen, but the tears ran like the Niagara Falls and she could not stop them. She felt she was not only crying for Clare, for the smashing up of their flat, their lives, she was crying for reasons she could not pin down, her tears were strangely universal; she wept for everything and had no need to put a name to her grief.

Joe put an arm around her and turned her towards him, held her close with her head buried in his white coat. She was shuddering and trembling in his arms, she was so weak she let her whole weight fall against him and the sensation of support gave her a tremendous feeling of relief.

When the tears slowed and dried up, she pushed away, searching blindly for a handkerchief in her handbag.

One was pushed into her hand. She kept her eyes down while she angrily blew her nose. Clutching the handkerchief tightly in her fingers, she muttered: 'Sorry about that.'

He gently uncurled her fingers and took the handkerchief. One hand lifted her face, his fingers firm as they held her chin. He wiped her wet face as if she was a sad child, with calm fatherly kindness.

'Feel better?'

Pamela tried to smile and didn't quite make it, her lips quivered and shook. 'I suppose so. Good for me, was it?'

'Definitely,' he said, half-mocking.

'I suppose it's the shock,' she said defensively, still not meeting his eyes.

'Leave the diagnosis to me,' he advised and she heard the smile in his voice with a new sense of shock, but a pleasurable one, this time. A little bleeping noise startled her but she realised what it was even as he stood up.

'I'll have to go,' he said.

She managed to smile, nodding.

'Have you had a cup of tea?'

She shook her head. She had not eaten either, but that hadn't even entered her head until now.

'I'll ask them to bring you some tea,' he said, moving away.

She heard him push through the ward door, heard it swing softly back with a shushing noise. A moment later he came out again and walked off down the corridor. Pamela looked up and watched his black head disappearing. He had a stethoscope dangling from one pocket, it swung to and fro as he walked. As he passed a window, sunlight gleamed on his hair and Pamela saw his elongated shadow etched briefly on the white-washed wall behind him.

'Miss Forrester?'

Clare opened her eyes reluctantly at the repeated question and looked at the woman standing beside the bed. She was slim, young, pleasantly dressed but she had an official manner Clare drew back from at once.

'I'm Detective Inspector Lucas. How are you feeling now? Can I sit down? I asked them to bring us some coffee, it should be here any minute.'

Clare watched as she drew a chair forward and sat down on it, smoothing down her skirt.

'I know you must be feeling lousy but there are just a few more things we have to know . . .'

'I've been through it all over and over again.'

'I know, it must be very upsetting for you.' The woman broke off as a nurse came through the curtains with a small wicker-edged tray on which were two cups and a plate of small, sweet biscuits.

'I could do with this, I'm parched,' the detective said, accepting a cup with a bright smile.

Clare took her own cup and held it, feeling the warmth percolating her skin, oozing through the chilled tissues and, as it permeated, making her even more aware of how cold she was, how withdrawn, how numb. She sipped and the coffee was very milky, very weak, sickly with sugar. She

56

normally drank her coffee black and sugarless but she sipped some more without a grimace.

'Can we go back to last night before you went to bed?' the detective asked. 'What time did you go to bed?'

'I'm not sure – around midnight?'

'You said you had a visitor for dinner?'

'Yes.'

'A Mr Thomas Prescott,' the woman said, consulting a notebook.

'Yes.'

'He's your boyfriend, is he?'

'Yes,' Clare said, wondering dully where all this was leading.

'I'm sorry to have to ask personal questions but it could be very important,' the other woman said in a polite voice. 'You cooked dinner and both of you ate it and then what happened?'

Clare looked up, frowning. Her mind was blank. 'What?'

'He's your boyfriend, you're on the pill, so presumably you're sleeping with him . . .'

'Tom's nothing to do with this,' Clare said. 'He had gone home ages . . .'

'Did you sleep with him last night?'

'That's none of your . . .'

'It could be important,' she was interrupted.

'I don't see what it has to do with . . . what happened later.'

'If intercourse took place with another man, it could be very important. There were no fingerprints left in the flats, so we might need to rely on forensic evidence relating to his rape of you, Miss Forrester, and it would be essential to our case to prove that his sperm had been found . . .'

'Oh, God,' Clare said, closing her eyes, and the cup rocked in her hand.

The detective leaned over and took it from her. Clare heard her put the cup down on the plastic-topped bedside table. The saucer chinked against the water jug and the woman coughed, settling back in her chair.

'I'm sorry, I know it must be unpleasant to talk about this sort of thing, but when it comes to court . . .'

'Please,' Clare said. 'Go away, please.'

'In a moment, Miss Forrester . . . can I call you Clare? It seems silly to go on calling you Miss Forrester. Clare, if you can just answer that one question I'll be on my way, I promise.' She waited and Clare didn't speak, her lids squeezed tightly over her eyes. 'Did you make love with your boyfriend last night?'

Clare shook her head jerkily.

'You're absolutely certain about that?'

'We didn't make love,' Clare whispered.

'We had to be sure,' said the level voice and she heard the chair creak as the woman got up. 'Thank you, Miss Forrester, I'll be on my way now.'

Clare kept her eyes shut and heard the rattle of the curtain rings as they were drawn and then pulled back to hide her from the rest of the ward.

In the corridor outside Pamela was drinking her tea out of a large white earthenware cup. It had been brought to her by a ward maid in a green uniform whose cap was stuck at a jaunty angle as if she were a sailor on shore leave. 'Here y'are, ducks, nice cuppa – drink it while it's hot. Dr Harper told me to put two spoons of sugar in, is that okay?'

Pamela had looked at her blankly, then realised whom she was talking about. Harper, she thought. His name is Joe Harper.

'Yes, that's fine,' she said aloud. 'Thank you, you're very kind.'

'Friend of yours, is he?' the woman asked. 'I'm Lily, ducks. You're waiting to see the poor little thing who come in last night, aren't you? Proper sight she is, one eye almost closed up, looks as if she's been losing a prize fight.'

Pamela's eyes lifted to survey her with hostility – the woman was in her late fifties, tall and skinny, with a face like a cheerful horse, her grey hair escaping in all directions from under her cap and her eyes an indeterminate grey, bright and beady and interested. She had the casual familiarity of an old acquaintance. Pamela could imagine that she had learnt to talk to strangers as if she knew them intimately from years of watching people come in and out of these wards, off balance, vulnerable, at a low personal ebb, unable to put up any protest about Lily's assumption of a right to talk as though she knew all about them.

'I'm waiting to see Miss Forrester,' she agreed, coldly.

'Poor girl, I think it's terrible what some men get up to. They should chop it off when they catch them, that's what I say.' Lily stopped talking as the ward door opened and the sister appeared. 'Just taking Miss Rawlings her cup of tea, Sister,' she said obsequiously and the other woman gave her a wry look.

'I could do with one myself.'

'Coming up, Sister,' Lily said, scurrying away.

'All right, Miss Rawlings?' asked the Sister and Pamela nodded without speaking. The woman went back into the ward and Pamela drank her tea.

Tom arrived ten minutes later; his face pale, freshly shaven, set in a heavy aggression which was continued down his body. His shoulders were hunched, his arms stiff, his legs moved jerkily.

'How's Clare?' he asked as he halted beside Pamela, his brows drawn. 'Is she okay?'

'I don't know how she is this morning but last night she was in a terrible state.' For the first time, Pamela felt no impatience at the sight of Tom; she tried to speak gently. He must be horrified, worried, angry, as she was, so she tried to smile reassuringly at him.

He sat down. 'I've been with the police for hours. They picked me up at my flat and kept me at the police station for hours, grilling me like a murder suspect. They kept asking the same questions over and over again, they gave me the feeling they thought I'd done it. They must be crazy. They only let me go because I demanded to see my lawyer. I'm not putting up with being treated like that, who do they think I am?'

Pamela felt rage beginning to build inside her like a tidal wave which was going to pour out of her at any minute and bury him, drown him, full fathoms five. His voice went on beside her; belligerent, resentful, self-righteous. He didn't care about Clare, he wasn't upset about her, he was upset about what had happened to him.

'I couldn't take it in at first,' he said. 'When they told me, I didn't believe it. They said it happened soon after I left the flat but I didn't see anyone hanging about. They weren't very forthcoming about what actually happened; they're a foxy lot, they have a lot of questions but they don't give many answers.'

'She was raped and beaten up,' Pamela said so loudly that a group of women in summer dresses walking past turned and stared and whispered with rounded eyes fixed on her. 'A bastard broke into the flat and smashed the place up and raped Clare after he had smashed her up too.'

'For Christ's sake,' Tom said, reddening. 'There's no need to bloody shout, I can hear you. You don't have to broadcast to the whole world.' He muttered it, his head bent but his eyes skidding after the women who were staring back over their shoulders as they reluctantly walked on.

'I'll bloody shout if I bloody want to,' Pamela said with her teeth together.

'You may be upset,' he began and she interrupted forcibly.

'Upset! My God, the mind boggles. Don't give me that pap – I'm not upset, I'm so angry I want to break things and so should you be, if you gave a twopenny damn about Clare.'

'Of course I do! What do you take me for?'

'Don't tempt me,' Pamela said.

'I wouldn't want to,' Tom came back and the hair stood up on the back of her neck.

'That's it, convert it into some sort of sexist joke . . .'

'I never had you down as a feminist,' he sneered.

'You'd make any woman feminist,' Pamela informed him. 'Your girl gets raped and all you can do is whine about police harassment?'

'I'm not saying they shouldn't do their job but I object to being suspected of something I didn't do – do you know they made me go through some humiliating physical examination? They took away the clothes I was wearing last night, too, to test them in their laboratory, they said. It's obvious they think I did it – has Clare told them I did?' He stared at her fixedly, his jaw clenched, and she looked at him with distaste.

'No, she has not – I don't suppose they think for a minute that it was you, you're just imagining it, unless of course you've got a guilty conscience.'

'What the hell's that supposed to mean?' he asked in a high, furious voice.

'I wouldn't know what goes on inside what you call your mind,' Pamela told him and he got up, knocking over one of the chairs which stood in a line against the wall. The clatter on the stone floor brought the ward sister popping out of the door like a rabbit out of a burrow, eyeing them reprovingly.

'Please! Not so much noise, you'll disturb my patients. This is a hospital, you know.'

'Excuse me,' Tom said, stamping over to her, 'I'd like to see Miss Forrester. When will . . .'

'Doctor hasn't done his round yet. Please, be patient, sit down, and I'll tell you when she can have visitors. It would be much better if both of you came back later, frankly, I'm not running a hotel, you know. We can't have people walking in and out of the ward as though it was Piccadilly Circus.' She had a way of sniffing in between each sentence which made Pamela want to laugh, but Tom didn't seem amused. Giving him a chilly look, the Sister went back into the ward and he scowled after her.

'I can't hang around here all day. They run these places for their own convenience. They don't seem to realise other people have to work.' He looked at his watch. 'I've got a meeting before lunch, I'll have to go. Will you tell Clare I'll be in to see her this evening?'

'Oh, sure,' Pamela said with sarcasm.

He turned his scowl on her, his eyebrows bristling. 'Look, I'm as concerned about Clare as you are.'

'Funny way of showing it,' Pamela muttered.

'I was knocked sideways when the police told me,' he said defensively. 'If I could get my hands on the swine – they'd better get him, that's all, but it seems to me they're

61

buggaring about, wasting time asking me stupid bloody questions. Why take my clothes away? Why would I rape my own girl?'

Pamela just sat there watching him. He looked at her for sympathy, his lower lip stuck out, but he didn't get anything but a direct, cool stare and his flush deepened hectically.

'I'd wait if I thought it would do any good, but she's in the best place, she'll feel more like talking to me later.' He looked at his watch again. 'I wonder if I'll get a taxi?' He turned to walk off. Pamela watched him with dislike and did not notice Joe's approach until he dropped into the chair next to her.

'Why the scowl?' he asked as her head swung in surprise.

'Men,' Pamela said, bristling, and he laughed. His laughter could have made her angrier, but it didn't. His eyes smiled as he looked at her, in a way quite different to the way he had always smiled in the past, with that wry, mocking little twist of the mouth. There was gentleness and warmth and sympathy in his eyes and she felt herself softening in the reassurance of that look, her body slackening from the bitter tension which had locked her muscles as she listened to Tom's self-obsessed whining.

'I'm very sorry about your friend,' he said, turning towards her with a twist of his body which had a strange effect on her. He put his elbow on the back of his chair and propped his chin on his hand, his gaze steady. 'I asked Sister Mack about her. I hope you don't mind, I was curious and I thought it would be easier for you if I knew without having to be told by you.'

Pamela nodded and gave a long sigh. 'I'm worried about her. If you'd seen her last night, when I found her – I thought for a minute she was dead. If you'd seen her . . .'

'I did,' he said gently.

She looked at him, eyes opening wider. 'You did? I thought you were off duty last night?'

'I was on call,' he said with a grin and a shrug. 'I had to come in to see a patient and I was in the ward when your friend was brought in. Of course, I had no idea she was your flatmate until I asked Sister Mack whom you were waiting to see. Did you find her when you got back from the party?'

She stared at him blankly – she had forgotten the party, all that had happened, and her face revealed as much. He watched her, one eyebrow curling up in wry understanding.

'Yes,' she said in a slow, quiet voice. So much had happened so fast. She had jammed all that into the very back of her mind while she coped with the events of the night, saying to herself: I'll think about that some other time, but now she flushed, right up to her hairline, as his carefully delivered insult came back to her.

He grimaced. 'Look, I'm sorry I shot my mouth off like that – I had no business talking to you in that way, put it down to one drink too many.'

Pamela saw the escape route he was offering her, the exit from her embarrassment and wounded pride, and was grateful. She was under no illusion – he had meant what he said and she could see that her own behaviour had laid her open to being insulted, however little right he had to do so, but the burglary and the vicious rape of Clare had altered the way she was seeing everything at the moment. She was glad of a chance to push what he had said aside, forget he ever said it.

'That's okay,' she said, shrugging. 'I wasn't exactly stone cold sober myself.'

'Parties bring out the worst in me,' Joe said and grinned at her. 'Three whiskies and I'm ready to fight anyone in the place.'

'I'll remember that.'

'I had quite a head when I was bleeped – I had to take two strong black coffees and a half-pint of water before I was up to going on the ward. Drinking and working don't mix.'

'A half-pint of water?' she repeated, frowning, and he smiled at her.

'Don't you know that cure? If you're a few degrees under, it helps to flush the alcohol out of your system if you drink as much water as you can manage – nothing sobers you up faster. Taken with some coffee it wakes you up fast, too.' He shot a look down the corridor as a little group approached. 'Oh, here he comes – the great man himself.' He stood up. 'When he's done his round you can see your friend.'

He briefly touched her arm and walked away to fall in with the white-coated young men following behind a small, wiry man with thinning grey hair and neat, rimless spectacles whose mouth had a compressed, faintly dyspeptic control. Pamela felt the dart of eyes behind those spectacles, then the group had passed through the ward doors and the corridor was empty.

She saw Clare twenty minutes later. It was a shock to Pamela all over again to see the bruising on her friend's face, the puffiness of her eyes giving her a Chinese look which made her barely recognisable.

Pamela sat down on the wooden chair. It creaked and Clare looked sideways, turning her head on the snowy white pillows quickly, with unhidden alarm.

'Hi!' Pamela said far too cheerfully, her voice sounded very loud in the silence around the bed.

'Hallo, Pamela.' Clare's hands lay flat on the bed, bloodless and still. They looked so cold, Pamela thought, and wanted to touch them, rub them until blood flowed back into them. She didn't like to touch Clare though; she felt with a stab of intuition that Clare would shrink if she did.

'How are you?' she asked, keeping up the bright tone, even as she wanted to kick herself.

'Okay.' Clare's lips moved reluctantly. To her they felt enormous and clumsy. She wished Pamela hadn't come. She did not want people looking at her like this. That was why she refused to let the nurse pull back the curtains. She wished Pamela would go away so that she could sink back into her empty, silent hibernation.

'Is there anything I can get you? Magazines, books?'

Clare shook her head. 'No, thanks, I'm okay.'

'Tom came along just now but they wouldn't let him see you so he's coming back tonight.'

Clare stared at the curtains and didn't answer. Pamela heard a trolley being wheeled past, the rubber wheels squeaking on the floor.

'How about some fruit?' she asked. Clare shook her head without looking at Pamela, who felt she had to go on talking, although what did you say, what could you say? 'I'll get in touch with your firm and let them know you'll be off sick for a while.'

'Don't tell them . . .' Clare broke out then the words were choked off and she sighed deeply. The police would have been in touch with her boss, no doubt, already, and even if they hadn't, it would have to come out sooner or later. She loathed the idea of everyone at the firm knowing but she couldn't stop them finding out. She closed her eyes, rejecting further thought. She lay so still, imitating sleep, that Pamela dared not speak to her again and just sat there, watching her in silence, feeling pity and anger forming on herself like brittle, brilliant scales, a new outer skin. For as long as she could remember Pamela had avoided feeling anything for anyone, she had lived alone inside herself, a cat walking by night on cold rooftops under a white moon. She knew her life had been altered dramatically last night. Her mind was charged with new ideas, her heart with new feelings but she wasn't ready to face up to them just yet. For the moment she was as much in retreat as Clare herself, sitting quietly by her bed and watching her while she mimed sleep.

CHAPTER FOUR

Clare heard the footsteps the minute the ward door was flung open and she knew who it was. She would never mistake that walk. Only one man in the world walked like that, charging at full speed into every second of the day, looking neither to left nor to right, but going like a bullet from a gun with his eyes fixed on a future nobody else could ever see.

She had been lying with closed eyes, locked away in that safe place where nothing could reach her, but as she realised who was coming, her eyes flew open and she was looking at the curtains as they were thrust back and he came through them. His arms were full of flowers. They spilled extravagantly in all directions as though they grew on him: fat pink roses with dusty golden hearts, shamelessly sensual, frilly white carnations, delphiniums whose blue was shadowy and smoky, like the dark images of leaves flickering in a sunlit wood, like the colour of a blackbird's wing as it flies in sunshine, rusty-pink hollyhocks with long, thick stems, feathery grass and purple iris, cool, fleshy wax-leaved lilies with the curling yellow tongues of their stamens like snakes. She did not look at his face, she looked at the abundance of flowers in amazement. He stood by the bed and heaped them on her, opened his arms and let them all tumble so that she was buried in beauty, her eyes peering out over the top, squinting down at the flowers.

He perched on the side of the bed casually and pulled a thin cheroot out of his denim jacket.

'You can't smoke in here!' Clare said and he gazed at her as he put the end of it in his mouth and struck a match.

'Like the flowers?'

'They're beautiful,' she said, her arms folding around them as if she thought he might be going to take them back. Fragrance rose up from their hearts, drifted around her nostrils; sweet, poignant, earthy, and in the shaft of light coming down from the window behind her, she saw hundreds of tiny golden particles of dust flying and floating as though the pollen was trying to penetrate the impervious glass and escape.

She looked back at him as he blew pale blue smoke up into the air. 'Larry, if Sister sees you . . .'

'What will she do? Smack me?' He grinned, his strong mouth curling back from his teeth.

'Anarchist,' Clare said wearily. It was an old office joke. The first day he arrived back from New York, he had come into the building in a black leather jacket and worn old jeans having arrived on a large, noisy motorbike, shocking the porter who had opened the door for him. 'He looks like an anarchist,' people had said. It was an image he did not reject. 'I'm here to put a bomb under this place,' he had agreed, and proceeded to do just that.

Looking at him, coolly sitting on the side of the bed blowing neat little smoke rings, Clare felt even more tired and even more like crying.

'You've got pollen on your nose,' he told her and she remembered what she looked like, her features battered into distortion and ugliness, and jerked the flowers up to hide her face.

'Don't look at me!' The words were hoarse, the rose petals brushed softly against her skin and she shut her eyes.

'I already have,' he pointed out without any inflection of any kind. 'I've seen worse – I once saw someone go through a windscreen, now that was much worse.'

'Are you trying to cheer me up?' Clare asked from behind the flowers, torn between hysteria and disbelief.

'No,' he said, sounding surprised.

They heard someone sniffing loudly, then the curtain was yanked aside and Sister stood there, an avenging angel in starched white, quivering incredulously.

'No smoking! No smoking is allowed on the wards! Please put that out at once!'

Larry regarded her curiously, his cheroot held between long, thin, powerful fingers.

'And kindly get off that bed! Really! Visitors are not allowed to sit on the patients' beds. Heavens, what do you think this is? Liberty Hall?'

Larry descended gracefully and without haste. He held his cheroot behind his back with one hand while he kissed the fingertips of his other hand and placed them briefly against Clare's forehead.

'See you,' he said and strode past Sister's agitated figure without a glance.

'Well,' Sister said, glaring at Clare as though she was responsible for him. 'Well, really!' Her eyes rounded as she took in the spilled flower garden behind which Clare was sheltering. 'Whatever next? Miss Forrester, what do you think you're doing with those flowers? You should have called Nurse to take them away. We can't have flowers all over the beds, heaven only knows what insects they may have in them, you'll be eaten alive by ants. We'll have to change the sheets, how very thoughtless.' She turned and called piercingly: 'Nurse Lunt! Nurse!'

The young, plump nurse panted into view, her starched apron top heaving over her full bosom. 'Yes, Sister.'

'Remove these at once,' Sister said and left in affront.

Nurse Lunt goggled. 'Good lord,' she said, looking help-lessly at the bed. 'You look like a funeral,' she said and then stood with her mouth open, her expression aghast.

Clare started to laugh in raw, painful gulps and couldn't stop. Nurse Lunt looked even more distressed and bent over her, saying: 'Ssh . . . ssh . . . Sister will hear you,' which only made Clare laugh more.

'You mustn't get hysterical,' Nurse Lunt whispered. 'Or Sister will slap your face – she wouldn't think twice, believe me.'

'Oh, I do,' Clare said, choking back her laughter. 'Sorry,' she said when she had finally stopped and had her breath intact.

Nurse Lunt started picking up flowers from the bed one by one, exclaiming over them. 'Someone's extravagant – your boyfriend, is it? Was that him went out just now? I call that sexy, he's just my type, the lean and hungry ones turn me on. I like a man who looks as if he might eat you alive.'

Clare looked at her with silent amusement. There was a lot of Nurse Lunt to nibble on, she thought, a meal fit for a king, in fact. Then she wondered if Larry's amazing appearance had left her a little light-headed because she felt a euphoric bubble forcing itself against her throat and had to swallow in case she started giggling again.

'Just look at these roses,' Nurse Lunt said dreamily, holding one out to her. 'They've got more perfume than Chanel – I wish I knew a man who'd bring me hundreds of flowers, all I ever get is a box of after dinner mints.'

'He's my boss, not my boyfriend,' Clare said.

Nurse Lunt looked disappointed. 'Oh, is that why he didn't stop long? I thought Sister had sent him out with a flea in his ear.'

'The lady who could do that to Larry Hillier has yet to be born,' Clare said. Larry had walked in and walked out again almost at once but her mood since his visit had been nervously high, she felt hot and excited. She must have looked it, too, because the nurse kept giving her a secret, assessing look.

In the evening Tom arrived, rather red, carrying a discreet bouquet of carnations. He didn't look at her as he pushed them into her hands, his eyes went everywhere but never met her own. He bent and kissed her cheek and Clare tried not to show the leap of tension with which she met his sudden closeness.

'How are you?' he muttered, sitting down on the chair next to the bed. Tom was embarrassed and uneasy, a man faced with something he did not know how to handle.

'Okay,' she said. The carnations were so perfect that they looked unreal, like flowers made out of crinkly-edged paper, their pink colour lifeless, their petals breathing no scent.

'Well, that's good,' Tom said too heartily, then he shifted, the chair creaking. 'The bastard, I'd like to . . .'

'Don't,' she said, shrinking from the violence in his voice. The raw male energy appalled her; from under her lowered lids she saw his hands curled into bony fists on his knees, striking them silently in furious frustrated desire to hit out.

He moved, turned his head away, she heard him breathing like a dog on a cold morning, struggling to get hold of himself. Suddenly he said: 'Good lord, who brought you all those?'

She looked sideways at the vases of flowers. 'Larry, Larry Hillier.'

'What did he do? Buy a flower shop?' Tom asked with a trace of sulky resentment.

'Beautiful, aren't they?'

'He's always been a bit of an exhibitionist,' Tom said and she felt him looking at his own flowers and lifted them to her face, inhaling.

'Yours are lovely, I love them.' The scentless carnations bristled on her cheek as if they had been cut out of foil, their edges stiff.

Tom talked about how busy he had been all day and how ghastly the traffic was on the way to the hospital. He had a headache, he said, all those petrol fumes, London was slowly poisoning itself with lead, and paying through the nose for the privilege.

'Have you eaten yet?' she asked and he said he would have a late supper somewhere on the way home, grab a hamburger or some kebabs.

He had talked non-stop but she knew he hadn't looked at her once. He avoided her face and let his glance slide in every other direction. She felt him fighting not to look at his watch, the flow of talk slowed now and then, and he would cough or move his feet. When the bell went, he would almost rush out.

'I'm tired, Tom,' she said. 'I'm sorry, but . . .'

'You want me to go?' He was on his feet, a sigh escaping, relief, guilt in his voice. 'I understand, it's been a terrible experience, poor Clare.' He bent towards her and she drew back involuntarily. Tom straightened without kissing her. 'Look after yourself, I'll come again tomorrow, anything I can bring you?'

'No,' she said. 'I'd rather you didn't come, I'll be home soon. I'll see you then, hospital visiting is so . . .'

'Well, if you're sure that's what you want?' He hovered uneasily. 'Well, take care, darling, give me a ring when . . .'

When he had gone she lay and listened to the unseen presences on the other side of her curtain; the coughs and shuffling, the murmurs and sighs of visitors. It was unvarying, a daily routine, the relentless cleansing and tidying of the ward before Sister opened the double doors and let the waiting relatives and friends walk in, their footsteps oddly laggard, uneasy. They brought with them flowers and fruit and embarrassment. The patients waited with an eye on the clock and when their visitors arrived, neither had anything to say, the conversation spurted and paused. They all watched the clock and waited grimly for a release from the boredom of it all.

Clare had not wanted Tom to visit her, she had not wanted Larry, or even Pamela. She felt like one of the untouchables of India, marked on the forehead, set apart. She did not want to talk about what had happened, it was bad enough talking to the police, at least their questions had a calm, official neutral ring to them. They sat there politely indifferent and wrote down what she said – they did not look at her as if searching for visible symptoms of what had happened.

Tom's sliding, sideways glances had told her how he felt about it. He made her feel guilty, as though she had invited the rape. He made her feel responsible for it all. She could pick up his resentment from his voice – she had involved him in this unpleasantness and Tom did not like ugly things, he didn't want any mud sticking to him. He dimly felt Clare had had no business getting herself raped, couldn't she have been more careful?

Her gaze moved to the rioting beauty of Larry's flowers and she wondered why he had come for so brief a visit? Curiosity?

Pamela dropped in at the hospital towards the end of visiting time with a small suitcase packed with Clare's nighties, make-up and a few other odds and ends which had occurred to her.

'I think she's asleep,' Sister said, taking the case. 'She's had a bad day, I don't think we should disturb her now.'

71

'I'll come tomorrow,' Pamela said. 'I just thought it might make her feel better to have her own things around her.'

'That was very thoughtful,' Sister approved, reminding Pamela of a schoolteacher who used to nod just like that when she was giving out marks for good conduct. It made Pamela feel suddenly much younger, she wondered if she should give the curtsey she had been taught to give at prize-giving.

As she walked back to the hospital gates she heard someone running behind her. 'Hang on!' a voice called and she turned in startled surprise to find Joe Harper panting up to her.

'Oh, hallo.' The sight of him made her nervous, his kindness in the hospital had overlaid the impression made by his blunt remarks at the party, and she no longer knew exactly how she felt about him.

'Been visiting your friend? How is she?'

'Asleep, I didn't see her, I just brought some things.'

'How are you getting back? Got a car?'

Pamela shook her head.

'I'm just going off duty, can I give you a lift?' Joe asked.

'That's very kind, thank you.'

'Car park over there,' he said, turning to the left and she followed him to where a large sign stated that only members of staff could park in that area. Joe's car was wedged in between two others, it took him some time to negotiate his way out. Pamela sat wearily in the seat beside him, her head drooping.

'You need a good night's sleep,' Joe said as he drove out of the hospital gates, getting a friendly wave from the porter on duty.

She shuddered. 'First I have to do something about the state of my bedroom.' Her voice held sick distaste and she felt him shoot her a quick look.

'Like that, is it?'

'Before he got to work on Clare, he wrecked the flat.'

'Isn't there somewhere you could spend the night? A friend? You should have booked in at a hotel or something.'

'I have to face it sometime.' Pamela was grimly determined to cope with the situation. She knew if she moved out now she might never move back in, she felt it would be cowardly to run away from what had happened; it would be allowing that bastard to defeat her.

She felt Joe watching her, but he said nothing and a moment later he pulled up outside the block of flats. Pamela looked out of the car window, swallowing.

'Like me to see you inside?' Joe was keeping his eyes on her profile, he saw the reluctance in her face.

'Would you? It's stupid but . . .'

'I understand, it isn't stupid, it's perfectly natural after what has happened. Anyone would be nervous.' He got out and Pamela opened her own door and shakily stood up. She found her key and walked across the pavement with Joe at her side. Her hand trembled as she put the key into the lock. The flat was dark, silent. Joe switched on the light and followed her inside the flat. Without a word he walked off and inspected every room. Pamela stood in the sitting room, listening. He came back a moment later, his face grave.

'You can relax, there isn't anyone here,' he said in a flat voice, then said: 'He certainly made a mess of this place, didn't he? Surprising your friend didn't hear what he was up to, surprising nobody seems to have heard anything.'

'This is London,' Pamela said with bitterness. 'Nobody ever hears or sees anything, or, if they do, they keep quiet about it.' Then she paused and said: 'I'm very grateful, you've been very kind.'

'Think nothing of it, will you be okay now?' He was poised to go and she did not want him to go; she was afraid of being alone here.

'I'm going to make some tea,' she said quickly. 'Will you have a cup?'

Joe visibly hesitated, his brows level and reluctant.

'Please,' Pamela said huskily, her face pleading. She didn't care what he thought of her, she only knew the flat was full of threatening shadows, she did not want to be left alone there yet.

Slowly, Joe said: 'Tea would be very welcome, thanks.' She quickly walked into the kitchen before he could change his mind, knowing that he had not wanted to stay.

When she went back with a tray of tea he had begun to clear the worst of the debris from the floor. The chairs had been turned right way up, he had filled the wastepaper basket with jagged pieces of record, piled the scattered books on to their shelves.

'Oh, you shouldn't have... there's no need for you to...' Pamela was taken aback, grateful, startled. Joe looked round at her, his hair flopping down like a spaniel's ears, making him look younger. Pamela's fingers itched to touch it, find out how it felt.

The phone rang and she jumped sky-high, going white. Panic surged through her, and Joe saw it, frowning.

'I'll answer it, shall I?' he suggested and when she didn't move or speak, walked over to the phone.

'Hallo?' Joe's voice sounded calm. Pamela listened, watching his profile, beaky, lamplight falling on the hard angle of his cheekbones and glazing his skin.

He turned, holding the phone out. 'It's Clare's mother.'

Pamela didn't move, staring. 'Clare's mother?'

Joe's face was gentle. 'I don't think she knows – she asked for Clare.'

'Oh,' Pamela said huskily.

'You'll have to tell her,' Joe said.

'What can I say?'

'Do you want me to do it?' His hand was poised, on the point of lifting the phone back to his mouth.

Pamela would have given anything to say: 'Yes, you do it,' but she met his quiet eyes and slowly moved towards him to take the phone. 'No, I will,' she said and he smiled at her.

She swallowed then said: 'Hallo, Mrs Forrester? This is Pamela.'

'Oh, hallo, dear, isn't Clare there?' Mrs Forrester sounded cheerful, and listening intently to her, Pamela realised Joe was right – Clare's mother hadn't been told what had happened.

'Well, no, Mrs Forrester, you see . . .'

'It doesn't matter, dear, nothing urgent. I just felt like a chat and I thought I might catch her in.'

'Mrs Forrester, I'm afraid I've got . . .'

'If I'm interrupting, dear, I'm sorry, tell Clare I rang and I'll ring back some other time.'

Pamela was afraid she was going to hang up. Rushing the words she said: 'Mrs Forrester, Clare's in hospital . . .'

'What?'

'It didn't occur to me that you hadn't been told or I'd have rung you.'

'Why is she in hospital? What's wrong?'

'Well . . .' Pamela tried to think of the best way to break it to her. She barely knew Clare's mother. They had only met a couple of times, very briefly. Pamela didn't think she would even recognise her if she passed her in the street. She had a vague image of someone in her early fifties with grey hair and a matronly figure.

'She hasn't been in an accident?' Mrs Forrester sounded alarmed and anxious and Pamela hurried to reassure her.

'Not exactly, don't worry, she's going to be okay, there's nothing to worry about. It's just that . . . last night we had . . . there was a burglary here, you see.'

'A burglary?' The question came sharply and Pamela could have kicked herself for the way she was handling this, she was making an unholy mess of it.

'I was at a party, Clare was here alone,' she said and heard the intake of breath at the other end of the line.

'What happened?' Mrs Forrester asked in a shaky voice.

'Clare . . . was attacked,' Pamela said unhappily.

'Oh, no . . .'

'I got back from my party to find the place turned upside down and Clare unconscious – but she isn't seriously hurt. I've talked to the doctor at the hospital, you mustn't worry.' Pamela was talking fast now, sensing that the woman at the other end of the phone was going to ask awkward questions if she allowed her to talk. 'They're only keeping her in hospital until the tests they ran on her have been examined. They said it was standard treatment for head injuries. She's had X-rays and there are no signs of damage to the skull. They're fairly sure she has nothing worse than a bump and a bad headache. But better safe than sorry, it won't hurt to keep her in for another day or so.' She had to stop at last, feeling Mrs Forrester dying to get a word in.

'Have you seen her today?' was all Clare's mother asked, though.

'Yes,' Pamela said heartily. 'And she's going to be okay, she was sitting up drinking tea.' May I be forgiven, she thought, aware of Joe watching her.

'I've told her until I'm blue in the face to keep the chain on the door,' Mrs Forrester said. 'How did he get in?'

'The window,' Pamela said.

'She didn't have it open?'

'It was so hot last night . . .'

'Oh,' Mrs Forrester breathed, speechless. After a moment she asked if anything had been stolen and Pamela with a sigh of relief told her about the stereo and the TV, dwelling on the destruction of the flat to avoid further questions about Clare, but in vain, since Mrs Forrester kept dropping in a difficult question about whether Clare had seen the man or if all that was wrong with her was a bump on the head. The more Pamela tried to avoid answering the more searching became the questions.

Beattie Forrester put down the phone and heard the click of it in the quiet little hall, jumping as though she had not expected it. Her husband was at a golf club committee meeting, she was alone in the house. She stood looking up at the darkened stairs, hearing the silence of the whole house beating around her in a menacing way, like the wings of a predatory bird, and groped her way along the wall hurriedly to switch on the light on the landing.

The news about Clare had left her trembling. She knew there was something Pamela wasn't telling her, she had picked it up – was Clare more seriously injured than Pamela wanted to admit?

She went back to the phone and picked it up again. She

rang the hospital and was put through to the ward sister who was calm and reassuring and uninformative. Yes, Miss Forrester was doing very well, she was asleep at the moment, there were no problems.

Beattie replaced the phone, her eyes moving around in search of familiarity, the reassurance of having her own home around her. Her heart was too big for her thin chest, it pulsed and throbbed against her ribs. Clare was her only child, her only living child. Her brow tightened at the word living – what did life mean, anyway? When someone died did they stop existing, how could they when you had them inside yourself, you thought of them and saw them in your mind's eye every day? Wasn't that life? You could keep them alive, like one of these new machines which replace a defective organ, a kidney or a heart, taking on the functions of it to keep the patient alive. So long as you refused to let someone die, they lived, she had told herself.

She walked past the grandfather clock, ticking sonorously at the foot of the stairs, the gleam of the polished brass face catching her eye. It had belonged to her father and, when he died, had been the only one of his possessions Derek would agree to let her keep – the rest had been sold in auction. Beattie had hated that, sitting in the shabby grimy auction rooms, hearing people's footsteps on the bare, dirty floorboards. Her father's belongings had looked so pathetic, so old and worn and sad, abandoned, tied up with string in untidy bundles or heaped together in wooden boxes with black numbers stuck to the sides. She remembered so many of them from childhood. They had been the bricks of her home, the surrounding, familiar objects she used and saw each day. People were like marine creatures which build themselves a shell with hundreds of tiny fragments, each nothing separately, yet together amounting to armour, a sanctuary, a disguise, which can resist the crushing pressures of the world outside, the vast, the incalculable ocean.

Beattie had wandered around before the sale began, in a floating tide of faces, bored, greedy, curious, scornful, all of them seeming to her hostile. She had hated them as they pored over her father's discarded shell.

In one box lay an orange tea-set her mother had once used all the time. Mary Ricci had loved bright colours, the gaudier the better. Set down in grey, smoky London after a childhood in the country, she had married an Italian whose very name seemed to conjure up the dazzling sunshine and bursting, shameless life of Italy.

Mary, herself, had been slow-speaking, warm and gentle. Her husband Salvatore had been short and broad and dark, explosively emotional, a family man, adoring children and always secretly sad that his Mary could have no more after Beatrice was born. Their house was full of love and colour and noise. People filled it, they loved to visit the Ricci family. Mary cooked huge, cheap filling meals of pasta and rich meaty sauces and Sal talked and laughed with little Beattie on his knee, his arm around her.

When Beattie was twelve, her mother surprised and alarmed her doctor by becoming pregnant again. Sal was overjoyed, he was a man who believed, a man of faith. He had lit candles to the Virgin Mary for twelve years for this and he was certain Mary would have this baby safely, it was a gift from the hand of God and what could go wrong? Doctors were pessimists, they expected the worst. Sal redoubled his prayers and had candles burning in the church day and night, he knew where to go for the help Mary might need.

'It will be a boy and we shall call him Nino,' he told Mary as she knitted little white garments and she smiled at him, her face radiant. Beattie had watched them and felt her heart hurting although why it should tighten inside her she didn't know. She believed, too, Mamma was going to be fine, Papa said so and Papa was always right.

Mary gave birth on a stormy November night when the wind made the branches of the plane tree outside the house rattle and squeak like creaking bones. The baby was beautiful, a girl with perfectly formed features and fine dark hair. Sal carried her in his arms to show Beattie while she was still asleep in bed. She woke up to find her father bending over her, his eyes wet, his smile excited, holding out the blanket-swaddled child. He had lapsed back into Italian, the words tumbling out.

They called her Donna because she had been given, she was God's gift. Nothing had gone wrong during the birth, Mary was sleeping peacefully and the baby was perfect.

Mary died a week later of puerperal fever and the joy went out of Sal Ricci. He aged overnight; moved slowly, spoke slowly, stopped going to the church. He turned his back on everything. He sat alone in his room at night and drank. The withdrawal lasted for a year and during those long months, it was Beattie who was left to care for the baby. She had help and advice from her mother's friends but it was Beattie who fed and bathed and looked after Donna. She left school when she was fourteen and ran her father's house. Sal emerged a little bit by bit from his grief but he was never the same man again. He took up old habits but without caring, he went through the outward motions of life but within him his spirit permanently mourned and it showed in his black eyes; they were lightless.

Beattie had aged as much, from being a happy, secure little girl she became overnight a woman with a baby to look after, a house to run. It wasn't until Donna was sixteen that Beattie allowed herself to think of men and, having realised that her thirtieth year had begun and she was unmarried and might now never have a chance to marry, she looked around her with a sudden sense of having been cheated by life. Within three months she had met Derek Forrester by accident in a dentist's waiting room, where they fell into talk largely because they were each so nervous, and had married him simply because he was the first man to ask her. It was then that she discovered inside herself some of her father's fire and possessive instincts. Derek was a very attractive man; he had never married because he liked women too much, he flirted and flitted on to the next, like a bee fumbling in and out of flowers. He wouldn't have thought of marrying Beattie if she had not thought of it for him, and if Derek, too, had not been recently aware of having waited too long to marry. Beattie was not beautiful, like Donna; she was sensually unawakened; her firm, rounded, healthy body had been uninitiated into the delight of sexual fulfilment and Derek sensed a stored pleasure which he could release. The first year of the marriage had been happy. Beattie rushed into sex like a parched woman released from a desert running into a pool of delicious, clear water. She found out so much about herself; tactile sensitivities engrossed her. She discovered her body with as much delight as Derek did. She enjoyed wearing pretty clothes, dancing, daring to walk around their bedroom in the nude while Derek watched.

Then she was pregnant, and she was frightened. She couldn't forget her mother's death. She lay awake at night and knew she was going to die, she was going to be torn away from the marvel and wonder of Derek's lovemaking, she was going to leave her newborn baby and vanish into the dark.

When she was alone, she cried all the time. She lost colour and weight, she couldn't eat. Derek was puzzled and their doctor was worried. 'Don't you want the baby?' he asked her and Beattie to her shame and horror heard herself saying: 'No, I don't want a baby, I don't want one.' She was aghast a second afterwards but it was out, it was said and she realised she meant it. The doctor prescribed some soothing anodyne; he diagnosed depression and said it was quite normal, it was common in pregnant women, she would get over it.

The baby was born and Beattie recovered rapidly but she found it hard to look at Clare. She was so ashamed of how she felt she couldn't even talk about it, she hid it from everyone but herself – and from Clare, whose blind blue eyes had looked up in puzzled reproach at the distance between them. Beattie might handle her capably, keep her beautifully clean and dressed in pretty baby clothes, she might feed her on the clock and take her along to the baby clinic to be weighed and admired, but the baby knew the hands which touched her held no loving warmth. Beattie did not talk to her all the time, as other mothers did, or pick her up even when she wasn't crying just for the pleasure of holding her close, feeling the soft little body against her heart.

When Clare was four, Beattie got pregnant again and

this time she wasn't frightened. She had been reassured by her easy first birth. She wanted another baby, to allay her own guilt about Clare, to feel the closeness she had always denied to Clare. She had something to expiate and she waited eagerly for the birth. The baby was a boy. She called him Ninian, but in private, Nino, and her heart almost burst as she held him in her arms.

Donna came to stay to look after Beattie and the new baby and little Clare, who adored her pretty young aunt, with her long flowing black hair and laughing black eyes. Donna was gay and spoilt and uninhibited, she made the house come alive. Derek laughed at everything she said. Clare sat on Donna's lap and sucked her thumb content-edly and wished her aunt need never go away. At night she dreamt of Donna and smiled in her sleep, nestling in the warm bed, but then the dream changed and she saw Donna walking away from her and began to cry. She sat bolt upright, sobbing, and the darkness was full of terrifying shadows. Clare slid out of bed and ran to the door. She padded along the landing in her bare feet and floor-length nightie, pushed open the door of Donna's room and the light fell across the carpet to the bed and showed her bodies jerking, pale flesh and hair.

She screamed and screamed, standing there. Her mother stumbled out of bed and ran out, her face startled from sleep. 'What is it?' she began and then she, too, looked across Donna's room and saw Derek and the girl. They were off the bed now. Donna had pulled on a robe and was white and staring. Derek was red. Beattie had put a hand on Clare's thin shoulder and pushed her back into her own room, put her into bed and gone out.

Derek had gone downstairs. Donna stood there, talking. Beattie didn't hear what she said. She stared at her mouth and a sort of spasm shook her. She screamed words she never heard, she ran at Donna with her hands curled, nails tearing the girl's face before Donna ducked past her and fled downstairs.

Beattie followed, shaking with rage and shock, moving stiffly because it was only a few days after the birth; her body still ached, and every time she took a step she felt a pull of pain between her thighs.

Derek was in the kitchen making tea. Beattie stared at him with hatred and he looked at her, shamefaced. 'It didn't mean anything, Beattie,' he said. 'A bit of fun, that's all.' Donna was sheltering behind him. Beattie saw her pale face over his shoulder and thought of her dead mother who had given her life for Donna, Beattie had given sixteen years of her life too: she had sacrificed herself and now she was almost forty years old. Soon she would be engulfed in middle age and the years of youth had been eaten up by this girl who stood there all big, dark eyes, having greedily snatched Beattie's man when she did not even really want him. It was nothing, it meant nothing, it was just a bit of fun.

Beattie picked up a carving knife and threw it at Donna with a force which sent it whistling so closely past the girl's head it almost took off the tip of her earlobe.

Donna screeched and shrank, babbling: 'Oh, God, she's mad, she's crazy, Derek, don't let her kill me.'

'You bitch, you selfish little bitch,' Beattie said hoarsely. 'I'll kill you, I swear I'll kill you . . .'

'Now, Beattie,' Derek said, watching her nervously as he began to advance. 'You mustn't get so excited, it will be bad for the baby.'

'I'll kill her, the bitch.' She put her hands up to keep him off. 'Don't you touch me, don't you ever touch me again. Get her out of my house now, tonight, I never want to see her again. If I do, I'll kill her, I'll kill both of you.'

She had been afraid to stay there in case she did kill them. She had felt as if she was on fire: her bones, her flesh, her hair shrinking from the heat generated by her passion. She had backed, stiff-legged, shaking, out of the door, her eyes staring at them through a red mist which she had thought she imagined until later, in her bedroom, looking in the mirror, she saw the bloodflecks on her iris. The doctor said next day she had slightly ruptured blood vessels behind the eyes.

Donna was gone in the morning. Clare did not mention her name again; she never came to the house and if Beattie thought she might meet her, she stayed away from the Ricci home. Even at their father's funeral the two sisters did not speak. Donna was there with her husband and two sons. She had become a ripe, sultry woman with a way of walking which turned men's heads, even in deep mourning. She hesitated, looking at Beattie, half-pleading, half-defiant, and Beattie looked straight through her as if she wasn't there. Clare, at seventeen slightly gawky, coltish, had avoided her aunt, too. Beattie had never mentioned that night to Clare yet she realised Clare remembered what had happened as she saw her daughter moving clear of Donna, her face averted.

Beattie had not allowed Derek back into her bed. They had lived together in that house ever since, polite strangers. She ran his home, she cooked his meals, she ironed his shirts and only spoke to him when she had to – from that night all the explosive feeling of her Italian parentage had been locked away behind a wall of ice.

For a year afterwards she had poured all her love into the baby, little dark-eyed plump Nino, with his soft warm arms and chuckle, his pleasurable delight in her cuddles and the sensual comfort of her full, white breasts. She fed him long after he should have been weaned. He thrived on it, both of them enjoyed a private world where they were alone; Beattie soaping his wriggling body and letting warm water trickle down over him, making him laugh with the surprise and marvel of it, drying him on her lap in a huge fluffy towel, playing games by hiding his face and then pulling the towel down and saying: 'Boo,' while Nino shook with laughter, his sweet-smelling flesh quivering like jelly. Dusted with talc, he would be crammed into his pyjamas and given warm milk to drink while she sang softly and rocked him.

One morning when she went into his nursery to pick him up and get him washed and dressed before breakfast, Nino lay still and cold. Beattie's heart stopped. She snatched him up, she said his name, she touched his face and felt the chill of his flesh like a nail through her hand. She would not believe what her brain told her. She ran to the telephone and called the doctor, clutching the baby, rubbing his back as if he had wind. Tears poured down her face. Demented, she tried to give him the kiss of life, she undid his jacket and tried to force air back into his lungs.

She had no memory after that. Derek spoke to her, Clare cried, the doctor came and tried to speak, tried to be heard. Beattie was too busy; she had to get Nino bathed and dressed, he would be hungry when he woke up.

When they tried to take the baby from her, she screamed like a mad woman. The doctor gave her an injection while she struggled and fought Derek's restraining hands. She slept for twelve hours and came out of it numb and dead and silent. She thought she would never smile again, never be happy. Her world had gone dark, but time worked a slow healing and in a few years she could think of Nino without feeling the tears burning at the back of her eyes, she could walk on a summer evening in the garden and listen to the piercing cry of a bird on the apple tree without agony. Her eyes could view beauty and her heart could lift in the surprise and delight of it while she wondered why it was that sudden beauty always causes that catch of the breath, that disbelief and joy.

The death of the baby did not soften her towards her husband. Derek had been as wrenched with grief as herself, even in her own misery she had known that. He had been pale and silent, his eyes had been raw with weeping, but the wall between them had held – Derek had gone out and got drunk a few times and then he had started spending all his time elsewhere. He had many friends in the neighbourhood. He was a popular man, attractive to women and a cheerful companion to men. He dressed well, was generous and lively, played golf and tennis and swam to keep fit. In the evenings while he was drinking and talking in the golf club bar, Beattie sat at home and watched television or read, and by the time he came home, she was asleep in bed.

They kept up an outward show in front of other people and since they never quarrelled even Clare was not aware of the depth of their division. As she began to grow up, she noticed more that her parents saw very little of each other, that they were oddly polite and distant when they spoke, as though her mother was the landlady, the housekeeper, rather than Derek Forrester's wife. During Clare's teens she and her mother began to quarrel inconsequentially, little flare-ups over trivial things which always came out of the blue. Clare was no longer a child, mutely obeying, unquestioning; she was exploring her own personal territory, herself, her newfound inner sense of being and she started to ask: why? when Beattie expected her to say: Yes, okay. From their arguments a delicate, nervous, prickly relationship had begun to grow as Beattie looked at this stranger who was her own flesh and blood through new eyes and abruptly, with shock, realised how many years she had spent ignoring Clare, feeding her and clothing her and housing her without knowing her.

Then Clare had left home and gone to London and the distance had opened up between them again. Beattie had stayed in the house with a man she almost never spoke to; shopping and cleaning and gardening and performing her daily functions as though that was all there was to life. She felt like a woman in a dark house who has herself shut every door, shuttered every window. She was alone because she had chosen to be so and she ached with the grievance of her own resentment. Derek seemed perfectly happy, no doubt he had a woman. Once she had caught sight of him talking to someone, driving past her in his car without noticing her walking along the pavement. Beattie had stared, feeling she was seeing a stranger; an attractive middle-aged man with a charming smile who looked happy. She had been so busy with the shock of looking at his face and realising all that, that she had not thought of looking at the woman who was sitting beside him. Her mind had merely registered the fact that it was a woman in the passenger seat, then the car had passed on, and she had walked automatically into the supermarket and gone around the shelves picking up tins of baked beans and packets of long grain rice and boxes of eggs while she was inwardly reeling with the shock of seeing that stranger who was yet so familiar to her, who was her husband. She had got so used to thinking about Derek only as she saw him in their home, separated from her by her resentment and his guilt. She had not seen him as a man for years, he was not a person to her at all. He was Derek, the cause of her empty life, the core of her brooding sense of having been betrayed. She had gone home that day feeling bewildered, conscious of some shift inside herself, the opening of a new angle of vision which puzzled her.

Now she was afraid and disturbed after the news of Clare. It was another shock, another breach in the wall which had separated her from life for so long. She went upstairs to bed, undressed and lay listening to the warm summer night, the air breathing like lovers' sighs in the trees. She couldn't get out of her head the suspicion that Pamela had omitted something when she described Clare's injuries. It was hard to put a finger on what had rung false. Beattie only knew that she had picked up something unspoken, and her anxiety about Clare spread through her, building up a new sense of guilt, a jabbing regret because she had let Clare drift so far from her without trying to hold on to her. Clare was her child, she wasn't a stranger, yet wasn't that what she had become? Beattie turned over heavily, with a sense of urgency, almost of desperation. She must see Clare, she must go to her tomorrow. For far too long her life had been filled with shadows, she was only now admitting to herself that life among shadows was cold and grey and empty.

CHAPTER FIVE

Clare woke up as the tea trolley crashed through the ward doors and lights snapped on overhead, making her blink. Where on earth? she thought for a second, totally disorientated, then she remembered and lay back against her tumbled pillows staring at the ceiling. They had given her sleeping pills the night before, her sleep had been deep and as far as she could remember, dreamless.

'Morning,' the night nurse said, coming over to take her pulse and push a thermometer under her tongue. 'How do you feel today? Sleep well, did you? Raining this morning, I hope our summer isn't over, I was counting on it lasting a bit longer than this.'

'Mmm,' Clare said around the thermometer.

'Tea, dear?' the nurse with the trolley asked, plonking a cup down on her bedside table.

The night nurse removing the thermometer asked casually: 'Want your curtains pulled back now?'

Clare looked at her calm, fresh-skinned face. She didn't look as though she had been awake all night. She looked as though she had just got back from a hike across windy moors; her skin blown into high colour, her eyes bright. As she dropped the thermometer into the plastic holder on the wall she smiled down at Clare encouragingly.

Clare suddenly felt like biting her, screeching at her. That sensible, smug face made her want to spit teeth. Who did she think she was? What business of hers was it if Clare preferred to keep her curtains drawn? Was there some law that said she had to put up with curious stares and insolent questions? She was so angry that she couldn't speak, trembling, and while she was trying to force out a reply, the nurse calmly started pulling back the curtains.

'No, I don't want . . .' Clare began and then stopped, finding herself suddenly exposed to the eyes of all the other patients, only their eyes seemed oblivious of her. Her own stare flashed around the ward. Women were lying in their beds, yawning, sipping tea with closed eyes, sliding out from between the covers to put on a dressing-gown and go to the bathroom, whispering hoarsely: 'Nurse, nurse, can I have a bedpan?' None of them were looking her way, none of them were interested in her.

The night nurse had gone on to the next bed. Clare picked up her cup of tea and drank it. Grey light seeped into the ward and she heard the sound of rain filling the gutters, gurgling and splashing.

Dr Harper came into the ward just as she was finishing her breakfast. He walked past her bed with the night sister and winked at her discreetly as he passed, to look at another patient. On his way back he paused.

'How was your breakfast?'

'I think I'll live.'

'Believe me, it's the best meal of the day!'

'Stop it, you're frightening me,' Clare said and he laughed.

'I drove Pamela home last night...'

'Pamela?' Clare interrupted, looking surprised.

'Didn't she tell you she knew me?' There was a wry amusement in his eyes. 'We have mutual acquaintances; I ran into her while she was waiting to see you yesterday.'

'I see,' Clare said drily, wondering how intimately they knew each other and then dismissing the idea that Pamela might be interested in this quiet, bony young man. He had a very intelligent face; his smile was distinctly aware of what she was thinking, irony in the curl of his mouth.

'I gave her a lift and went in to check out your flat. Pamela was understandably nervous.'

Clare looked down, tensing, and he continued in a calm voice: 'While I was there, your mother rang. Pamela told her the flat had been burgled and you'd been attacked.' Clare looked up, very pale. 'She left it at that,' Joe added. 'She didn't go into details. Your mother said she would visit you today.'

'I'd rather not see her,' Clare said in a shaky voice. It took her quite an effort to sound as calm as that; she felt her eyes burning, tears pressing at the back of them, an irrational, confused rush of feeling welling up within her.

Joe showed no surprise, nor did he ask questions. He nodded, his hands pushed down into the pockets of his clean, stiffly laundered white linen coat.

'She's coming a long way,' he pointed out neutrally.

'I don't want to see anyone,' Clare said on a note which held the threat of hysteria. She couldn't face the thought of seeing her mother. She felt that Beattie would blame her for what had happened, be convinced that she had invited the rape. Her mother was rigidly puritanical about sex. Clare could imagine how she would look: thin-lipped, frowning, icily reproving. Her mother was encased in disapproval; she always had been for as long as Clare could remember. Clare had never dared ask Beattie anything about the facts of life, her mother's attitudes had made that impossible.

'It might help to talk to her,' Dr Harper said, watching her distressed face.

Clare shook her head, wishing the curtains were still drawn around her bed so that she could be alone and cry if she wanted to. How could she cry with all those strangers lying around, listening and watching? There was no privacy, you lived in public. She hated it here.

'When can I go home?' she asked. 'How much longer do I have to stay here?'

'That isn't my decision,' Joe Harper said. 'You'll have to wait and ask my boss. He does the hiring and firing.' He smiled at her coaxingly. 'Don't you like us? We're very nice once you get to know us. Even the food improves on acquaintance.'

He was humouring her, as if she was an idiot. Clare wouldn't smile back at him. She was thinking about her mother, about her father. She had just disinterred an image of bodies moving in the dark, spotlit briefly, with herself in the doorway, screaming. Had it happened? Or had she just imagined it? The memory had surfaced without warning from the dark waters of the past. Clare hadn't thought about it for years, but now she remembered how frightened she had been. Her mother had come, but Beattie had been angry, she had not comforted Clare. Bewildered, guilty, worried, Clare had been thrust back into her bedroom by her mother as though she had done something wrong. Huddling in her bed, she had lain listening to the angry shouting, half-believing that she had caused the violent quarrel between the parents.

'Would you like me to talk to your mother?' Joe asked, watching her with a gentleness that she hated. She did not want his sympathy or his watchfulness because of what caused them, she wasn't going to be pitied any more than she intended to be blamed. When she didn't answer he added: 'Somebody has to – after coming all that way, she has to have some explanation.'

'Do what you like,' Clare said in a hostile voice. 'Suit yourself, I don't care what you do. I won't see her, that's all.' She turned on to her side, her back to him, and closed her eyes, her head digging into the pillow.

She heard him walk away and opened her eyes slowly to find the woman in the next bed watching her. Clare stiffened, meeting the glossy blue eyes. One of them closed in a wink.

'You tell 'em,' the other woman said. 'I can't stand doctors, liars the lot of them.' She was a very pretty woman in her late twenties with a lot of coppery hair and enormous eyes which dominated her thin face, the iris permanently shiny as though covered by a film of water.

Clare didn't answer but neither did she turn away and the woman started to talk about the operations she had had during the past eight years. She looked frail, her skin very pale and fine, and if her recital was anywhere near the truth, it was amazing she was alive at all, she must have an indelible desire to live.

'Most of me's not me own,' she said. 'One of these days I'll look in a mirror and I won't know meself at all.'

'What beautiful eyes you've got,' Clare said. It was the only thing she could think of to say, her mind was dazed by what she had been told although it had all been narrated in a gossipy, cheerful way which made it sound as normal as buying tea in a supermarket.

'They 'aven't got round to me eyes yet,' the other said, laughing, with her mouth wide open and her false teeth demonstrated in all their National Health glory.

Pamela had just got up when the phone went. She stifled a yawn as she answered. 'Hallo?'

'Don't tell me you're still in bed?' Joe's voice teased.

She came wide awake. 'Oh, hello.' She had dreamt about him last night. It was the first time in her life that she could remember dreaming about anyone and she felt herself blushing like a schoolgirl. She was both alarmed and incredulous. Pamela had not so much outgrown the blushing stage as never entered it – she had been a cynical, worldly wise teenager with a permanent, scornful smile, watching the idiocy of the adults around her from a distance, clothed in superiority and contempt. What on earth is wrong with me? she asked herself as she caught the sound of her own breathless voice and could have kicked herself for behaving like this.

'Sleep well?' he asked and there was a smile in his voice, a soft intimacy in the question which made her feel like someone in a lift which abruptly drops several floors at great speed. Her stomach plunged and her fingers tightened around the phone.

'Fine,' she managed to say with a pretence of cool amusement she hoped sounded convincing.

'No bad dreams?' he asked.

'Not that I remember.' The thought of the dream she did remember made her voice curt.

Joe had stayed until eleven, working hard. Pamela had been amazed to see how good he was at housework, how deft and rapid in everything he did. He had even managed to clean all the dirty words off the walls, scraping with a kitchen knife and scrubbing with a nail brush, only pausing once to say: 'Limited vocabulary he had,' grinning at her and somehow taking some of the nasty taste out of her mouth because if you could laugh at it, even briefly, it made it seem less threatening.

When they stopped work, they had some cocoa. Joe

91

made that, too. Pamela looked at it with a grimace.

'I haven't drunk cocoa for years – Clare keeps it for Tom, I think.' She stirred the thick mixture with a spoon, nose wrinkling. It looked like melted face pack.

'Drink it, it will help you sleep,' Joe said. 'Will you be okay here or would you like me to sleep on the couch tonight?'

Pamela had looked at him through her lashes, involuntarily raising her eyebrows. He couldn't mean that. 'Why sleep on the couch when there's a bed available?'

'Clare might not like me to use her room,' he said calmly.

'Who said anything about Clare's bed?'

He just looked at her, levelly, and suddenly pink was pouring up her face and she got up and said: 'I was joking, I'll be okay, there's no need to stay. I've got over my attack of the jitters now the flat's looking almost normal.'

Cool as a cucumber, he had left, giving her his phone number and saying: 'If you do get worried, ring me. I'm used to emergency calls, so remember, it won't bother me.'

She would have died sooner than yell for help to him. She was furious with herself. Twice she'd made a heavy pass at him and he had turned her down – what was she? A masochist? She had to be a glutton for punishment to make the same stupid mistake twice in so short a time, but when he offered to stay the night she had thought . . . but she should have known better. Joe Harper meant what he said, no more, no less. He had offered to sleep on the couch in case she found it hard to go to sleep alone in the flat, he hadn't been making an oblique advance.

She had gone to bed so angry with herself that she hadn't been thinking about the fears which had disturbed her earlier. She hadn't had the energy to spare for fear – she was too busy fuming and fretting herself to sleep.

Now he told her: 'I've been talking to Clare, she refuses to see her mother. Don't they get on?'

Puzzled, Pamela said: 'As far as I know, but we've never really talked about her family. Clare isn't one for confidences. She keeps her private life very private. I've met her mother a couple of times, so they aren't having a feud.'

'Maybe Clare's afraid of her mother's reaction to the news about the rape.'

'Yes,' Pamela said. 'That I believe.'

'I'll see Mrs Forrester when she arrives, put her in the picture, but if Clare doesn't want to see her, we can't do much about it. Clare's an adult. But it would be a good idea for her to stay in London in case Clare changes her mind. Could you put her up at the flat?'

'Of course,' Pamela said. 'She can have Clare's room – if she doesn't mind sleeping in it.'

Joe hesitated. 'You could swap rooms,' he said without any intonation in his voice at all.

Pamela felt a cold trickle down her spine. She half-sighed. 'Okay,' she said and heard him laugh so softly she almost felt she had imagined it. All right for him, he wasn't being asked to do it!

'It won't be so bad,' he said. 'Her room is immaculate, just don't think about what happened there.' He paused briefly. 'I'll talk to Clare again later today – it will make it much easier for her to come home if she knows you've been using her room.'

Pamela made a ferocious face at the telephone in her hand, then said to him bitterly: 'As you say, Dr Freud. Anything else you'd like me to do while we're at it?'

'I'll take a rain check on that offer,' he said and hung up. She hung up herself slowly. What had he meant by that?

Beattie Forrester sat in the small office with her untouched cup of strong, hospital tea in front of her and stared at the thin young man in the white coat.

'Oh, my God,' she said for the third time, her eyes half closing as though to shut out the realisation of what he had told her. 'Oh, my God.'

The young doctor leaned over the desk and pushed the cup closer.

'Drink your tea.'

While she sipped, her cup clattering in the saucer because her hands shook so much, he leaned back and studied the notice board behind her as if he had never seen it before. It flapped with pinned lists of duties and days off, fluttering whenever the door opened or shut.

'Why won't she see me?' she asked and he looked back at her.

'I thought you might tell me that.'

She looked blank. Joe Harper studied her, assessing the neat navy blue dress with the white piping around the throat and the hem, the white shoes, very sensible and well-made, the handbag which matched. Clare's mother was a woman well into middle age; hair grey, eyes dark and rather sad, the skin below them stretched into a web of thin fine lines, an indefinable feeling of remoteness about her which reminded him of Clare herself. There was little physical resemblance, only that tantalising similarity of expression, and he had seen too little of either of them to be sure he wasn't imagining it.

'Do you get on well?' he asked, and saw the way her eyes moved aside.

'We . . . haven't seen much of each other since she came to London to live. She's very busy, you know, she doesn't often come down to see us.'

'Have you any other children?'

Beattie shook her head and the sadness in her eyes intensified. Joe watched intently, wondering what caused that tremor around her mouth. Did she regret never having had any other children?

'How does she get on with her father?' he asked.

The woman looked blank. 'Well enough,' she said and he wondered: well enough for what?

'Are they close?' he pressed and she shrugged.

'I don't think you could say that.' She put down her cup of half-drunk tea. 'I don't think you could say Clare was close to either of us,' she added with honesty and her eyes suddenly filled with tears. 'It's all my fault,' she said and scrabbled in her handbag for a handkerchief. Joe got up and came round the desk. She was crying into her smoothly ironed white handkerchief like a child, her shoulders shaking. Joe patted her back, bending over her.

'Don't upset yourself, Mrs Forrester, of course it isn't your fault.'

She blew her nose violently, head averted, and he walked back to his chair. She dried her face and cleared her throat. 'I'm sorry.'

'Don't be silly, don't apologise, I understand how you must be feeling.'

'Do you?' she asked with a trace of irony which baffled his watchful attention to her every reaction.

'Mrs Forrester, I suggest you stay in Clare's flat tonight – her flatmate is expecting you, I've spoken to her. She's proposing to put you in her room while she uses Clare's – is that okay with you?'

Beattie got up, nodding. 'Thank you, you're very kind. I'm very grateful for your tact, Dr Harper. It was good of you to give up so much of your time . . .'

'Not at all, my pleasure. Can I get you a taxi? I'll ask the porter to ring for one.'

'No,' Beattie said. 'I'll walk to the bus stop. I need some air.'

She left the hospital, walking stiffly, and kept on going without noticing where she went, her mind constantly repeating what Joe Harper had told her, trying to absorb the pain of it, aching for Clare, for the terror and misery she must have been through. Guilt dogged her everywhere she went. She hated herself for the years when she might have been cushioning Clare against this moment, building up a sense of love and security which might have buttressed her so that the shock of what happened might not have been so destructive. She had no real idea how Clare would have taken the rape – what emotional and psychological damage might have been done to her. Anger and pain and guilt churned inside her as she found herself by the Thames and stood on the Embankment by the grey stone wall staring into the oily dark water. The rain had stopped, the skies were slowly clearing, but the day was still dull and the river flowed sullenly between the restraining banks.

Across the water she saw the white concrete blocks of modern buildings, the windows blank with no sun to reflect. A few gulls quarrelled above the driftwood tossing on the surface. Beattie looked at the blank windows and thought: that is what my life has been, I have been dead in life for so many years without noticing, without caring. She felt ashamed, she felt the weight of her own deliberate atrophy on her conscience. She had let her feelings diminish and waste away through lack of use, she had sat and sulked because life had not been as perfect as she had thought she had a right to expect.

No wonder Clare wouldn't see her! When had they ever talked about anything important? If they had ever been close, Clare would need her now, she wouldn't refuse to see her, but even a small child is aware of the absence of love. Clare had probably known from babyhood that she was not loved or wanted. A mother's smiles, touch, the caress of the voice, is understood at the deepest level of awareness, and the lack of love is known in the same way.

Beattie looked at the past with new eyes and could find no forgiveness for herself – she had mourned Nino all those years and ignored her living child. How could she have been so blind?

'I'm sorry,' Detective Inspector Lucas said, blowing her nose in a paper tissue neatly with a deprecating air. 'I've got a cold. God alone knows why I always get them in the summer, my husband says I'm just contrary, maybe he's right.' She tucked the tissue into the plastic bag suspended by a clothes peg from the back of the bed. Clare had been stuffing damp tissues in there all morning. She kept crying silently when she wasn't expecting it. It was so stupid, it made her angry, to feel tears trickling down her face, as though she had a secret leak from her eyes. It wasn't like a real crying, she hardly noticed it, until the wetness on her face alerted her.

'They tell me you should be able to leave here tomorrow,' the policewoman said.

'Oh,' Clare said, startled. They hadn't told her.

'We'd like you to come along to the station to look at a line-up.'

'A . . .' Clare's body stiffened. She sat upright in the bed.

'We've picked up somebody who might match your description.'

What description? Clare thought and the detective shrugged, as if aware what she was thinking.

'We'll send a car for you. It won't take a minute.'

'I . . . do I have to? I mean, I didn't even see his face.'

'We'd like you to watch a few people walking past a window, that's all. Nothing to worry about, you won't have to face him, he won't even know you're there.'

'But . . .'

'There were just a couple of other points I wanted to ask you about,' the other said. 'Are you sure he didn't say anything? You didn't hear his voice?'

Clare shook her head. Detective Inspector Lucas sighed.

'Did you notice – was he wearing gloves?'

Clare's mouth twisted in a spasm of disgust. 'Not . . . not while . . . no, he wasn't.'

'You struggled, you say . . .'

Clare nodded.

'Did you hit him? Scratch him?'

'I tried.'

'Where did you scratch him? His neck?'

Clare closed her eyes and nodded again, holding her mouth steady. The policewoman got up, her chair creaking. Her voice sounded thick and snuffly, oddly toneless.

'Sorry about my cold,' she said. 'Thank you, Miss Forrester, I realise how painful this is for you but we're just doing our job.'

When she had gone the nurse came back and whisked the curtains back so that Clare was part of the ward again, not safely hidden in her little sanctuary, but faced with the stares of the other women who had been eating a tea of thinly sliced brown bread and butter with jam and a tiny currant-dotted fairy cake.

'Fancy your tea now?' the nurse asked.

Clare was about to say no when the woman in the next bed shifted heavily with a sigh. Clare said: 'Yes, please.' She was never sure why, but when her tea was brought, she sat up and ate it all, less with hunger than with a resentful determination.

'My word,' the young nurse said, removing it later. 'You made a good job of that, nothing left for me and I was relying on you.' She laughed, to show it was a joke.

Pamela came in as soon as the doors were opened for visitors and brought her a pile of magazines and some paperbacks. 'Your mother's staying with me,' she said casually.

Clare didn't look up. She flicked the glossy pages of one of the monthly magazines. 'Oh?'

'I gave her my room, it's bigger than yours. I'm using yours, you don't mind, do you?'

'No,' Clare said, and her face had no expression, Pamela could not work out what she felt. There were ugly blue bruises blotching her skin, drying scratches running red and angry-looking down her throat. She still looked Chinese, the puffiness of eye and mouth had not faded. 'I gather they may let me go tomorrow,' she said.

'That's great,' Pamela said, smiling.

Clare glanced up and ran an eye over her. 'That's new, isn't it?'

'Yes.' The dress was silky and sleek, a flattering cream which made Pamela's amber eyes glow like traffic lights and it looked as if she had had her hair done that day. Just looking at her made Clare feel like hiding from sight. 'Got a date?' she asked.

'No. I'm cooking supper for your mother.'

'That's nice of you, thanks.' Clare felt uncomfortable. Pamela obviously knew that she had refused to see her mother, and no doubt was speculating on the reason, but she couldn't face the thought of trying to explain, even if she had understood the reason herself.

'I'm glad of the company,' Pamela said, glancing down the ward as someone came through the swing doors. Clare caught that look and was reminded of something.

'I like your Dr Harper, he's nice,' she said and Pamela looked furious.

'He isn't my Dr Harper. I just know him casually, that's all.'

Clare looked surprised. 'Sorry.' Pamela was being oddly touchy about him; it made Clare curious. 'He's got a soothing bedside manner,' she said and that seemed to make matters worse.

'I wouldn't know,' Pamela informed her tightly, then the man who had just entered the ward halted at the end of Clare's bed. Clare looked at him with a wry, tired expression, smiling faintly.

'Hallo, Larry.'

'You're looking much better,' he said, putting down a brown paper bag on the bedtable. 'Cherries,' he explained. 'You can spit the pips at that little Hitler they call Sister.'

Clare moved her head on the pillow. 'Thank you.' She looked at Pamela, gesturing. 'You know Larry Hillier, don't you, Pamela?'

'We have met,' Pamela said with ironic emphasis and Larry turned his head to grin at her, a thick strand of black hair falling over his forehead. Clare watched the light glinting on a single silver hair and wondered: where has that come from? She had never noticed any silver in his hair before. He would look very distinguished when the silvering had advanced even further, she decided, it would give him a touch of class.

'Hallo,' he said to Pamela, who was assessing him as a male animal through her thick, false eyelashes.

Clare saw the slight cynicism in Larry's eyes as he gave Pamela a smile. They exchanged a look of recognition. They're two of a kind, she thought, envying them their certainty about themselves, their odd air of being self-sufficient. Trying to track down exactly what they had in common, she realised it was that they were both hunters – they padded, sleek and glossy and dangerous, through a jungle filled with weaker creatures than themselves and went after what they wanted with a purr of self-satisfaction.

'You're a model, aren't you?' Larry asked Pamela who nodded.

Clare watched him as he leant on the end of the bed; a tall man, leanly built, his waist and hips narrow, his legs very long but his shoulders and chest powerful. As he talked he always seemed to give off electric sparks, they flicked from his fingertips, flashed in his eyes. He was too restless to sit down for long, he moved impatiently. She could imagine he had been a fidgety child, she could just picture him getting scolded for it in school or at home. Clare had always been a mute, still child, watching the world from behind cover, wary and apprehensive of what it threatened. Larry Hillier, like Pamela, met life from an attacking position, ready to take it by the throat if it did not give up what he wanted.

'Your firm is really going places, isn't it?' Pamela said and Larry laughed, arrogant self-assurance in his face.

'You'd better believe it. We've only just started, keep your eyes on us and we'll take your breath away.'

Pamela looked amused. 'No wonder you're doing well, you really sell hard, don't you?' There was a trace of sarcasm in her voice but it had no effect on him, he merely grinned at her.

'You know the saying – if you've got it, flaunt it.' His eyes flicked over her and came back to her face, mockery in them. 'I'm sure you've heard that one.'

Clare lay back wearily, wondering if he fancied Pamela. It wouldn't be surprising if he did, most men fell for her at first sight. The two of them would make a matching pair. It meant nothing to her whether Larry dated Pamela or not, but somehow the sight of them smiling at each other like that made her feel more depressed than ever.

Larry leaned over to pop a cherry into her mouth, holding the stem. 'Taste it, they're delicious,' he said, and she reluctantly bit into the sweet, white flesh. He dropped the stone into her fruit bowl and ate some of the cherries himself.

'I think we've finally got some good copy and artwork for the Purewash ads,' he told her. 'I had to bang a few heads together first, though.'

'I bet you enjoyed that,' Pamela murmured.

He laughed. 'Bitch,' he said with casual enjoyment. 'If I didn't keep them all on their toes, nothing would ever get done.'

'I'm sure you'd even get the trains running on time,' Pamela mocked.

Clare wished they would both go away, especially Larry; he was too vibrant, too vital, that play of brilliant energy in his face made her feel very tired. He was so alive, so confident, and Clare felt like something which has been washed up on a beach. The contrast was dispiriting. She was relieved when they left a few minutes later.

Next day Pamela arrived with her suitcase and Clare got dressed behind the curtain, feeling stupidly weak-legged.

'Pity to leave those fabulous flowers here,' Pamela said, touching a lily with one finger. A trace of pollen yellowed her pink skin and she pulled a tissue from the box on the top of the bedside table. 'I'll ask the nurse to find us some paper to wrap the stalks with and we'll take them, shall we?'

They took a taxi to the flat. Clare held Larry's flowers in the crook of her arm, nursing them like a baby. She thought wildly that she must look like a woman coming home after being in a maternity home, only there was no baby, only the fantastic profusion of Larry's flowers clutched to her breast. The dead air of the hospital had killed their perfume but now it was coming up in heady waves to her nostrils: she inhaled it, with closed eyes, like someone standing in a crowded garden with dozens of flower scents besieging their senses.

'Here we are,' Pamela said, nudging her.

Clare climbed out unsteadily and hurried into the building, her head bent, afraid of seeing someone, being seen. She felt like a criminal returning to the scene of the crime; she should have a blanket over her head.

The front door of the flat opened as she reached it and her mother stood there. Clare couldn't look at her, she wished fiercely that her mother had not stayed. She had never been able to talk to her mother about anything, she certainly didn't want to talk to her about what had happened now. Every time Clare thought about it, she mentally skirted the word rape. It was a taboo word, she couldn't even think it in relation to herself; it was a dirty word, it left her feeling dirty.

'I've just put the kettle on,' Beattie said, smiling far too cheerfully. 'Tea won't be long. What wonderful flowers, I've never seen so many, who gave you those? Tom?'

'Hallo, Mother,' Clare said. She wanted to have a bath. She didn't want to go into the flat at all. She looked past her mother down the corridor and saw the door of her room, it was closed, and behind it hid things she wanted to forget, wished she need never admit had happened. It wasn't so much that it happened to her, she thought, it was that everyone knew. If only Pamela hadn't come back when she did, hadn't seen, hadn't called the police – nobody need ever have known, she could have kept quiet about it. Feverishly her mind struggled with painful thoughts as she sat down on the couch in the sitting room, still nursing her flowers. The walls had been stripped of paper, they were down to the bare creamy plaster, the room looked strange but tidy. Pamela had been very busy.

'It won't take long to put up some more wallpaper,' Pamela told her, looking around the room. She was wearing skintight jeans and a white silk shirt and she looked beautiful. She didn't look as though she had spent several hours stripping wallpaper, her curved nails were pearly and immaculate. She'd have worn rubber gloves, Clare thought inconsequentially; Pamela was always very careful about her hands.

'Here's the tea,' Beattie Forrester said, carrying a tray into the room.

Pamela discreetly took her cup and left the room, saying she had to write a letter.

When she had gone Clare and Beattie sat in a silence thick with unspoken words; they beat around the room like moths, darkening the air.

Too late, too late, Beattie thought, holding her cup between both hands and trying to think of something to say. Words were supposed to build bridges between people but they formed walls instead. They're so clumsy, she thought, trying to say what you really feel with them is like trying to pick up a hair with a pair of coal tongs. What did she want to say to Clare? I'm sorry I've been no sort of mother to you at all; I'm sorry we've never got to know each other, you're a stranger to me; I don't know what sort of person you are at all but I want to know now, at last, I need to reach you and find out who you are inside your head, won't you give me a chance; I know I don't deserve one, but forgive me for what I've never done and said before and let me try again.

'It's a lovely day,' she said.

'Yes, isn't it?' Clare said. 'I think I'll have a bath,' she added, getting up.

As she walked to the door, her cup in her hand, Beattie said: 'Clare . . .'

'I won't be long,' Clare said and went out. She had heard the appeal in her mother's voice but she could not bear to turn and face it, she could not accept feeling from anyone, her spirit was as raw and sensitive as burnt skin, the weight of a feather brushing past it would make her wince and scream out. She wanted to be alone, it was safer.

In the bathroom she ran the water until it was scalding hot, and climbed into it, gritting her teeth. Using a nail brush she scrubbed at herself meticulously from head to foot, almost scraping the skin off – she had had several baths yesterday but she could not get clean.

She heard the telephone ringing as she was climbing out. Her mother came to the bathroom door while Clare was towelling herself roughly.

'Clare?' At her little tap on the door, Clare wrapped herself in her robe and reluctantly answered.

'I won't be a minute.'

'That was the police,' Beattie Forrester said. 'They're sending a car to pick you up. They want you to identify someone.'

CHAPTER SIX

Clare stood beside Detective Inspector Lucas in the police station, and watched through a window as a line of men shuffled into position in the yard outside. A uniformed sergeant holding a clipboard was talking to the men, walking up and down inspecting them as if they were on parade.

'There's no hurry,' the Inspector said. 'Take your time and look hard at each one. Try to remember the height, the general appearance of the man, see if any of them ring a bell. Don't worry about the face, as you didn't see it, just look at his eyes and . . .'

'I know,' Clare interrupted, having heard it all before. She was shaking with nerves, she wanted to turn and run away. Her skin was clammy, her mouth dry, her stomach churning with nausea. She didn't know how she was going to get through the next few minutes. She did not want to go out there and look at those men, feel them watching her. All she wanted to do was block out the memory of what had been done to her, she wanted to pretend it hadn't happened, it hurt too much to remember, but nobody would let her forget. People kept trying to force her to remember. Couldn't they understand how she felt? It had been a nightmare from which she had struggled to awake, yet she was being asked to go through it again, and she couldn't, her mind screamed with bitter refusal each time she tried to make herself remember.

'I think they're ready now,' the Inspector said and opened the door.

Clare had already watched the men through a two-way mirror without recognising any of them. Apologetically the Detective Inspector had asked her to take a closer look.

'It's very important, Miss Forrester, you understand that, of course,' she said, and Beattie Forrester had looked angrily at the other woman.

'Can't you see how painful this is for her? You might leave it for a few days.'

'We can't, I'm afraid,' the Inspector said patiently.

They had begun to argue and Clare had interrupted, her face tired. 'I'll do it,' she said, because sooner or later she would have to face up to it and it might as well be now.

She wanted the whole episode to finish, she wanted to get away. She was afraid she might throw up any minute. For the first time in her life she had fear stalking at her heels day and night. She could never relax because her mind kept giving a spasmodic jerk of remembered shock; she would look up, trembling, waiting for someone to leap out of darkness. Every time anyone moved unexpectedly her nerves shrieked.

'Clare, are you sure you want to do this?' her mother asked and she nodded.

'Yes.'

She made herself look at them as she walked unsteadily down the line. They were all of vaguely similar type, height, build and age. One had acne and thick, pale eyelids, one had stubble on his chin and smelt of drink, one had been eating garlic, it made her queasy as she smelt it.

She was waiting with bitter tension to recognise him, to know those eyes, those pale, glittering eyes. Her eyes skimmed over them and lifted briefly each time, with screwed up courage, to search their faces.

When she went back to the Inspector her face was chill with beads of sweat. She shook her head, swallowing. 'No.'

'You're sure?'

Clare nodded. 'None of them even reminded me . . .' It wasn't strictly true – they had all reminded her. The hair on her neck had been bristling with terror and distaste as she walked past each one.

The ordeal wasn't over. The Inspector asked her to come back to her office and another of those slow, patient interrogations began; the details repeated, queried, sifted.

'We have to keep asking these questions,' the Inspector said. 'You might remember some vital point.'

Clare only wanted to forget – she did not want to sit here and remember. Her mother was sitting outside on a bench, waiting for her. A bluebottle was buzzing around the window, trying to get out. Sunlight glittered on the row of windows opposite, Clare saw people in other offices moving around, heard the traffic in the distant streets humming and purring. Life was going on out there in London and she did not want to sit in the cluttered, little office facing a polite woman across a desk piled high with papers, dragging out the memories she only wanted to forget. She wanted to put it all behind her and somehow pick up the shattered pieces of her life and glue them back together.

When she was leaving, the Inspector said: 'We'll get him, Miss Forrester, don't worry, we'll get him.'

Clare somehow smiled, she could hardly say: I don't want you to find him, I'm sick with fear at the idea of going through a court charade, repeating all this in a witness box, feeling curious eyes watching me as I'm cross-questioned by some defence counsel. She had already had enough questions to last her a lifetime. She did not want any more.

On the way back to the flat, Beattie Forrester said: 'Why don't you come home for a week or two, Clare? You won't want to go back to work for a while.'

'I don't know,' Clare said, slowly. She did not want to go home. The house had not been a home to her since she was a child.

'Some sea air would do you good, the atmosphere is much more restful than London would be for you just now.'

'I'd have to talk to Larry.'

'Would you like me to speak to him?'

Clare shook her head. 'I'll ring him in the office tomorrow.'

'Would you like me to stay in London? I'd be happy to stay, your father can manage without me.' Beattie heard herself say that with bitter irony. Derek hadn't needed her for years, why had he stayed with her? Habit? Had he never quite got up the nerve to walk out?

'I'll be okay, Mother,' Clare said, then she looked at her mother quickly. 'Does Dad know? Have you told him?'

'Not yet,' Beattie said. 'I just left a note saying I was coming up to London to stay with you for a few days.'

'Don't tell him! Don't tell him what happened,' Clare said harshly.

Beattie frowned. 'I can't keep it from him, Clare!'

'I don't want him to know!'

'Sooner or later he's bound to find out, and then he'd be furious if we hadn't told him, he'd feel a fool.'

'I'm sick of talking about it, sick of people knowing – how can I forget when everyone around me knows?'

Beattie heard the note of pain in her voice and sighed. 'All right, I won't tell him yet.' She could understand how Clare felt, it was natural, and, in a way, Beattie was relieved not to have to break the news to Derek. How would he feel when he heard? She didn't know, and that was a painful idea, too, because she ought to know. He was the man she had lived with for a quarter of a century but she didn't know him at all.

'I can sleep on the couch, Clare, it looks quite comfortable,' she said, hoping Clare would let her stay, but Clare averted her face, frowning.

'You can't sleep on that thing, the springs dig in your back, and, anyway, you'll want to get back home. It would be best . . .' Clare was too used to living on her own terms, she would only get back to normal when everything around her was normal, the way it had been before. She had to build her life again, brick by brick, and she couldn't do that with her mother around.

Beattie would sap her weak store of strength and make it even harder for her to fight her way back to normal life. Her mother was not merely offering comfort and love, she was asking for it in return, and Clare wasn't up to giving what her mother wanted.

'I'll try to get down to see you soon,' she said uneasily. 'A week by the sea would be fantastic.' Maybe when I'm feeling stronger, she thought, maybe I can cope with my mother when things look better. She did not want to think about all that at the moment, she had enough problems to worry over.

Beattie left almost at once; she forced herself to go quickly while she could still pretend to smile. Had she been hoping for miracles? Had she thought she could just walk in and offer Clare her love, get Clare's love in return? Her daughter's eyes told her she had been over-optimistic. Life isn't so easy, you can't erase a lifetime of neglect and indifference with a few words, a gesture. In the train going back to her silent little house, her absent husband, she sat upright and stared out at the English landscape as it faded into soft twilight; green elms and cows, lush green pastures and little villages.

It surprised her to find Derek at home when she let herself in at the front door. He came out, a newspaper in his hand, frowning.

'Oh, you're back,' he said, hovering as she took off her jacket and automatically tidied her hair with one hand. 'How was Clare?' he asked. 'It's a long time since we saw her down here.'

'She's in hospital,' Beattie said.

'In hospital? What's wrong with her? Why didn't you let me know? Is she ill?'

'Someone broke into her flat and attacked her, she was knocked unconscious, but she's okay now, she's back home. She was only in hospital for a couple of days, it wasn't serious.'

'Good God, Good God, what's happening to London these days? My God, Clare... have the police caught whoever did it? Was the flat burgled?'

Beattie made a pot of tea, talking, and he listened, newspaper still in his hand, interrupting now and then with angry sentences.

'All these muggings in the streets, burglaries, you can't even feel safe in your own home! Why didn't you bring Clare back with you, she shouldn't be left alone in London after that.'

'I asked her to come but she decided against it,' Beattie said. 'She's a grown woman, Derek, not a child; her flat's her home now.'

'And this isn't much of a home anyway,' he said bitterly. 'It never was, was it? We didn't give her much of a child-hood. I don't blame her for staying where she is...'

Beattie sat down at the kitchen table with her cup of tea. 'Neither do I,' she said. 'It was my fault. I was no sort of mother.'

'No sort of wife, either,' Derek said, turning on her, his voice rising.

Beattie didn't answer. She stared into her tea, feeling old and tired. He was right, she couldn't deny what he had said. If he had said that to her a year ago she would have erupted into angry denials, she would have been incoherent with disbelief at the suggestion that she had ever been in the wrong, she would have reminded him bitterly that it had all been his fault.

'I don't know why I stay,' Derek said, his hands clenched at his sides. 'This isn't a home, it hasn't been for years.'

Beattie did not know what to say to him. She didn't know what she was thinking or even feeling. Her body sat in the chair, slumped and defeated.

Derek turned and walked out, slamming the door.

Clare was watching a film on television. Larry had sent along a new set to replace the one which was stolen, and, when she thanked him, had shrugged offhandedly and said: 'That's okay, I got it from that guy who's just taken us on to mount a campaign for his TV shops. No charge, a freebie, I thought you could use it.'

She hadn't been sure she believed him. It was typical of Larry to do good by stealth, he shook off impatiently any suggestion that he might be soft-hearted. It was bad, he felt, for his image. So she had smiled at him and said: 'Well, thank you, anyway, it was very thoughtful,' and Larry had changed the subject, almost scowling.

The shrill of the telephone made her jump. Pamela was working and she was alone in the flat, and although it was broad daylight her nerves prickled at the unexpected sound. She got up unsteadily and went over to pick up the phone, her hand clammy with perspiration.

'Hallo?'

'Clare? It's Tom. I rang the hospital to find out how you were and they told me you had gone home, why didn't you let me know?'

'I only came home yesterday,' she said.

'How do you feel?' His voice was guarded and she heard the uneasiness she had detected in it before.

'I'm fine, how are you?'

'Up to my ears in work,' he said heartily. 'If I'd known you would be back at the flat I'd have kept this evening free, but I was asked to take some foreign buyers out to dinner and it's too late to cancel now, I'm afraid. I wish I'd known. Could I come round for a quick drink just to see how you are?'

'Tonight?'

'Around six?'

'Well, would you mind if I left it for the moment, Tom?' she said. 'I'm still tired, I'll go to bed early.'

'Yes, of course,' he said, very cheerfully, and after a few bright remarks about work rang off – she almost heard the sigh of relief with which he put down the phone. Tom was a very conventional man, he found the situation painful and unpleasant, he was disturbed by what had happened to her but with him, his own feelings came first. Tom did not love her, he fancied her, he enjoyed going to bed with her, but his real emotions had never been engaged. She had begun to realise that, before she was raped; she had begun to see that in her desperate need for love from someone, anyone, she had been prepared to let Tom treat her as a doormat. He was a selfish, spoilt man who saw life from his own point of view and did not want anything ugly intruding on his private territory. Their relationship had been entirely based on Tom's expectations from a woman and her weak-kneed desire to be loved at any cost.

She went into the kitchen to make herself a cup of tea and was about to carry the tray into the sitting room when the doorbell went. She froze, her heart in her mouth. Every time she heard a sound, every time the phone went or they had an unexpected visitor, Clare found herself sweating. The ordinary small surprises of life had become violent shocks her system could not cope with, and she went slowly to the door and opened it, keeping the chain in place.

'Yes, who is it?' she asked in an unsteady voice, peering through the crack.

'Larry.'

She unchained the door and opened it. 'Oh, hallo, what are you doing round here?' She had flushed with relief and embarrassment because of course Larry must have heard the tremble in her voice just now.

'Do I have to have a reason for dropping in?' he asked, walking past her with his usual impatient lope; the smooth, aware grace of a dangerous animal which can move at speed while keeping a predatory eye on the jungle around it.

Closing the door she followed him into the sitting room to find him surveying the television set, his hands in his pockets and his face wry.

'Killing time?'

'Why not? I love old films, they don't make them like that any more.'

He leant forward and switched off Humphrey Bogart whose lip writhed with irritation as his face faded from sight.

'You're here on your own?' he asked and she nodded, her eye avoiding him.

'Pamela's working. I've just made some tea – want some?'

'Tea?' he repeated as though she had used a rude word.

'Tea – the stuff that comes in packets.'

'And turns your insides brown,' he said. 'I'd love some.'

Clare went back to the kitchen to get the tray, added another cup and saucer and found some sweet, dry biscuits which her mother had bought, she imagined – Pamela certainly didn't buy such dangerous temptations. They rarely had a biscuit in the house. When she got back she found Larry crouched by the bookcase running a long index finger over the rows of books. Most of them were hers – Pamela wasn't into reading books, except the latest fat best-selling paperbacks which she bought when they were hitting the news and glanced through merely so that she would know what people were talking about.

'You like poetry, don't you?' Larry asked, getting up.

She poured the tea, nodding.

'How long do you think you'll be off work?' he asked as she handed him his cup.

'I had an idea this wasn't a social call,' she said, sitting down. 'I meant to write to you. I'm resigning, Larry.'

He stood over her, his eyes narrowed. She wished he would sit down, he made her nervous looming over her like that. Larry had always made her nervous; that swift, almost demonic energy of his was tiring and alarming. Everything he did, everything he said, the way he moved and spoke, pulsed with the deep, assured power which was his special characteristic. Larry Hillier was a man who was going places and did not mean to let anything get in his way. Most people, when you meet them, are easy to type and place; you know their limits and how far they are likely to climb, but Larry was open-ended. So far as she could guess he recognised no limits and was going to climb far out of sight.

'Why?' he asked curtly and she looked down at her cup, shrugging.

'Oh, let's say the job's beyond me. I'm way out of my depth these days – you'd do better with someone else.'

'Would I?' he asked drily. 'I see.' He drank his tea in silence and put down the cup but did not sit down. That didn't surprise her – Larry thought best on his feet, she knew that perfectly well. He often paced to and fro in his office, from wall to wall, like a panther in a cage, until he came up with the answer to whatever was bothering him.

'This is because some swine broke in here and raped you,' he said tersely, biting the words out between his teeth, his lip curling in a derisive line.

'No! It's got nothing to do with that.' Her face had whitened and she glared at him bitterly. She might have known that from Larry she would get a punch below the belt – he never did mince words, he came out with what was in his mind without caring what his directness did to anyone on the receiving end, unless, of course, he was talking to a client who had a huge account to bring them, when he would begin by using his considerable charm. It often amazed Clare to watch the way Larry could get clients eating out of his hand. The staff in the agency saw him when he wasn't bothering to charm. They saw the dangerous jungle animal, all teeth and claws. Clients were taken in by

the soft purr of his voice, the coaxing gleam of his dark
eyes, especially female clients. With them Larry had a
walk-over.

'No?' he queried, one eyebrow lifting.

'No,' Clare denied. 'I've been floundering for weeks.
The pace is killing. It may suit you but I'm not made of iron,
I get tired . . .'

'Who doesn't?' He took her up quickly. 'Do you honestly
think I don't?'

'I've never seen any signs of it, you thrive on work. The
more you have to do the more you seem to enjoy it.'

'I thought you enjoyed it, too.'

She hesitated and he watched her intently. 'I used to,'
Clare admitted. 'It was exciting at first.'

'But it isn't now?'

Clare didn't answer and Larry sat down again. 'You
didn't mention anything about resigning before. I think this
is just part of the backwash from what happened, you're
depressed, that's all.' He smiled at her. 'You love the job,
you know you do.'

Clare sighed. 'Larry, you're exhausting to work for. I
don't know how I'll cope with you when I come back to the
office. I feel like someone being dragged behind a speeding
chariot. You never stop. I used to work eight hours a day,
now I often work twelve hours. I can't take the pace you set.'

Larry considered her, his head to one side. 'You need a
holiday. Why don't you go away for a few days?'

'I'm not in the mood.' Her voice was irritable, she was
frowning, she felt that he was pressuring her and at the
moment she found Larry's vibrant energy more than she
could stand. She was wincing with unbearable sensitivity.
She wanted him to leave her alone, she did not want him
trying to run her life.

'My mother has a cottage on Romney Marsh,' Larry
said. 'It's a quiet little place, very isolated. She loves to
have visitors. Why don't you go down and stay with her for
a few days?'

'I can't land myself on your mother! She doesn't even
know me.'

'You forget, she's a shareholder; she knows more about you than you think. She's very interested in everything to do with the firm.'

'I couldn't possibly,' Clare said with an obstinate expression. Larry was still trying to change her mind as he left, but she wouldn't budge.

Clare was slicing cucumber for the salad supper she planned when the telephone went. She put down the knife, wiped her hands on her apron and went to answer it. 'Hallo?'

Nobody answered. Clare waited a few seconds, frowning. 'Hallo?' she repeated. The line was open, she could hear the faint, hissing noise and then something else – breathing, low, careful breathing.

'Hallo? Who is that?'

The breathing got louder, whoever was at the other end had moved the phone closer to his or her mouth. Clare felt the hair on the back of her neck bristling, she was icy cold. Hands shaking, she slammed the phone down and stood there staring at it, her knees almost giving way. It rang again and she gave a violent start. Every nerve in her body was jangling. She picked up the phone, swallowing.

'Hallo?' Her voice sounded tiny, high, like a frightened child's. For a few seconds she listened to the thick breathing then she flung the phone down again and ran out of the room.

Her hands were trembling too much for her to be able to carry on slicing cucumber. She began pulling lettuce apart under a running tap. Who had it been? Was it a coincidence? Or had it been the man who . . .

She violently cut off that thought, her teeth grating together. She still couldn't bear to think about what had happened, every time the word rape came into her head she veered away, sweating. Her head hammered with pain. At times she forgot about the bruises which had been left on her, but now they were throbbing and aching. She felt sick and frightened, she wished Pamela would come home.

The phone rang again. She stiffened, listening. She wouldn't answer it. She waited for it to stop, counting the rings, praying for the noise to end. When it did and silence flowed back she sank down on a chair, weeping, her hands full of wet lettuce.

Dusk was slowly settling over the city, moths tapped at the lighted windows of the flat, their powdery wings leaving glistening marks on the glass. The throb of London had steadied to a hushed roaring like the sound of the sea in a shell.

Clare had cried herself out, she was dry-eyed now. She got up and looked in bewilderment at the crumpled lettuce she still held, then brushed it off her hands into the wastebin. She went down the corridor into the bathroom to wash her hands and face. The crying jag had made her head ache and the fading bruises swell with dark blood.

Who was ringing her? What did he want? To frighten her? He was doing a good job, she was terrified, her hands were shaking; she held them under warm water to get the circulation going again, her fingers were blue with cold, despite the sunny weather they had had all day. She dried them, beginning to get angry now. If she knew who was doing this she would . . . She broke off as the phone began to ring again.

'Damn you, damn you,' she screamed, shaking with rage and fear. She ran to the sitting room. She wanted to smash the phone into fragments, she wanted to hit someone, pound them into the ground, she was sobbing and trembling as she reached for the phone, but just as she picked it up, the ringing stopped.

Stiffly she walked back to the bathroom. She flung the towel she still held down on to the side of the bath and washed her face again. She felt dirty, there was sweat glistening on her forehead. She didn't hear a sound above the running water, but when she turned off the tap she heard someone moving and her body jerked in panic. She froze on the spot, listening. Had she imagined it? There was a rustle, a stealthy footstep. It was someone out there, there was someone in the flat.

* * *

Pamela was sitting perched on a crumbling sea wall, huddled in a fun fur while she waited for the photographer to
set up the shot he wanted. A force eight gale was blowing
her blonde hair into a wild tangle, her teeth were chattering, her ears had turned blue and she was dying to go to
the loo.

'Hurry up, for pity's sake,' she muttered under her
breath as Chris prowled up to her with a light meter and his
assistant scurried around from box to box sorting out
plates.

Chris looked up at the cloud-heavy sky, hissing between
his teeth. 'What a day. The light keeps changing, it's gone
up again. Andrew, make me up a Polaroid, would you? I
want to get an idea how it will look.'

'I want to go to the loo,' Pamela said, fidgeting and
feeling a jagged bit of rock digging into her behind.

'In a minute,' Chris said absently, moving back to stare at
her. 'Your hair's a mess. Fix it, will you, Molly?'

The make-up girl darted forward, brush in hand, and
Pamela groaned. 'It's this wind, couldn't I sit somewhere
else? I'm almost being blown away up here.'

'Where's the product?' Chris asked, ignoring her. 'Give
it to her, Molly. No, left hand. Get that coat off, Pamela.
Molly, take it.' Pamela sulkily allowed Molly to remove the
coat, shivering melodramatically as she felt the sea wind
knifing her through her flimsy dress. Why am I doing this?
she asked herself as she gazed at the camera. Was it a sane
way for an adult to earn a living? Her job seemed so idiotic,
so pointless. She had been posing for these advertising stills
ever since ten o'clock that morning, she was bored out of
her skull and she wanted to go home.

Should she have left Clare alone today? She had hesitated about going to work but Clare had insisted she would
be okay; she had practically forced Pamela out of the flat.
Maybe I should have ignored her, maybe I should have dug
my heels in and stayed, whatever she said, Pamela thought,
trying not to shiver as Chris studied the Polaroid he had
taken.

Looking up, he said: 'Okay, that's fine, we'll do it like

116

that, it's just the picture I want.' He focused on her again, his eyes on his camera, watching her image inside it. 'Keep that hand up, let's have the product well in shot, chin up, you're drooping, that's fine, lovely.'

His assistant re-loaded the camera a few minutes later and Pamela said: 'I have to make a phone call, I won't be long.'

Chris grinned at her. 'You mean you want to go to the loo.'

'I want to do both,' Pamela said, sliding down off the wall and exclaiming irritably as she felt her tights snagging. 'Oh, hell, another pair gone west!'

Tights were a big expense. They had to be fine quality, which meant they only lasted a few hours. Pamela wore jeans whenever she got the chance, it saved on tights.

She went into the public phone box down the road and dialled. The phone rang and rang but nobody answered. Pamela waited, frowning at her reflection in the tiny mirror above the phone. Why wasn't Clare answering? Had she gone out? Maybe Larry Hillier had whisked her off to lunch to cheer her up, she decided, putting the phone down, but as she paid a quick visit to the distinctly disgusting public convenience nearby, she felt even more worried. Maybe she was imagining it, she was still feeling nervous about what had happened, but she had a nagging feeling that something was wrong. The sooner she got back to the flat, the better.

As Clare realised that the footsteps were coming down the corridor, she pulled herself out of her frozen trance of fear and ran to the bathroom door. Slamming it shut, she fumbled with the bolt and as she heard it slide into place, she slumped against the door, her ear to the panel, trying to hear what was happening outside but half-deafened by the chaotic beat of her own blood.

'Clare?'

Stiffening, she lifted her head. Someone banged on the door and she jumped.

'Clare, what the hell are you up to? Are you all right?'

'Tom?' A wave of relief flowed over her.

'What's going on? I've been ringing you and not getting any answer. You had me scared. I jumped into the car and drove round to see you right away.'

'How did you get in?' she whispered, her hand on the bolt.

'How do you think? I used my key.' He was irritated, his voice snapped. 'Are you coming out of there? What on earth's wrong with you? Aren't you dressed? I've seen you without your clothes before, for heaven's sake.'

'Why didn't you ring the doorbell before you let yourself in? How was I to know it was you? I heard someone creeping about, I didn't know who it was . . .' She slid back the bolt and Tom's eyes peered at her through the door as she opened it.

'I thought you might be asleep, I didn't want to wake you up if you were.'

Now that Clare was no longer so frightened she was angry, her face flushing. She had had a bad shock and she looked at Tom with resentment. He had been the cause of some bad moments and she was still off balance; she felt like hitting him, her dilated pupils hard and glazed.

'Are you okay?' he asked, frowning. 'You look terrible.'

'You scared me.'

'I'm sorry, I didn't mean to.' He sounded aggrieved, Tom couldn't stand being criticised, being blamed for anything he did. 'I was worried about you,' he said reproachfully. 'I came round to check if you were all right. Why didn't you answer the phone?'

She walked out unsteadily, running a hand over her hair, smoothing it down. It felt damp, it had been splashed with water when she washed her face.

'I've been getting some weird phone calls.'

'What? Who from?' Tom asked, looking startled and annoyed. 'What do you mean, weird? Obscene, you mean?'

'Heavy breathing,' Clare said, and Tom swore.

'Bastards! Have you told anyone? The police?'

'Not yet. Anyway, what could they do? Everyone gets

calls from nuts now and then, what would be the point in telling the police?'

'It could be the same man,' Tom said uneasily. Didn't he think she could work that out for herself? She was too angry to answer.

'I'm going to make some coffee,' she said. 'Want some?'

'I'll ring the police for you.'

'No!' She almost screamed the word, then bit her lip. More quietly, she said: 'No, leave it for now, Tom.'

'But . . .'

'I don't want to see the police again just yet,' Clare said harshly. 'Can't you understand that?'

'You'll have to tell them sooner or later, have some sense,' he said as he followed her into the kitchen, and watched her getting down the coffee jar.

'Leave it.' She plugged the electric kettle in and spooned instant coffee into two mugs.

'They'll be furious when they realise you've delayed calling them. If it is the same man . . .'

'Stop talking about it!'

Tom moved closer and put his arms around her. 'Hey, you really are in a state,' he said. 'I know it must be pretty scary, but don't you see that's just why you should call the police? Who knows what's behind these calls? You shouldn't be here alone.'

Clare felt his hands just below her breasts, he had pulled her back against him and was resting his chin on her shoulder. She felt her skin crawling as though there were insects under it, she had difficulty not crying out in disgust.

'I'm okay,' she said stiffly. 'The kettle's boiling.' She tried to get away and Tom held her. He began to kiss her neck, his mouth moist. She could smell the faint scent of perspiration on his skin mingling with the pine smell of his aftershave.

'Let me go, Tom, I want to make the coffee,' she said, controlling her impulse to break away, standing rigidly in the circle of his arms.

'I've missed you,' he murmured. 'Have you missed me?

119

You'll get over this, Clare. It makes no difference to us, you know, I don't think any the less of you . . .'

In a violent reaction she jammed her elbows backwards into his ribs and broke away. 'Don't touch me, don't touch me!'

Tom stumbled backwards, swearing, and almost fell against the sink. 'What the hell's the matter?'

'I'm sorry, but don't touch me, I can't bear being touched.' Couldn't he make the effort to put himself in someone else's place just for once? Did she have to explain everything to him as if he was a child? Hadn't he any idea about how other people felt?

'I was trying to comfort you,' he said like a sulky, rejected child, his lower lip stuck out in that typical movement. 'Did you have to push me away like that? I'm not to blame, why treat me like an enemy? I love you . . .'

'You don't love me! If you did, you'd be able to understand how I feel, I wouldn't have to tell you. You'd spend a little time thinking about what's going on inside me. You'd understand me better, you wouldn't need to be told it makes me sick to my stomach to have a man touching me just now.'

'I'm not any man, I'm supposed to be the man you love, or so you kept telling me, but you haven't wanted to know lately, have you?'

'Oh, for God's sake,' Clare said wearily, turning away. 'Go away, Tom, please, just go away.'

'You're being bloody unfair,' Tom grunted. 'I came rushing round here because I was so worried about you. How do you think this has affected me? Don't you think I've been sick with worry?'

'I'm sorry you've been worried and I'm sorry to sound ungrateful, but I want to be alone for the moment. I need to be on my own.' She couldn't talk to Tom, he wouldn't listen, he was rigid, fixed, he wouldn't alter for her. He didn't understand and he never would.

'All right, I'll go,' he said. 'If you want me, you know my number.'

He left, closing the front door very quietly, and Clare

began to shake with hysterical laughter. Oh, she knew his number all right. She knew it now, it had taken quite a time for her to get it but in the end it had dawned on her.

She poured herself a mug of coffee and sipped it. It tasted bitter, she grimaced, then she heard the phone begin to ring again and her hand shook so much that she dropped the mug, splashing her legs with scalding coffee.

CHAPTER SEVEN

The evening seemed to drag by; Clare kept looking at the clock and wondering feverishly what had happened to Pamela. Wasn't she coming back here after work? Had she gone on to one of her parties? Normally, Clare wouldn't even have thought about it. Pamela had always been erratic, coming and going as she chose, and Clare had barely noticed, but tonight she was on tenterhooks, desperately aware of being alone in the flat.

Should she ring the police?

She stood, hesitating, looking at the phone, but the thought of facing new questions, spending hours in the stark police waiting room, made her reluctant to do anything. Perhaps if she stopped answering the phone, the calls would stop; he would give up.

The phone rang. She jumped, her body as taut as stretched wire. 'Oh, God,' she whispered, not moving. The ringing went on and on. When it cut off Clare stood in the growing darkness, shuddering. When she could move, she went round the flat turning on all the lights. She was afraid of the dark for the first time in her life. Going into the kitchen she turned on the radio and listened to some pop music, drinking her coffee, her mind besieged by fears.

Was it the man who had broken in here? Was it him? Her hand went to her mouth which was still slightly swollen, shadowed with bruises. She winced as she touched it.

If it was him, how did he know it was her answering the phone? Why was he ringing? Then another thought flashed into her mind and she sat up jerkily. What if he lived nearby? What if he lived so close that he could see the flat, could watch her coming in and going out? Had he rung just now because he knew she was alone? Could he see her? Her eyes went to the window, terror in them. Could he see her now? Was he watching her?

She sprang up and went round the flat again, turning out

all the lights, as if she was on a brilliantly lit stage with menacing eyes watching her from the outer darkness of the auditorium.

She stood by the window staring out. There were buildings all around – other blocks of flats, old Edwardian terraced houses rising four storeys high, divided into bedsits, smaller houses jammed close together, office blocks.

How many of them? Her eye ran around the whole vista, appalled by the number of people who must be within eyeshot. How many people could see her moving about in the flat when she had the lights on? She had never thought of it before. She had felt safe, invisible, private once she was in her own home, but now she knew that you weren't safe anywhere.

Was he watching her now, perhaps through binoculars, from an office or a flat? Or in the street, behind a tree, or a parked car?

She felt her heart beating fast, sickeningly close to her ribs, she could almost feel it pumping; she put her hand there and the heavy rhythm went on under her palm. She had never been so aware of the physical motions of her body: the blood passing along the veins, the lungs filling and emptying with air, the nerves passing messages to the brain's central sorting office to decode. That body now was in a state of panic.

She had never been so aware of being alive. She was afraid of dying, in the dark, alone. She was afraid of the faceless unknown out there whose hatred was so motiveless and so terrifying. If she had known him, if she had understood why he wanted to kill her, why he hated her, what his face was like, what sort of man he was, she wouldn't have been so panic-stricken. It was the unknown that was so frightening.

A key grated in the lock of the front door. The little noise made Clare gasp, spinning. The door was pushed open. Light blazed, blinding her.

'Clare?'

Pamela came through the kitchen door and switched on the light in there. She looked at Clare quickly, anxiously, questioningly. 'What is it? What's happened? Why are you in the dark?'

Clare was trembling, her teeth chattering with shock. She could hardly speak. 'Ph . . . ph . . . phone,' she stammered.

'Phone who? What's happened? Who do you want me to phone?' Pamela dropped her handbag on the kitchen table and came over to Clare. She put an arm round her and led her to a chair, made her sit down, a hand on her shoulder. 'What's wrong, Clare?' she asked gently.

'Ph . . . phone calls. I'm sure it's him, I know it is . . .' Clare's voice had risen and had a wild edge to it.

'What does he say?' Pamela felt anger rushing through her as she looked at Clare's white face, the tic going under her eye, beside her mouth. Early that morning Clare had begun to look almost normal. Now she looked like a woman on the verge of breakdown.

Clare shook her head like an automaton, hardly knowing what she was doing. 'He doesn't, he never says anything, he breathes, he's listening to me, trying to scare me. He's going to kill me, I know he is, he's going to kill me. He wanted to last time, that's what he was going to do, if you hadn't come back, he'd have killed me, he wants to kill me.'

She was hysterical, Pamela thought, she broke into the high-pitched stream of words, putting her arms around her. 'Don't!'

'He's going to kill me, he hates me, he . . .'

'Clare!' Pamela shouted. She shook her violently. 'Stop it!'

Clare's head went back and forwards like the floppy head of a rag doll. Her eyes were wide, staring, her skin white and drained of blood. Pamela crouched down and hugged her and felt that icy skin against her own face, shivering.

'Don't,' she said again very quietly. 'I'm here, he won't hurt you, I won't let him.'

Clare began to cry silently. Pamela didn't hear a sound but she felt the wetness against her face.

'Sit there, don't move,' she said. 'I'm going to ring the police.'

Clare moved but did not speak. Pamela waited a moment

then got up and went out. Clare stared at the floor. She heard Pamela talking in the sitting room, she heard a car accelerate outside in the street. I can't stay here, she thought, I have to get away before he kills me. If she stayed in the flat, she would never have a moment's peace. She would never know when he was coming to get her.

Pamela came back just as Clare stood up. Clare felt Pamela looking sharply at her and tried to smile. 'I'm going to ring Larry,' she said and Pamela did a double-take.

'Larry? Hillier? Why?'

Clare didn't answer, she went into the sitting room and clumsily dialled Larry's number. He picked the phone up and said: 'Yes?' in a discouraging voice. In the background she could hear Mozart, a pure high sound. It seemed a million miles from what was happening to her, she sighed as she listened to it, and Larry said again, impatiently: 'Yes, who is that?'

'It's Clare. Larry, I would like to go down to your mother's, if the offer's still open.'

'Of course it's still open,' he said and she picked up the note of query in his voice. 'Are you okay, Clare? What changed your mind?'

'I'll tell you later,' she said. 'Can I go at once? Tomorrow?'

'Sure, I'll drive you down myself.'

'There's no need, I could . . .'

'I'll drive you.' Larry used the voice he used when he did not intend to give way about something. It was a tone Clare had often found infuriating in the past, it had made her want to hit him, but now she found it comforting. She accepted it.

'If you're sure you can spare the time.'

'I'll pick you up at nine,' Larry said. 'Pack your swimsuit, you'll need it. Nothing much to do down there except swim and sunbathe.'

'Sounds heavenly. Thank you, I'm very . . .'

'See you,' Larry said, hanging up.

The police arrived ten minutes later. They were two total strangers. They did not seem particularly interested although they asked a lot of questions, and it soon dawned on Clare and Pamela that they would merely hand the information on to Inspector Lucas in the morning. They had just happened to be on duty that night, it wasn't their case.

'I expect they'll have your phone tapped, try to trace the calls,' one of them said. 'It takes time to set up a phone tap. In the meantime, hang up if he rings. Someone will come and see you tomorrow.' They drank the coffee Pamela had made and departed cheerfully, obviously pleased to be able to pass the case to someone else.

Pamela slammed the door after them. 'Well, they were a lot of help!'

'I expect their work load is heavy enough already,' Clare said with weary amusement. 'I won't be here tomorrow, anyway. I'm going to stay with Larry's mother on Romney Marsh.'

'Oh, are you?' Pamela asked, eyeing her wickedly, but Clare was in no mood to respond to that sort of needling.

'I'm going to bed,' she said. She felt like something washed up by the tide; white bone bleached bare by the salt sea. She was empty, hollow, exhausted, but at least her hysterical panic had subsided now. That was something. On her way to the door, she stopped, frowning.

'You don't mind if I go away, do you?'

'Why on earth should I?' Pamela asked.

'You'll be alone here.'

Pamela grimaced. 'I'll manage. I doubt if he'll pay a return visit.' She saw Clare's face stiffen and groaned. 'Sorry, that was a daft thing to say. Take no notice of me. I'll be fine, I'm not a jellybaby. I shan't stay awake half the night worrying about being alone.' She grinned. 'In any case, I won't have any trouble finding someone to keep me company if I do get lonely.'

Clare nodded and went to bed, half envying Pamela. She was so self-sufficient, so independent. Pamela had much in common with Larry. He didn't take life or the opposite sex seriously, either. Whenever she saw him with a girl, it was someone new, his relationships never lasted. He wasn't the marrying kind, he proclaimed from the housetops. Monogamy was a dead bore, an outmoded institution from more primitive times. The pill had put a stop to the need for marriage, he said.

Larry believed in travelling light in life. He wasn't dragging a wife and children behind him, they merely slowed you up, cut down on your options. He had told Clare so many times. Larry made no secret of his views.

Clare began to think her own attitudes had been stupid; her mind had undergone a sea change lately, new ideas, new realisations kept flashing into her head, and it had not merely been the violence which had broken into her life which had changed her. The change had begun before that. What had happened over the past week had merely accelerated the process.

Pamela didn't seem to want love; sex was enough for her. She was too self-sufficient to need to feel that someone else cared about her. That was a freedom Clare had not wanted, had even dreaded. It hadn't looked like freedom to her – it had looked like loneliness, and she had run from it into Tom's arms. Now she saw that she had not found security or love with Tom. She had found only the loneliness she had run from because Tom had not cared about her; he had merely accepted the love she poured out to him without giving anything back. Maybe that was all anyone ever did. Perhaps love was a one-way current, and never aroused an answering feeling. There is always one who kisses and another who is kissed, but was it possible to have an equality between lovers? Could love be exactly balanced on both sides?

She thought about the man who had raped her. She had been keeping him out of her mind. He had invaded her body, she wanted to shut him out of her head, but he had been there, all the time, buried in her subconscious, like some foreign body she tried to eject and could only wrap round and round with shielding tissues to lessen the infection he brought. Thinking about him made her feel sick and scared. He had hurt her, her body remembered and winced, her mind screamed, but she made herself think about him. In a twisted way he had come closer to her than anyone in her life before – that was a strange thought, not a pleasant one; it made her stomach clench as though some-one had hit her there.

He had cared about her, his feelings had been real: he had hated her – that was the strongest emotion anyone had ever shown her. She could still feel the flames of his hatred, they scorched her and she shrank from them, but they had been powerful. The moments while he was hurting her, using her, had been so private, just the two of them alone in a dark world and she had known that his entire attention was focused on her. What had made him the way he was? Why had he wanted to do that to someone he didn't even know?

Or did he know her? She hadn't seen his face, heard him speak, but perhaps he had seen her in the street, perhaps she had seen him. It might be someone she knew casually. He might have been one of the men in that line-up, how could she have recognised him when all she remembered was his eyes and his emotion?

It was painful to think that the first person who had ever really tried to reach her had been someone who loathed her, someone who wanted to hurt and humiliate and degrade her, but although he had left her shaking, terrified, sick, something else had happened that night. The cold shell she had lived in for so long had been smashed apart. She was suddenly exposed, naked, aware of herself as never before and in admitting that he had got through to her, she couldn't help wondering if she, herself, was warped, or whether after a lifetime of indifference from everyone around her she had responded powerfully to that act of hatred because anything was better than indif-ference. Was that why some women put up with a husband who beat them up? Did they prefer being battered about by a violent man to being ignored by a kindly one? Reading about such things in newspapers she had marvelled that any woman could put up with such treatment, but who knew the inner processes of another person's feeling and thought? Not thought, she told herself. It was feeling; raw, instinctive feeling, a blind response the mind couldn't touch. Her own mind told her that what had been done to her had been brutal, terrifying and sick but what did her feelings tell her? She turned on to her side heavily, refusing to think about it any more.

Pamela helped her to pack, but then had to go to work before Larry arrived. Clare sat in the flat, wishing she need not walk out to the car. Her face was still bruised and misshapen, people would be bound to stare.

When Larry rang the bell she jumped and went reluctantly to let him in. He was wearing a black leather jacket, the collar up around his face, and his hair shone with drops of rain.

'A sudden shower,' he said. 'Got a brolly?' He took her case and went ahead down the path to put it into his car. Clare came behind, having locked her flat, sheltering beneath an umbrella and invisible to people in the flats. The street was empty. She was in the car and able to relax a moment later. It had all been much easier than she had feared.

Larry drove like a bat out of hell. He was one of the cut-and-thrust school of drivers, he took every spare inch of the road left open to him and zoomed past every car they met as soon as he had the chance. It was nerve-racking to watch him.

'Do you have to drive so fast?' she asked and he slid her a satisfied grin.

'Yes, I enjoy it.'

They left the urban sprawl of London behind far sooner than she had expected and headed into the rolling green Kent countryside. The road was wet and black with rain but as they got to the Medway, the sky cleared and the sun came out, turning the grey river to a glittering blue. She looked down from the bridge and saw little boats bobbing with gaudy coloured sails on the water.

'Want to stop for coffee?' Larry asked and she shook her head. She did not want to walk through a crowded cafeteria and feel people staring at her disfigured face. She carried the mark of what had happened to her so visibly, like a stigma.

Larry threw her a shrewd look. 'Just as you like,' he said, then leaned forward and flapped down the glove compartment of the car; he drew out a pair of sunglasses and tossed them into her lap. 'Put those on.'

She flushed and obeyed. In the wing mirror she caught a brief glimpse of herself, he was right, they made an immediate difference, why hadn't she thought of that before? The swelling on her mouth had already lessened, the blue and yellow stain of bruises on her cheeks couldn't be seen quite so clearly through heavy make-up and the glasses took care of the rest. She brushed her hair down over her forehead and almost felt normal.

'You ought to talk about it, you know,' Larry said, his eyes fixed on the road. 'If you shut it all inside your head, it will fester, get out of proportion. You won't get over it until you've come to terms with it.'

'It's not a subject people want to talk about,' Clare said. 'Tom goes beetroot red every time he thinks I might bring it up.'

'Tom!' The car put on speed, the tyres screaming on the wet tarmac, and she gripped the edges of her seat.

'Hey! This isn't a race track!'

He slowed. 'I've never understood what you saw in Tom Prescott, but maybe you have a masochistic streak that enjoys being made into a doormat.'

'I was in love with him!'

'Was?' he repeated quickly, turning to look at her.

Clare was silent, her eyes hidden behind the sunglasses.

'Why the past tense?' Larry asked, looking back at the road. 'Is it over? The deathless romance finally died, did it?'

'Don't sound so gleeful,' Clare muttered. 'You may not believe in love, but I do, old-fashioned though it may seem to you.'

'Not old-fashioned,' he corrected, laughing softly. 'Rather sweet, like believing in Santa Claus – we all do when we're kids but we grow out of it.'

'Well, I haven't grown out of believing in love,' Clare said but her voice had, she knew, a defiant, unconvinced ring. She was trying to assure herself, as much as him, that love existed.

'I suppose it's all a question of what words mean,' Larry said in a thoughtful tone. 'I believe in the chemical process which most people call love – some women are instantly attractive to some men, they get the hormones going, you take one look and start working out how long it will take you to get her into bed.'

'Charming,' Clare said, half laughing, half irritated. 'That may be how men think, it isn't how women think.'

'Again, that depends on your definition,' he said. 'Pamela, now, she wouldn't disagree with me for a second – I've seen her look round a room and think: hmm, he's nice, and an hour later they leave the party together bound for bed.' He lifted an eyebrow in her direction, his face mocking. 'True?'

'Pamela's a law unto herself,' Clare said.

He shook his head. 'I wouldn't put it like that – I'd say Pamela was one of the new breed, a woman who doesn't think life begins and ends with marrying and having children. She may marry some day, she may have kids, but she won't make the mistake of thinking that's all there is to life for a woman. Pamela's got a brain inside that very lovely head. When she gets past her peak as a model, I might give her a job with us. She's clever, she's ambitious and she's quick-witted. I think she'd be a natural for our business.'

'You may well be right,' Clare said slowly. Was he dating Pamela? she wondered. He seemed to know a lot about her, he had obviously been thinking about her.

'The pill's liberated women,' Larry said. 'Sex is no longer a dangerous pleasure for them, they can have it on demand without fear of consequences, just like a man.'

'Except that women aren't men, either physically or mentally, and they tend to get emotionally involved with anyone they make love with – how are they going to get round that in your brave new world?'

'I didn't make the rules,' Larry said. 'I'm just reporting what I've noticed going on. When I was twenty, there were two sorts of girls: those who did and those who you'd have to marry if you talked them into it and they got pregnant. That no longer applies.'

'It strikes me that for all this talk about liberating women, it was the men who got liberated,' Clare said with a tinge of bitterness. 'They no longer have to pay for sex – either with money or marriage.'

He laughed. 'It was women who demanded equality and liberation – now they've got it, all they do is complain.'

'Maybe they've realised just what they've had to pay to get it,' Clare said. 'I suppose it's okay for women who get the exciting jobs – top executives in big companies, models like Pamela, actresses, but what about all the women slaving away at boring jobs in offices and factories who wish to God they could afford to stay home and run the house and cook the dinner? My mother's never worked, her generation didn't unless they had no other option. When I got back from work, it was me who cooked Tom's dinner while he sat and read his paper. It didn't matter how dead beat I was . . .'

'That was your own fault,' Larry said drily. 'Don't whine to me about letting him use you as an unpaid servant. You have a tongue in your head, you should have told him straight that it wasn't on, if he couldn't go fifty-fifty with you, he could hit the road and not come back.'

She was silent for a minute. 'I did,' she said. 'In the end I did.' She started to laugh. 'He was flabbergasted.' She remembered Tom's aggrieved, incredulous face. 'He said I sounded like a fishwife.'

Larry gave her an amused look. 'Well, I'm glad you came to your senses at last – I was afraid you were going to marry him and hand in your notice to go off and build a cosy little suburban nest with two point five children and two cars and plastic gnomes in the pocket handkerchief garden.'

'Snob,' Clare said, grimacing as she secretly admitted that her dream of marriage to Tom had not been unlike the picture Larry just conjured up, in his wickedest voice.

They had turned off the motorway now and were winding their way through the maze of narrow country lanes leading into the marsh. High-banked hedges stood on either side, their foliage so thickly set that you caught only rare glimpses of the lush green pastures behind. On tall stems blew pink willowherb and occasional purple foxglove and when they slowed to turn a corner, Clare saw among the rough, wild coils of grass tiny red strawberries like jewels, scattered casually. The air grew heavy with the salt smell of the sea, the wind freshened and whipped her hair around her face. As they descended nearer to the coast the land flattened, they saw sheep grazing on the short turf and the villages they passed had ancient churches with tapering spires which soared skywards. The road still wound drunkenly in serpentine deception, so that you never seemed to get anywhere, you seemed to be going round and round in circles.

'How much further?' she asked Larry.

'Not far.'

'Are you sure you know the way?'

'Do you mind? I've driven along this road a million times.'

'But do you ever get anywhere on it?' Clare asked and he gave her a grin.

'Hungry?'

'Yes,' she said, looking surprised. She hadn't realised it until now, but she was definitely hungry.

'It's the sea air,' he said.

'Are you sure your mother doesn't mind being landed with me?'

'If she did, she wouldn't have you. My mother doesn't do anything she doesn't want to do.'

'So that's where you get it!'

'That's enough cracks from you,' he said with laughter in his voice. 'I'm your employer, remember, I expect to be treated with respect!' He paused for a moment, then added wryly: 'Especially in front of my mother, she has a low enough opinion of me as it is.'

'I can see I'm going to like your mother.'

'I told you, you'll find you have a lot in common.'

'Including our opinion of you.'

Larry shot her a look from under drooping lids, his eyes gleaming dark with silent amusement.

As they turned into a narrow gateway a few moments later he said: 'I'm glad to see you haven't had all the spirit knocked out of you, Clare.'

She was too taken aback to answer and stared ahead at the small cottage she could see through a leafy tangle of trees. A rough, gravel drive ran through them, the surface bumpy and full of shallow depressions into which the car ran with a grating of springs which made Larry swear under his breath. White-washed stone walls, an uneven pink-tiled roof, windows with diamond-leaded panes beneath which ran green-painted troughs planted with pink and scarlet geraniums – the cottage was almost picture-postcard pretty but the wilderness of the garden gave it a very different atmosphere.

Larry parked with a scrunch of rubber on gravel and got out of the car. Clare climbed out and stood by the car looking around her curiously at the overgrown garden – it looked as though it was never touched yet it had a distinct charm, as though the wild clusters of bushes and trees, the blowing grass, were planned, were intentional.

Larry picked up the brass lion's head knocker and crashed it down, making her jump. Nobody came. 'She may be round the back,' he said, and walked off leaving Clare standing in the windy sunshine. She watched a heron slowly move across the sky, shading her eyes to follow it out of sight. She had never seen a heron before – she recognised it immediately and was filled with excitement. A heron! She couldn't believe it.

Suddenly through the trees darted a tiny figure, waving its arms and shouting. 'Shoo, scat, go away, if I catch you here again I'll cut off your tail and ears . . .'

Clare stood open-mouthed, wondering if the threat was aimed at her.

At first she found it hard to decide whether she was watching a man or a woman, or even, perhaps, a child. Well under five foot, wearing a blue-and-white checked shirt, old faded jeans and a yellowed straw hat, the figure wove its way towards her, waving vigorously. Only at the last minute did her presence apparently dawn. That zigzag flight paused, she felt eyes pinning her down, then Larry came round the side of the cottage.

'What's all the yelling about?' he asked and the figure moved towards him, stood on tiptoe and kissed him on the cheek.

'Hallo, Larry – cats.'

He removed the straw hat and the sun shone on hair the colour of spun silver, thick and as shiny as new-minted coins.

'Cats,' Larry repeated, looking amused.

'A big ginger one and a tabby – I think they're living wild in the copse on the other side of that field, I've seen them every day this week. I won't have cats in here scaring off my birds.' She took her hat out of his hand as he absently fiddled with the brim. 'Do be careful, Larry, you'll ruin it, I've had this hat for years.'

'I know, I remember it,' he said. 'You ought to give it to a jumble sale and get a new one, this is a disgraceful object.'

'It's a perfectly good hat, it functions, keeps the sun off my neck and shades my eyes.' She had a clear, precise voice, each word issuing like a drop of water from a slow tap, in crystal perfection.

Larry looked towards Clare. 'Come and meet Clare, Mother.'

Clare looked into bright blue eyes which betrayed no hint of an ageing process, they were almost as clear as a child's, their regard wide and thoughtful. They shook hands and Clare smiled.

'It's very good of you to have me here, Mrs Hillier. Are you sure it's no trouble to you?'

'No trouble at all. I have two spare rooms, take your pick. I eat very sparingly and never cook. If you want to have hot meals you must cook them yourself, use the kitchen at liberty, make yourself at home, cook whatever you like but always leave the rooms tidy, that's all I ask. I like the house to be clean and tidy.'

'You should have been a seaside landlady,' Larry said and his mother gave him a calm stare.

'Are you criticising me, Larry? Is he, do you think,

135

Clare? He was an objectionably critical child, he had a way of looking down his nose and making pointed remarks that really irritated me. Some people are never children, they sit in their prams and feel superior – Larry was one of those. You could tell just by the way he wouldn't open his mouth for a spoonful of prunes that he was passing judgement on everything around him.'

'I don't recall you ever feeding me prunes,' Larry observed.

'Don't be so literal-minded,' his mother said.

'I don't recall you ever feeding me anything, come to that,' he added. 'I must have been one of the last of the nanny-reared generation. It was a ridiculous expense because we were hardly in the millionaire class.'

'It was not an expense, it was a necessity,' Mrs Hillier said. 'I had no idea how to look after a baby and I was too old to learn.'

How old was Mrs Hillier? Clare wondered, studying her discreetly. Impossible to tell – her skin was weatherbeaten, wrinkled, but oddly soft, like a crumpled roseleaf, and her body was so thin as to be sexless, her movements still rapid and agile. She could be anything over sixty and under eighty.

'You didn't like babies,' Larry said and Clare wondered if he was accusing his mother of neglect until she saw the smile in his eyes. He was teasing his mother, but there was no malice in the game.

'I'm not rising to it,' Mrs Hillier said calmly, 'come along indoors, Clare, and have some tea.'

'Thank you,' said Clare and Larry moved beside her, his long legs keeping stride without strain.

'Be warned, her tea is undrinkable stuff – made with nettles or dandelions,' he said.

'Very good for you,' his mother informed her. 'You look as if you need some iron, Clare.'

'My mother is a herbalist,' Larry explained.

'Oh, really? How fascinating,' Clare said as she followed Mrs Hillier into the cottage. The rooms had low ceilings, painted white, but with the dark veins of old oak beams running across them, the wood pitted with ancient worm holes. Bowls and vases of flowers stood everywhere – glossy dark red peonies which had shed a few petals to lie on the polished wood of a table like gouts of blood, spiky delphiniums, round white daisies with flat yellow buttons in their centres, towering hollyhocks and stock which scented the air heavily, tight bunches of sweet william crammed into narrow jugs, orange marigolds and willowherb. The curtains were well-washed faded chintz, the furniture was old and comfortable and shabby.

'Sit down and I'll get the tea,' Mrs Hillier said, walking through to the back of the house while Larry steered Clare through a door into the sitting room. She sat down on the sagging sofa, looking around her. The air was sweet and musky with summer flowers, lavender polish and heat.

During the drive she had been almost animated, talking to Larry in something approaching her old liveliness, but suddenly she was tired, grey, depression was seeping back into her and she wished she had not agreed to come here to stay in this strange house with a woman she did not know. She had been crazy to agree to it, she would give anything to be back in her flat in London alone. She had never realised how much she needed to be alone at times, how essential it was to her. There was a world of difference between loneliness and being alone – the difference between being on a desert island in the middle of a trackless ocean and being in a room in a busy house with the door shut and firmly locked.

Larry's mother brought in a tray and Clare absently accepted a cup of cloudy greenish liquid. She sipped it, nose wrinkling involuntarily. Larry observed her face with apparent amusement. He was talking to his mother, their voices ran through Clare's head like whispers around the dome of St Paul's – strange, disturbing, worrying. She drank some more of the herbal tea. It wasn't actually unpleasant, merely odd. She would have loved a cup of strong black coffee.

'Why don't you go to your room and rest?' Mrs Hillier asked, taking the cup from her.

Clare started, eyes puzzled.

'You're almost asleep,' Larry said and pulled her to her feet. She stumbled and he put an arm around her. Clare's nerves jangled like fire alarms, she stiffened and jerked away, feeling him looking at her sharply.

'I'll show you the rooms and you can choose which you like best,' Mrs Hillier said, moving to the door. Larry had let his arm fall. Clare followed his mother, angry with herself. It made her feel sick to be touched by a man in that intimate way, if she had realised Larry was going to put an arm round her, she could have prepared herself, but he had done it suddenly and her reaction had been instinctive, a leap of alarm, a shiver of rejection. She hadn't been able to help it. She should apologise to Larry, he hadn't meant to be anything but kind, yet she couldn't say a word. What could she say? Don't touch me unless you signal your intentions well in advance? How absurd, she'd feel a real idiot saying that.

'Both rooms are east-facing, you'll get the first sunlight to wake you up,' Mrs Hillier told her, opening a door.

Clare looked at the sparsely furnished little room. The floorboards were polished to a shine like trapped sunlight, by the narrow monastic-looking white bed lay a large round mat in a dozen different colours.

'I made that,' Larry's mother told her. 'Out of old clothes – rag rugs are very soothing to make, you buy some hessian and cut up any old clothes you have into strips, then poke them through the hessian with a sort of whittled down wooden clothes peg so that they form a knot on one side of the hessian. When you've completely covered the hessian like that, you trim the long tags of rag so that they're uniform – and you've got a rug.'

'Oh,' Clare said. 'How . . . how wonderful, it certainly saves money on carpets, doesn't it?'

The other room was almost identical but it was full of books and on the walls were prints of famous paintings, watercolours on cartridge paper, wall posters, shelves holding a clutter of objects from lumps of jagged rock to sea-shells and twigs in jars. It looked like a room to live in, unlike the other, which had echoed emptily.

'I'd like to use this room, if I may,' Clare said politely.

'By all means,' Mrs Hillier said. 'Larry will bring your case up. Make yourself at home.'

The door shut, Clare was alone. She walked to the window and looked out at the leafy treetops. A bird was singing among the shadowy branches. Clare listened and found tears filling her eyes, she wept without knowing why, her mind desolate.

Pamela was working on a television advertisement and the director was a real bastard. He had made his name in international films and on the first day announced that he wasn't taking any crap from anyone, they were going to make the little film a work of art and everyone was going to work their backsides off from him downwards.

'Everyone got that?' he had asked and they had all made suitable noises, waiting for him to turn his back before they mugged at each other ferociously and mimed pulling guns and shooting him right between the shoulderblades.

Pamela was always happier working with a tough professional, you felt better when you knew you were doing something worthwhile, but this guy was a sour individual who really fancied himself. She couldn't stand him. He kept them in the studio until midnight, endlessly repeating one simple scene.

'It's going to be perfect,' he said. 'You want it to be perfect, don't you?' And they agreed they did, stifling their yawns and feeding each other aspirins with paper cups of black coffee.

By the time she got back to the flat, it was almost one in the morning. One of the cameramen dropped her off and she stumbled into the building, head buzzing. She pushed her key into the lock and the door swung open and then she froze, every hair on her head prickling. Ahead of her the flat lay dark and silent as the grave, but she felt there was someone there, waiting, in the darkness, she felt she was being watched, she was not alone.

CHAPTER EIGHT

After the first shock, her mind worked quickly. She slid her hand down the wall and switched on the light. Her eyes flashed down the hall. All the doors were closed. Had she left them closed? She thought back to that morning. Yes, she thought. Clare had been gone two days. Pamela had been sleeping badly, she kept hearing noises and waking up, alert, tense. When she went out this morning, she had carefully shut all the doors although it was stupid, because if someone broke in, what difference would it make if the doors were open or shut?

A weapon, she thought, I need a weapon. She stepped sideways and opened the kitchen door, groped for the light switch and quickly looked round the room. A carving knife?

Too dangerous, she thought – it might end up in me. She opened a drawer and found a rolling pin made of Italian marble which she had brought back from a working trip to Tuscany. It weighed solidly in her hand. She gripped it firmly and began to search the flat, leaving the front door wide open in case she needed to bolt for it or scream for help. The rooms were empty, she left the light blazing in each.

As she got to her own bedroom she distinctly heard a sound behind the door.

She stood still, dry-mouthed, straining to hear another sound.

At last she tired of waiting and flung the door open, the rolling pin raised in case someone hurtled out of the darkness at her. Nothing happened. She switched on the light, her hand shaky. As she did so she heard a rustling, flapping sound and saw the curtain blowing against the wallpaper. The wind had got up outside, and although the window was shut, there was a draught through the frame which had warped slightly away from the wall.

Pamela sagged, her forehead cold with sweat. She went back to the front door and shut it. In the kitchen she turned on the radio and got some low jazz on a late-night show. She made herself some black coffee, she wouldn't sleep anyway, not now, so what did it matter if the coffee kept her awake?

She was just about to drink it, the marble rolling pin close to her hand, when the phone rang.

Her hand trembled, coffee spilled across the kitchen table. Pamela swore.

She got up, weak-legged, snatched up the rolling pin and went to the sitting room. The clamour of the phone sounded shrill and menacing. Who on earth could it be at this hour? Something must be wrong. Clare? she thought with piercing anxiety. Had something happened to Clare?

'Hallo?' she asked huskily.

There was no answer, only a thick, deliberate breathing, as if someone was panting into the phone.

Pamela flung down the phone, waited a moment then picked it up again and dialled the police. 'He just rang again!'

'Did he say anything this time?' Inspector Lucas asked.

'Not a word, just made those awful noises. He must be crazy, he's got to be a straitjacket case.' Pamela was shaking and that made her angry, it maddened her to admit she was scared. 'I thought you were tapping the line? Didn't you arrange for the calls to be traced? What are you doing about it?'

'If he rings again, try to keep him talking,' the Inspector said calmly without bothering to answer Pamela's irritated questions.

'He never talks, just breathes.'

'Try to get him to say something. Talk to him, say anything, just keep him on the line for as long as you can. He may be calling from a private number. If it is in your district, it won't take long to pick him up. If he's calling from long distance we'll have problems, it could take quite a time. But if he rings again, talk, keep the line open for as long as you can manage. Whatever you do, don't hang up.'

'You don't have to stand there listening to him. It makes my skin creep.'

'I can imagine,' the Inspector said drily.

'Do you think it is the same man?' The idea of that was making Pamela very nervous.

'Could be.'

'What if he . . . comes again?' Pamela said, swallowing.

'Keep your door on the chain, don't let anyone in unless you know them.'

'I won't,' Pamela said with emphasis. She rang off and looked at the clock. She couldn't stay there in that silent flat. She was going out. One of the other models was having a party that evening. Pamela hadn't intended to go, she wasn't in a party mood these days, but now she decided on impulse to take a taxi round to Helen's flat. She needed company, the livelier the better.

It was only as she rang Helen's doorbell that it occurred to her that Joe Harper might show up at the party. The thought sent a little flicker of excitement through her. She hadn't seen him since Clare left the hospital, she had tried to put him out of her mind. He had made it quite clear he wasn't interested in her, and Pamela wasn't the type to pursue a reluctant male. There were plenty of other fish in the sea without fishing for something so elusive. Yet she kept thinking about him.

She found herself glancing around the crowded room quickly as Helen handed her a drink. 'Glad you could come, you don't need any introductions, do you?' Helen was a tall, dark girl with a hauntingly fine-boned face which was usually to be seen on magazine covers. She was very popular in fashion photography. She could make the most outlandish garment look chic and desirable.

'I'll find people to talk to,' Pamela told her, smiling.

'I just bet you will.' Helen winked and darted off to meet a new arrival, and Pamela began to circulate. She didn't get very far, a broad young man in a pink shirt put an arm around her and kissed her ear.

'Pam, darling, where have you been all these years? I

haven't seen you around for so long I thought you must have got married or something equally depressing.'

'No, I've been working hard, that's all,' Pamela told him, detaching herself.

'Don't use words like that,' he groaned. 'They have the most horrific effect on my metabolism. My father is always advising me to do some, but then he's a very dull boy indeed.'

'Do some what?' one of the others in the little group asked with a puzzled expression.

'Work,' Pamela said ironically. 'Mark has never done any in his life.' Mark Filton didn't need to work, he was the heir to a large fortune built up by his small, grey, hard-working father.

'I should say not,' Mark agreed complacently. 'I'd rather die.'

'Let's hope you're never faced with the choice,' Pamela informed him and walked off, her mouth wry. Mark Filton annoyed her, he seemed to lead a pointless existence, drifting through life without purpose. She helped herself to another drink, frowning. A year ago she had seen quite a lot of Mark, they had had a number of dates and she had enjoyed helping him spend his father's money. She had thought him witty and good company, then. He hadn't changed, but Pamela had, without noticing it until now. She stood with her drink for a moment, staring around the room. There was no sign of Joe and Pamela's spirits fell, she felt herself sinking inside like a soufflé taken out of the oven too soon. Suddenly the party seemed boring, a waste of time, the people seemed silly and noisy and childish. She felt like going home, but if she left she would only find herself back in that silent flat, alone, and she couldn't face that either.

'Pamela! What a super dress,' someone said behind her and she turned with a bright smile, pushing away her depression.

It wasn't until the early hours of the morning that she got back home and she only had a few hours' sleep before she had to get up again, dress and get to work.

'Been burning the candle at both ends, again?' the director asked nastily as he studied her face and she gave him a defiant glare.

'I'm fine.'

'If you say so,' he muttered, sniffing, and she put out her tongue at him as he walked away, but took care to work hard and stay alert throughout that day's shooting. He wasn't having any excuse for criticising her!

They stopped work at six and several people went off to have a drink. Pamela drifted with them through sheer inanition. She sat on a bar stool limply, now and then remembering to pick up her glass. Somebody dropped a crate somewhere at the back of the bar and Pamela's nerves went crazy, her hand jerked and her glass crashed. She grabbed at it as it fell and several jagged pieces were driven into her palm.

'God Almighty,' someone said.

'Pamela . . .'

'Are you okay? Don't move or the glass will be dug further in.'

'She ought to go to hospital, she ought to have a doctor look at that.'

Pamela lifted her hand very, very slowly, like a wooden puppet pulled by a string, and stared at the dark red blood flooding out of her skin.

She clumsily got down from the stool. 'Hang on,' one of the men said. 'I'll drive you over to St Aidan's – the casualty ward will take the glass out and give you some stitches in there.'

'I've cut my hand,' she said stupidly.

The others exchanged glances. 'Shock,' one of them whispered.

'Come along, Pam, we'll get you to the hospital.'

She sat in the car with her hand palm upwards on her lap watching the blood oozing round the pieces of glass – they felt enormous but they were only just visible. She remembered reading a story about a knight who had a lance tip in his side. Would they give her an anaesthetic before they removed the glass? It would hurt like hell if they didn't. It hurt now, it throbbed red hot there, but she felt oddly calm about it. She wasn't afraid or upset. She was removed, detached, it wasn't happening to her. She was an observer watching some other girl sitting there, pale and cold, losing blood from a tiny wound.

Casualty was crowded. She saw a nurse who asked her to fill out a card.

'I can't write,' Pamela said. 'It's my right hand.'

The nurse sighed irritably. 'I'll do it, then,' she said and asked her a string of questions. Then Pamela was told to sit down and wait. There were rows of chairs full of people with the bored, patient faces of people who know time has no meaning. Every now and then they shuffled along to a new chair as patients were seen and new patients arrived.

It was an hour and a half before Pamela had the glass taken out of her hand, and three stitches put in to keep the wound together.

She slowly walked out of the hospital and looked around for a taxi. Her friends had dropped her and left. It was nearly nine, the rush of patients was almost over. The hospital was quietening down for the night. She looked up at the rows and rows of lit windows, wondering if Joe was in there somewhere. A pierce of emotion went through her to her amazement. She felt tears filling her eyes.

She had always told herself that women who let one man take over their whole lives were fools, they were old-fashioned, sentimental idiots who had let themselves be taken in by male propaganda. She had been irritated by watching Clare waiting on Tom after she had been working flat out all day. Pamela had despised her. She laughed scornfully at the idea of romantic love, it didn't exist. All there was between a man and a woman was sheer sex drive. Human beings were animals who needed to release their sexual energy. Pamela had often liked one particular man, enjoyed his company, gone to bed with him and had fun out of it, but without confusing her enjoyment with the rapture romantic poets waffled on about.

She didn't understand why she was crying now at the thought of Joe Harper, she didn't want to feel like this, what was happening to her?

Her hands curled up at her sides and she winced, feeling the drag of her injured palm. The nurse had bandaged it tightly, too tightly, Pamela could feel the gauze sticking to the torn flesh.

She brushed one hand across her wet eyes, furious with herself. She must be tired, it was the only explanation, or the nervous tension of the last few days was catching up with her perhaps. She just wasn't herself.

She began to walk away, hearing a car coming behind her. When it slowed and drew up beside her, she automatically jumped back from the kerb, looking round towards the car, her eyes wide, her nerves jangling.

'Pamela?' The voice sounded surprised, curious, uncertain, and she felt a jab of surprise herself as she recognised it.

For a moment she had thought the driver was going to make a proposition and she had been about to run for it, but now she relaxed in relief and a sudden confusion.

'I thought it was you,' Joe said. 'What on earth are you doing at the hospital?'

'I've been in casualty, I'm just on my way home,' she said, sounding far too breathless, and Joe leaned over and opened the passenger door.

'Want a lift?' He sounded polite but cool and by contrast Pamela was trembling like a schoolgirl with a crush on a teacher. She got into the car clumsily, her skirt sliding up over her knee almost to the top of her thigh. Joe's eyes observed her long, smooth legs without a flicker of expression.

She pulled the door shut with her good hand and Joe's brows lifted. 'What have you done to your hand?'

She turned, extending the bandaged shape. 'Cut it, I had to have some stitches.'

He switched on the light and took her hand between both his, staring at it although the bandage covered the wound. Pamela felt her fingers trembling as they lay against his skin. She was so aware of being touched by him that she had to look down like a little girl, her face hot. His thumb softly trailed across the tips of her fingers and her heart hurt.

'How did you do that?' he asked.

'I dropped a glass.'

'I see,' he said drily and she looked up with anger.

'I'm not drunk! It was an accident.'

He looked at her oddly. 'Okay, calm down.' He let go of her hand and turned to start the engine again. 'Did you have to wait long?'

'Hours,' she said. 'The place was packed to the doors – you should sell tickets, you'd make a fortune.'

'We're not in it to make fortunes,' he said, turning out of the hospital gates into the thick streams of traffic. 'Have you eaten tonight?'

'No.'

'Hungry?'

'Yes.'

'I've got a flat near here – how do you fancy some spaghetti?'

'I'd love some,' she said, trying not to sound too eager.

'I do a good spaghetti,' he said. 'The secret's in the length of time you cook it – it has to be just right, al dente, not too firm, not too soft. At this hour, we'd better not have a sauce that's too rich. I suggest bacon and mushroom, that shouldn't be too indigestible.'

'Sounds marvellous,' Pamela said.

His flat was smaller than the one she shared with Clare. He had two rooms in a rather ramshackle old house which was like a rabbit warren of shabby rooms with yellowing cards stuck on the doors. Joe picked up a pint of milk as he let them into the flat. Pamela stood looking around her curiously. Books, she noted, books everywhere – on rows of wooden shelves along the walls, on piled tables and on the floor. There was a sagging couch and a table and dining chairs and at the end of the room a tiny kitchenette with a dark green curtain half drawn across it.

Joe pointed to a door. 'The bedroom's through there – there's a bathroom in it, if you want to use it while I get the supper.'

She wanted to see his bedroom. She went over there and closed the door behind her, eagerly looking around. The bedroom was monastic – a bed, a bedside table with a clock and a telephone on it and an old wardrobe along one wall, a chest of drawers against another. The carpet was dark grey, the walls were pale cream. The bathroom was almost a cupboard. The bath was squeezed in from wall to wall, big enough for a dwarf or a child. There was a W.C. and a little wash basin. A clean white towel hung on the wooden towel rail. She stood looking at the shaving things, the toothpaste and toothbrush. She had a bizarre desire to pick up the toothbrush and use it, to taste Joe's mouth on it. She felt herself reddening at the thought. She had to be going out of her mind. Maybe she was more shocked by what had happened to Clare than she had realised – this was all a reaction, it wasn't real.

She went back into the other room to find the air fragrant with the smell of frying bacon. Joe was moving about behind the curtain.

'Can I help?' she asked and he told her to sit down and read a book, he could manage. There wasn't room for two in the little kitchenette anyway.

She browsed along the shelves. Medical text books, large volumes of anatomy drawings, art books full of glossy illustrations, poetry, novels, she looked at them all, trying to learn something about him from them. She pulled down a big book on the Pre-Raphaelite artists and sat down with it, turning the pages slowly and staring at the girls with limp, crimped golden hair flowing down around pale, remote faces – they remined Pamela of Clare, those girls: she had seen Clare look just like that at times, ethereal, out of this world.

'Supper's ready,' Joe said, carrying a huge earthenware bowl of spaghetti to the little table.

Pamela got up, closing the book, and he looked at it and smiled. 'Like the Pre-Raphaelites?'

'When I was at school, I hated them, we had them pushed down our throat. Now I'm fascinated, I'm not sure why.'

'It's very romantic stuff,' he said, holding a chair for her.

She slid in between him and the table, feeling rather like

148

one of those limp, wistful girls, enjoying the sensation of having him push the chair gently once she had sat down. 'Are you romantic, Joe?' she asked as he sat down, too. Her question was a little teasing, she didn't expect an answer, but he surprised her.

'Yes, sorry.'

'Why are you sorry?' she asked, taken aback.

'You think romance is old-fashioned, don't you? You're not alone, most of the guys I know would agree with you. When I was ten years younger, I'd have agreed too, I thought sex was the only thing that mattered then. I couldn't get enough of it, I spent most of my waking moments chasing it and I had some pretty technicolour dreams, too.'

'But you've changed your mind?'

He began to lift great creamy whirls of spaghetti out of the dish and drape them on her plate. The sauce slid through slowly, bacon and chopped mushrooms and onions. The smell was delicious.

'There's a lot more to life than orgasms,' Joe said, offering her a little tub of parmesan cheese.

'Such as?' Pamela asked, shaking the little red-yellow drifts of cheese liberally over the spaghetti.

'Maybe I'm getting old,' he said, mocking her, his sideways smile gentle. 'I want someone to talk to, someone to share life with, not just a body in a bed for an hour or two and then goodbye.'

'But you haven't married.'

'That's what I meant about being romantic,' he said, deftly looping spaghetti around his fork. 'I found I couldn't bring myself to marry cold-bloodedly. I wanted to find someone special – a dream, I suppose. I ought to have more sense, I know romantic love doesn't last, it's just an illusion, but although my mind tells me it's crazy to harbour dreams, I find life's rather grey without them, so I go on dreaming.' He lifted the spaghetti to his mouth and Pamela watched, enthralled, as though everything he did was beautiful, riveting, she could watch him for hours on end without getting tired of it.

He looked at her, his mouth full, and his eyes held

laughter. He leant over and took her fork and twirled spaghetti round it, put it into her mouth, his face inches from her own.

'Good?' Joe asked a moment later.

'Fabulous,' she said, and he laughed. 'What did you do before you became a doctor?' she asked.

'I was working in my family business in the City,' he said. 'My father's on the Stock Exchange. I went up to university and I had no idea what I wanted to do so Dad put me in his office. I stuck it for a couple of years but it was deadly dull. You either find money exciting or you don't – I didn't. I need the stuff for eating and having a roof over my head, but I can't get hooked on the glamour of world finance. Then I had a car crash – I was badly injured. It was six months before I was fully recovered and by then I'd realised what I wanted to do – I wanted to be a doctor. Of course, my family thought it was just shock and the experience of being in a hospital for so long, they humoured me but they thought I'd soon forget about the whole idea. I think they were staggered when I finally passed my exams and qualified.'

'Have you any brothers or sisters?'

'One of each,' he said.

'What about your family?' he asked her a few moments later. 'Have you any brothers and sisters?'

She shook her head. 'No, there was just me.'

'And your parents?' he pressed.

She hesitated, her lips twisting in a little grimace of reluctance. What could she say about her mother, her father? 'We didn't get on all that well.'

He surveyed her shrewdly. 'Which did you dislike? Your mother? Or your father?'

She half-smiled. 'I had a pretty low opinion of both of them. My mother was a doormat and my father was a brute. Some evenings he didn't say a word to her, he came in each night, sat down in his armchair with his paper, shouted if his meal wasn't ready five minutes later, sat down at the table and ate then got up and went back to his chair until he went to bed. He shouted at me a lot, too. I put up with it while I

150

was at school because he hit me if I answered back, but as soon as I could, I left. It wasn't a home, it was a place you were stuck until you could escape.'

Joe finished his meal without commenting. 'I've got some fruit,' he said. 'Would you like an apple or an orange?'

She shook her head. 'No, thank you, I'm absolutely bloated as it is . . . thanks, the spaghetti was wonderful.'

'Fancy some coffee?'

'Love some.' She got up and he shook his head at her as she went to clear the table.

'No, you're a guest – sit down and look at the Pre-Raphaelites while I get the coffee and clear the table.'

Over the coffee they talked about art and he asked her about her job. She told him how tiring it was, working sometimes for fourteen hours at a stretch, how worrying it was if you didn't have a job for several weeks and were running low on money, how boring it was putting up with some of the men who thought a model was easy game and got nasty if you refused to go to bed with them.

'I decided right at the start that if I wanted to go to bed with someone, I would, but that it would be me who did the picking, not them.' She waited for the distaste to come into his eyes again but he just looked at her steadily without a flicker of thought visible in his thin features.

She risked another honest remark, encouraged. 'It was a bit of a shock to my ego to have you turn me down flat the way you did. It had never happened to me before.'

'There has to be a first time for everything,' Joe said coolly.

They had talked like friends, she had begun to feel hopeful. There was often a smile in his eyes when he looked at her. Hope was a tenacious plant, it kept on crowding again no matter how many times it was cut down. She was finding that hope was an indivisible part of this feeling to which she was so new – her mind told her all the time to cut her losses, forget him, but every tiny shred of an excuse she got she seized eagerly.

'If you don't fancy me, you don't,' Pamela said unsteadily.

Joe was sitting on the couch next to her. He put his elbow

on the bulging, squashy cushions at his back, turning her way, his thin body twisting to half-face her.

'Who says I don't?' he murmured and Pamela's breath seemed to stop. She looked into his eyes, feeling sick. 'You're very beautiful,' he said. 'But I gave up grabbing every pretty girl I saw a long time ago and I don't like sharing, either. I want my woman to be just that – mine and nobody else's. I'm the jealous type. I wouldn't put up with other men hanging around. I want a strictly one-to-one relationship. As I said, I'm old-fashioned.'

Pamela was watching his mouth. Her eyes were cloudy, her pupils enormous and very dark. She was breathing unsteadily. She moved and her hand touched his cheek. Joe just sat there, watching her. She stroked the hard, muscular line from cheekbone to jaw, feeling her fingertips prickling from the stubble on his skin, then she bent forward and kissed him.

His lips were firm and cool, and did not move. She knew he was giving her no response, but she moulded them with her own, her hands catching his head to hold him. It was only now that she felt his mouth touching hers that she realised she had wanted to kiss him badly. A fierce, primitive, burning thrust of desire went through her, she heard herself groaning, her arms went round his neck and she kissed him with passion and pleading, trying to get from him the response she needed.

Joe unlocked her arms and pushed her away. Trembling, she opened her eyes with reluctance.

'It wouldn't work,' Joe said. 'We're not the same sort of people and I'm not starting something that can only end badly. Call it self-preservation if you like, I don't want to get hurt so I'm not getting involved with you, Pamela.' He got up. 'I'll drive you home.'

CHAPTER NINE

Clare had been at the cottage in the marsh for over a week before she said more than a few words to Mrs Hillier. The old woman rarely put in an appearance, she was up and out of sight before Clare got up and she went to bed early. From the first day, Clare found herself settling into a pattern, a routine – which was yet a million miles from what that word usually meant, since no two days were the same; each began and ended with a different feeling, and between dawn and dark stretched hours of changing experience unlike anything she had ever known before.

For a start, Clare was alone throughout most of the time, and yet she found herself never lonely. She had companions everywhere she went – from the white gulls with their wide, powerful fringed wings, floating effortlessly on warm currents of air like swimmers on the surface of a sunny sea, to the trees which surrounded the house, never still, never silent, trembling and swaying in the wind, their branches creaking, murmuring, whispering, their shade full of birds which made plaintive little cries or emitted sharp alarm calls or sang with liquid mystery. The trees, the grass, changed with the altering light; now dark, now silver, sunlit or moonlit, or mere breathing shapes in the profound blackness of moonless night.

She had never noticed such things before with such intensity. Since she was raped, depression had lain on her spirit like a cold mist on low ground, clinging, damp and pale and insubstantial. She could only wait for it to lift, for a new wind to blow it away. Her food had no taste, her moods were dull and grey, but now and then it would seem to be gone, just for a few moments, and she would come alive and awake and remember how it felt to be happy. She did not want human companions; she did not resent Mrs Hillier's silences and absences, she concentrated her whole being on the natural world around her. It made no demands on her, it pursued a life apart, self-absorbed, self-sufficient and since she lacked the courage to look ahead into her own future, she focused with an emotional myopia on the constantly varied foreground of the landscape.

She sat on the grass and watched the ants scurrying like the White Rabbit along paths between the rough blades; she watched the bright green grasshoppers springing with all the surprise of a jack-in-the-box from stem to stem, she caught them mid-leap and held them, vibrating angrily, in her cupped palms, then let them go and heard them whirring out of sight. She put twigs in the path of caterpillars and watched them writhe and slide over, their furry, compartmented bodies shuffling along like the dragon in Chinese New Year celebrations. The garden was full of butterflies, pure white or cream, brown or purple, their powdered, glistening oily wings dotted and blotched with colour, their antennae twitching and flicking as they perched on a leaf, picking up signals inaudible to the human ear.

As the sun sank, the moths came out blundering against the windows, infatuated with the light, great dusky soft things with peering, pleading eyes. Clare walked at night in the garden and felt them brush against her, a delicate tickling like eyelashes on a cheek, but their wings left a glitter on your skin, and if you touched them, they sank, flapping helplessly, wounded to death by your lightest touch, and never flew again.

The birds fed richly on insects and nets of nuts which Mrs Hillier hung up in the trees, on coconut shells full of melted bacon rind and meat fats mixed with seeds which she cooked for them and left to harden before she hung them up, on scattered crusts of bread and chopped fruit. Clare saw her at work, hanging her little larders from branches high enough to discourage cats, she saw the birds coming to swoop and swing, pecking, looking round to check that no predator was in sight before taking another stab at the food, squabbling crossly with each other for possession of some titbit, tumbling in mid-air as they fought with beak and claw. She learnt that the big black crows were raucous bullies, the thrushes aldermanic, stately, the starlings back-street thugs who ganged up on all the other birds and waged noisy war to get more than anybody else, the tits cheeky and quick, the swallows rarely seen as they flashed with forked tails in dazzling loops through the air.

All around her life was in full tilt with summer: multiplying, feeding, growing, blooming, things seeded and blossomed and perfumed the air. The year was at high tide, the grasses and trees with all their inhabitants richly occupied with living.

She walked further afield after a while and discovered a narrow path across low fields which ran down to the sea and a flat, curving beachline of pale sand which the wind heaped up in dunes and drifts like the Sahara with tough marram grass growing among them. Few people came there early in the morning although as the day wore on the beach would be invaded by sunbathers and swimmers. If Clare got up early she could swim alone in the delicate morning mist, watching the skyscape slowly changing colour as the sun rose and the first grey dullness gave way to a bright, silvery light which turned pink and coloured the floating islands of cloud, then became blue, a blue so vivid, so clear, so piercing that her heart lifted to watch it.

On the shore road there was a wooden café which took down its shutters around ten o'clock. Sometimes Clare stripped off her wet swimming costume in the shelter of one of the grass-tuffeted sand castles which hid you from anyone on the beach, and slipped on a thin cotton dress and sandals before walking back to the road and stopping for a cup of coffee at the little café.

She rarely had any companions at that hour. The woman who ran it was matter of fact and polite and never seemed to notice Clare's fading bruises. She handed over the cup of coffee and took Clare's money and went back to reading her woman's magazine. Sometimes she listened to the radio, playing pop music but not at a volume which blasted Clare out of the place. Clare would sit by the window looking over the sea and feel clean and new, the rough caress of the waves left a salty bloom of delicious freshness on her whole body.

As her physical bruises faded and her body grew healthy again, her depression showed faint signs of lifting. As with any recovery from illness she grew irritable at first, she lost patience with herself when she failed to walk straight along the wooden groynes dividing the beach, preventing the sand from eroding and washing out to sea, or when she couldn't swim strongly for more than a few minutes. She felt angry when she saw people coming down on to the lone, empty sands which she loved to have to herself; she wanted to snarl at them when they waved or called, 'Good morning,' and smiled. She attacked inanimate objects which would not do as she wished; she kicked chairs which maddeningly appeared in her way, pummelled pillows which maliciously dug into her neck as if they had developed sharp corners, swore at the stiff buckles on her new sandals, cursed the intrusive, ever-present sand which crawled between her breasts, filled her hair, her ears, got between her toes and under her nails, fell in pale showers like the tribute of the Gods to Danae whenever she undressed at night.

She walked faster, felt energy crackling in her as she combed her hair, the sparks flying blue in the twilight of her room in the evenings. She was no longer happy to lie in the long grass and watch the insects, she wanted to run and swim and unleash the anger into the atmosphere. There was no place for that anger to go except in exercise.

One morning as she was finishing her coffee in the café, three young men came in, leaving their motorbikes propped up outside. They were in their late teens, wearing black leathers, the backs of their jackets studded and carrying menacing designs of eagles. They wore black leather boots which went up to just below the knee. They swaggered, their black helmets under their arms, and said: 'Coffee, doll,' to the woman behind the counter who sniffed as she put down her magazine to get their coffees.

A newspaper lay on the counter. One of them picked it up and stamped over to the table next to Clare to sit down and flick through it.

''Ere, that's mine,' the woman shouted after him and his friends leaned on the counter threateningly.

'Keep your 'air on, you'll get it back.'

'I'd better,' she said, slapping their cups down. She held out her hand for the money.

Clare stared out of the window, the hair on the back of her neck bristling.

The motorcyclists sat down beside their friend. She felt them staring at her but ignored them.

'Hallo, darling,' one of them said, leaning her way.

Clare went on watching the waders, the small black and white birds with red legs, scavenging at the tide's edge, taking a few running steps before abruptly ducking their heads to dig into the damp sand. Where they had been, they left a trail of fine, triangular marks like ancient arrow heads, like the fossils of flowers, the prints of those delicate, soft-stepping feet. In a few hours the tide would swallow up every sign of their presence, their prints would vanish, eaten up in a few minutes. Human beings were in the same predicament, they moved and fed and reproduced, and in the flick of time's finger they were swallowed by the advancing tide.

'Stuck-up bitch,' one of the boys growled.

'Know what she wants,' another one said and they all laughed loudly.

'You read about that vicar?' the boy reading the paper asked and started to read aloud, slowly, his finger following each word.

'Dirty old man,' one said. 'Pass the sugar, Dave. Call this coffee, washing up water, that's what this is, look at them grease spots on the top.'

'That guy that raped the secretary got off,' the boy with the paper said and Clare's body stiffened in shock.

'Course he did, she asked for it, didn't she? Goes away with him for a weekend and then claims she thought it was a business trip. Who does she think she's kidding?'

'He didn't pay her enough, that's why she went to the cops, you bet, she thought she'd get a nice bonus. Ask me, girls who get raped always ask for it. If they didn't want it they wouldn't be where they could get raped, see what I mean.'

Clare got up, trembling. She felt red mist clouding her eyes, the anger inside her was choking her throat. She tasted the bitterness of bile, she wanted to kill them, her hands curled at her sides, like talons, like claws, to scratch and savage. She saw them looking up at her but she saw them from a long distance obscured by her burning rage. For a few seconds they sat there and stared at her and she stood by their table, shaking, on the point of hitting them, screaming, tearing out their eyes.

Then the rage began to ebb a little and their faces came swooping into focus: young faces, with a town pallor over-laying the sharpness of their features, that stupid animal brutality which did not think. She saw them, looking from one to the other, and realised they were frightened, her expression had alarmed them. They looked so young, so vulnerable, so nervous, all the noisy aggressive swagger gone.

Clare picked up the sugar bowl and emptied it slowly into the cup of the young man reading the newspaper, the one who had said girls who get raped have always asked for it. All three watched, open-mouthed. They didn't move.

Clare turned and walked out. The woman behind the counter caught her eyes and winked, grinning ear to ear. As she closed the door she heard the boys, recovering from their surprise, start yelling.

''Ere . . . bloody sauce . . . what'd she do that for?'

'She crazy or something?'

'Bloody looney, look at my coffee . . . I can't drink that.'

Clare walked calmly back through the fields in the morning sunshine feeling the springy turf beneath her feet, the warmth of the sun on her back, the rough kiss of the wind as it blew against her bare, sandy legs.

She had half expected the boys to follow her but as she climbed the stile into the field she had glanced back and seen them all with their helmets on, climbing on to their bikes, their faces hidden by the smoky visors, looking like dangerous space men. They had roared off down the road and she had begun to trek back to the cottage feeling strangely triumphant.

That evening Clare was boiling some speckled brown eggs for her supper when Mrs Hillier came into the kitchen, barefoot, in an old well-washed cotton dress whose pattern of poppies had faded so that you could hardly recognise the flowers. Her feet were flat and brown and hairy, she looked like a faun in drag, her grey hair tucked back behind slightly pointy ears, her thin arms weathered and muscled. She washed her hands at the sink vigorously, using a wooden nailbrush to scrub her nails, and the water running down the sink was discoloured with earth.

'A good day?' Clare asked, lifting the eggs out of the water carefully in a big spoon. There were bantam hens running wild in the garden. They were shut up each night inside a wire-enclosed run with a little wooden hen-house, but during the daylight hours they scratched and squawked and nested in the trees and tried to lay their eggs where no human could find them. Mrs Hillier knew all their favourite places but sometimes she let one hen nest and hatch her eggs to encourage the others to keep producing. Clare had been a little nervous of them at first. They had wild, mad eyes; they pecked savagely when you came close, ran about hysterically as soon as they saw you coming, but they were beautiful. She had learnt to enjoy watching them. Their feathers were so soft, so downy, rich and brown and deckled and freckled, the fanlike edges tinged with other shades of colours, brown and black and white. Their eggs were strongly flavoured, gamey, the yolks very yellow, the whites very clear.

'I had a very busy day, how about you?' Mrs Hillier said, drying her hands on a rough buttercup yellow towel.

Clare had carried her eggs to the table. She sat down and cut off the top of one with a vicious slice. 'I had an adventure,' she said and told her about the boys in the café.

Mrs Hillier laughed. 'I'd love to have seen their faces.'

'They looked scared,' Clare said.

'Big boobies.'

'That's what they were! They thought I was going to hit them – I thought I was, for a minute. I wanted to, I've never wanted to do anything so much. I can't remember ever having been so angry.'

'How did it feel?' Mrs Hillier asked curiously and Clare paused for thought, a slice of wholemeal bread and butter in one hand.

'Terrific,' she said at last, laughing.

'Anger is pure energy,' Mrs Hillier said. 'Larry's angry all the time.'

'Isn't he? Isn't he just? Was he always like that?'

'I think he was born in a temper. He knows how to use it, though. He gets things done by getting angry – I asked him to help me dig out an obstinate clump of weed once. The roots were as thick as an arm, I couldn't shift them. Larry got so mad he wrenched them out in the end. He was purple in the face with temper but he did it.'

'Oh, that's just what he's like in the office! He's like an earthquake – the ground rumbles and glass shatters when he erupts. He's always on the move, I never know what to expect next. He seems to operate best in the middle of commotion – the more difficult things get, the more Larry enjoys himself. I can't cope with it all. I never seem to get my breath. I feel like a cork bobbing along in the wake of a speedboat, I toss about, feeling helpless. I don't know why he hasn't fired me – it must be obvious that I can't do that job.'

Mrs Hillier surveyed her, head to one side, with the bright curiosity of one of the little bantam hens. 'If Larry didn't think you could do that job, you'd be out quicker than you could say knife, don't worry.'

'Half the time I can't get on with my work anyway because I have to soothe down the people Larry has knocked over and trampled on.'

'You're tactful, are you? I've no doubt Larry appreciates that.'

'Larry knows as much about tact as he does about life on the moon!'

'Larry has a genius for finding square pegs for square holes – I'd say it sounds as if you fit nicely into yours.'

'I don't know about that, but I do know I'm exhausted after a day tidying up after he has caused chaos and confusion. It's no wonder I never find time to get anything else done.'

'Have you talked to him about it?'

'I've tried – he brushed the subject aside, said I should wait and see how I felt later.'

'Then I should take his advice. Maybe you haven't looked at the problem in the right light – try looking at it from Larry's angle. What does he think your job demands? It sounds to me as if he's using you as some sort of Red Cross, to follow him and patch up all his victims. If you don't see yourself doing that for a few years, hand in your notice and get another job. You're obviously a bright girl. You could do any number of things. The main thing is to decide what you want to do, and do it. It's your life, nobody else has the right to tell you what to do with it. But if you're afraid of falling down on this job with Larry, ask him if he thinks you are before you go leaping in with resignations.'

Clare spent the next few days thinking about her job, trying to decide whether she wanted to go on doing it, whether she enjoyed it, whether her worries about it were justified. She kept on walking in the salty, windy fields, swimming each morning early and enjoying the glistening stretch of wet sand which looked like a mirror to the arriving day, the clouds and the sunshine reflected in ever-changing beauty; reading in the garden on the grass, borrowing Larry's books one by one, curious about his tastes and amused by the schoolboy books on the flyleaves of which a scrawling hand had written his name and address. Larry Hillier, his book, they often said. Larry declaring that possessive, insistent nature even in boyhood, making her laugh.

She was re-assessing herself all the time now, looking back over everything that had happened to her from this point of time, like someone who has arrived at a hill during a long trek through winding countryside, and can see backwards across the landscape she has journeyed through. All her life, she saw, she had had a negative attitude to herself, a poor self-image. She carried a load of guilt because her parents had not loved her, and beneath the guilt a smouldering resentment.

She went through moods of anger towards them, towards

Tom, towards Larry, but most of all towards herself for her craven defeatism, her inner hollowness. Where was the use in blaming herself, or blaming anyone, she thought one day, as the anger turned on itself, like acid eating internally. You might as well blame life.

Her parents had never deliberately ignored or neglected her – they had been too busy locked in their own struggle with living to realise what they were doing to her. They weren't weak and wicked, they were human. Her mother had been cheated by herself, by those around her, too. Her life was full of failure and misery. To try to put her in the dock and accuse her was futile, was to lose the struggle towards maturity. She had to come to terms with her mother or she would never move on into real adulthood, she would drag around inside her for ever the whining, accusing child which had already bedevilled her life so far. She had to evict that child, grow up, before it was too late.

She had to learn to stand on her own two feet without needing an approving, parental pat on the hand; she had to stop looking to others for assurance, for confidence, for a framework within which she could live. All this time she had been telling herself that Tom had used her, he was selfish and spoilt – and, of course, that was true, Tom was no more an adult than she was – but in another sense she realised that she had used Tom. She had clung to him like a weak plant to a strong stake, afraid of losing him by opposing his slightest wish, by arguing or demanding that he start treating her as an equal. She had allowed him to impose on her the standards his mother had taught him. She hadn't believed them, she had resented cooking and waiting on him when she was tired after a difficult day – why had she let him take advantage of her like that? It had not been Tom who was to blame, it was herself. She should have been firm with him from the start, she should have put a value on herself if she wanted Tom to value her.

Once she had arrived at that point, she thought about her job again and realised that she was not worn out by Larry, she could cope with him. All she needed was humour and firmness and the ability to take him lightly when he bellowed, bellow back, tease him. She had done it many times before without realising that it worked. When she was on a high she could take Larry without blenching, it was only when she was tired and depressed and low that he was too much for her.

She walked along the sea's whispering shallows, the waves curling around her bare feet, blanching them, crinkling her skin until it looked like a pale prune, and she felt strong and alive. She felt immortal. The wind flung her hair back around her face, it wrapped her cotton skirt against her bare legs, it filled her lungs and made her skin tingle. Life was a wind, it blew you about like a leaf from an autumn tree, it battered and wailed at you, it wrenched you from your moorings and sent you far from home, but if you faced up to it, squarely, shoulders back, standing your ground, it sent a shiver of exultation through you which was worth the struggle.

Pamela had just washed her hair when the phone rang. She stood in the bathroom, listening, with water dripping down her back, a towel in her hand, and couldn't bring herself to move. The calls had come all day. She had nerved herself to stand there, listening, while her stomach churned and she wanted to scream, hoping that finally he would stay on the line long enough for the police to trace him. It was a Sunday. She wasn't even sure the police phone tap would be in operation on a Sunday. She was alone. She wished Joe was there, but she couldn't ring him and even if she did, she couldn't be certain he would come round, why should he?

In the end she forced herself to move, and picked up the phone. 'Hallo?' Her voice sounded hoarse, the war of nerves was getting to her. She felt she was under siege in the flat, he was out there, the bastard, silently sniping at her from cover. She couldn't see him but she could feel him watching her from somewhere.

The breathing, the breathing... she closed her eyes, cold trickles of water running down the indentation of her spine where tiny hairs were raised in prickling anxiety.

Suddenly she got angry. Why should she put up with this? Why should she have all this crap from anyone?

'Why don't you come round?' she said furiously. 'Let's see you face to face, you bastard, you rotten swine, you make me sick, what sort of lowdown, sneaking coward are you, ringing up every five minutes to make noises like a drowning hippopotamus. If you've got anything to say, say it, come round here and let me see your face. If you had any guts you'd show yourself, but you haven't, have you?'

She stopped only to draw a rough breath and started off again, her voice louder, angrier, more positive. 'Can't you pull a bird, is that it? So ugly the girls laugh at you if you try it on? Is that why you have to make dirty phone calls to people you don't even know? Well, I could do with a good laugh, come on round and let me see what you look like, I bet you couldn't make it anyway, you're probably not even capable of it, no bloody balls at all . . .' She was waiting for him to snarl back, to start using even nastier language than she was, to shout or hang up or something, or anything other than just listen and breathe.

She ran out of insults in the end, she was exhausted, empty. She stood there, listening to him, hearing him listen to her, then the phone clicked and he was gone.

Pamela sat down and cried, on the floor, tears dripping through her fingers.

Clare and Larry walked along the shore talking, their shadows flung in wavering outline on the wet smooth sand. They had left their sandals among the dunes and their footprints ran behind them, already filling with water as the tide flowed in. Looking back Clare saw a shivering little wader standing in one of Larry's footprints and laughed at the way it was digging at the print of his toes.

'I'm ready to start work again,' she said, her hair whipped back by the morning breeze, giving her face a pure, clear outline.

Larry smiled in satisfaction. He turned his windblown head and his expression both amused and annoyed her.

'Don't look so smug and don't say I told you so!' she warned, grimacing at him.

'I'm tempted,' he said.

'Fight it!'

He took her hand lightly in his. 'Race you to the end of the point,' he said, then let go and began to run before she could react. She was slow in starting and had to drive herself to catch up with him. They ran through the water, their bare feet splashing and sending drops of crystal clarity in all directions. The milky blue of the sky ran to the horizon in unbroken light, no clouds, a calm and endless beauty. A dog began to chase after them, barking excitedly. Larry stopped as they reached the place where the land pushed out a sharp finger into the sea, and Clare almost bumped into him, her breath coming pantingly, her skin flushing from the exercise. He put an arm round her to steady her instinctively and she tensed. He gave her a sharp look, feeling her body shrinking from his touch. Clare made herself relax, her eyes apologetic.

'Sorry, I can't help it . . .'

'Still uptight?'

'It just happens. Every time . . .'

'A man touches you?'

She nodded.

'That isn't surprising,' he said. 'Don't worry about it, I understand.' He didn't take his arm away, though. He held her casually while he bent and picked up a flat white stone and sent it skimming across the waves. The dog apparently decided it was a game for his benefit. He plunged in, barking, and swam in a clumsy dog paddle, splashing noisily, to where the stone had sunk.

'He's going to be disappointed,' Larry said and Clare laughed helplessly, although it wasn't really funny, but having started to laugh she couldn't seem to stop. She just reeled against Larry, gulping and shaking in a paroxysm of amusement.

He put both arms around her. 'Okay, calm down now,' he said as if to a child, his tone firm and yet soothing. 'It wasn't that funny.'

'Sorry, sorry,' she spluttered, tears in her eyes, but still laughing. She leaned back against his supporting arms to look at him, choking back the wrenching gasps. 'I'm . . .'

'I know,' Larry said. He pushed back a windblown flurry of hair from her face, looking at her gently. 'Don't worry about it.'

'There's a hell of a lot I mustn't worry about,' Clare said, on the verge of laughing hysterically again.

'Including me,' Larry said and kissed her. His mouth was warm and firm, it didn't insist, yet it was confident, and just as Clare was aware of a sense of panic, he lifted his head again and gave her a cool smile, watching her flushed face.

'You see? No problem, you're as safe as houses with me.' Without haste he dropped his arms and moved off. 'Time to get back, I think,' he said over his shoulder, and Clare slowly followed, not quite certain how she felt. Why had he done that? To reassure her? Because he wanted to? To prove to her that he wasn't going to make a heavy pass at her without warning? He had had some reason – Larry Hillier never did anything without a very good reason.

They walked up through the garden to the cottage and found Mrs Hillier grating cheese in the kitchen. A huge bowl of salad stood on the table. She smiled at them and said to Clare: 'Your friend rang, she asked you to ring her back. It's urgent.'

Clare felt a pang of alarm. She went to ring Pamela at once.

'How are you?' Pamela asked.

'Fine, how are you?'

'Okay,' Pamela said, but she didn't sound okay, she sounded tired and flat. 'Clare, when are you coming back to London?'

'I was just talking to Larry about it. Soon, I hope, why?' Clare picked up something, she wasn't sure what. She only sensed that Pamela was off balance. 'Is anything wrong?' she added quickly.

'Well . . .' Pamela began uncertainly, then in a rush said: 'They've caught him, Clare . . .'

'Caught him.' Clare's voice died away. She went pale.

'All I had to do was try to keep him on the line long enough for them to trace the call, but that took days. He didn't stay on long enough at first, then I realised I wasn't talking to him and I started... that's when they caught him. He stayed on just long enough.'

'How can they be sure it's the same man?'

'He had some of our things in his house.'

Clare leaned against the wall. She was afraid she was going to fall down; she felt waves of bitter bile coming up in the back of her throat. She could not face it. She would have to go through one of those identity parades again, she would have to see him this time, the man who had beaten her and hurt her and raped her like an animal. She had thought she was over it, she was strong and able to cope, but back came the weakness, the fear, the trembling shock of what had happened that night and she was powerless to hold it back, that drowning wave of remembered pain. Her mind flashed beyond the immediate future – she foresaw it all, the trial, the questions, the courtroom and the staring eyes, the full extent of what had been done to her discussed in public by strangers. It would be another rape, this time in public, with curious, gloating voyeurs to watch her being humiliated and degraded and defiled, and for the second time she would be helpless to avert it. No matter how much she fought, how much she struggled, it was going to happen to her.

CHAPTER TEN

'You're quite sure?' pressed Inspector Lucas

'I'm certain. I told you, I didn't see his face. It was dark and he was wearing that thing over his head. I've told you.' Clare got angry suddenly, she had been in a state of nerves ever since Pamela's phone call, she hadn't slept well and she was tired. 'How many times do I have to say it? I haven't any idea what he looked like. Do you think I noticed anything about him? Do you think I want to remember...?'

'Calm down, Miss Forrester,' the other woman said, breaking into the tumult of words. 'Can I get you a glass of water? Some tea?'

Clare slumped back, defeated by the neutral tone. It made her rage seem silly, it made her feel childish. 'I'm sorry,' she said. 'All the men in the line-up looked...' How had they looked? She tried to think but her mind wasn't working very quickly or clearly. She rephrased it. 'I didn't feel I knew any of them, they didn't seem familiar.'

'Well, never mind,' the Inspector said. 'He has been charged, anyway. It would have been useful if you had given us a positive identification, though.'

'He... he admits it?' Clare asked shakily.

The Inspector surveyed her. For a moment Clare didn't think she was going to answer, then the other woman said: 'He's agreed to cooperate with us by making a statement about a number of offences which we have reason to believe he committed.'

Clare frowned impatiently. 'What does that mean? Does he admit it was him who... who broke into our flat?'

'Yes.' Picking up a ballpoint pen the Inspector let it roll down the desk, watching it as if fascinated. 'Once he realised how much evidence there was against him, he decided to talk – if he's cooperative he is likely to be more favourably viewed by the court.'

Clare swallowed. 'Will... shall... I have to give evidence?'

'I'm afraid so, but don't worry, your name will not appear in connection with the case – it is illegal for the press to print a report which names a rape victim.'

Clare's breathing was heavy in the silence which followed, she tried to slow it down, breathe more easily. When she felt able to, she asked: 'But I will have to answer questions? I mean, what will they ask? Will . . .'

'It won't be as embarrassing as you think, don't worry. Look, Miss Forrester, put it out of your mind for the moment – frankly, it could take months to reach the lists. There's a logjam of cases waiting to come up, this one may not get to court for six months or so.' The Inspector smiled wryly. 'The legal system in this country's nearly as bad as the National Health, waiting lists for everything, and the cases drag on for days, tying up my officers when they already have far too much to do. I'm afraid we're all being strangled in red tape and government forms.'

Clare forced a tired smile. 'You think it will take six months before I have to give evidence?'

'At least – we still have a number of investigations to make. He had done a string of burglaries, they'll all be taken into consideration.'

As she was leaving, Clare said: 'Why did he keep ringing the flat? I don't understand . . .'

'Who knows?' The Inspector shrugged. Her face was cynical and indifferent. 'I gave up trying to explain what makes these people tick a long time ago.'

Larry was parked across the road from the station. Clare climbed into the car and he turned to watch her, his arm along the seat.

'Okay?'

She nodded, wishing he wouldn't look at her. She felt as if the ambiance of the police station hung around her like a rotting odour. She did not want anyone looking at her until she had had a bath.

'Did you pick him out?'

Clare shook her head.

'But he's being charged?'

She nodded again.

'Has he admitted it?'

'Yes,' Clare said and the word crawled from between her lips, she didn't open her mouth to let it escape.

Larry started the car. The window was open and through it Clare breathed the decaying smell of the river in warm sunshine, the scent of roses in the Embankment gardens past which they were driving, the summer smell of flowering privet and the acrid fumes of petrol, a poisonously heady bouquet which made her head ache. The traffic was choked, bumper to bumper; horns blared, buses inched along, crammed to the doors, the men were in shirt sleeves and light-coloured trousers, the women in summer dresses. Clare longed to be back in the quiet fields in the marsh. She closed her eyes and yearned for silence.

'I can't understand why he kept ringing...' she said, to herself, yet speaking aloud almost without realising it.

It was a shock to her when Larry answered and she knew she had spoken aloud. 'Some men are like that, they enjoy hurting, frightening...'

'Why?' Clare asked without expecting an answer, it was not so much a question as a cry of protest.

'It turned him on,' Larry said and she went first red, then white. She wondered how Larry would look at her if she told him what she had dreamt last night. She had woken up with a gasp of fear and lain here, shaking, while she remembered her dream. It had been so vivid that she had thought for the first few seconds that it had just happened, it was no dream at all. She had been back in the flat, in the dark bedroom, with that man – struggling, screaming, trying to hit him. Then she had stopped screaming and fighting. She had felt it. She had felt what he was doing to her, she had given in. When she came out of the dream with that cry she had been vibrating in the throes of orgasm.

She had slid out of the bed, trembling, and crept into the bathroom where she washed from head to foot in cold water. She had felt dirty, she had loathed herself, and when she did go back to bed, she dared not let herself fall asleep

170

again in case she met those monsters of the mind, the unrecognised desires she had never suspected and even now refused to admit existed. She had lain awake for hours, anguished, examining herself like a prosecuting counsel trying to force her reluctant memory to give an answer to a question she hadn't even thought of asking herself before. Had she had an orgasm that night?

She had refused to remember the details of what happened. She had told the police so starkly, so barely, she had not been asked what she now asked herself. Oh, they had asked: did you struggle? did he have orgasm? did he force you to have oral sex? Their questions had been both crude and polite. They had asked painful questions as if it was a matter of course. No intonation had given away what they felt. They had not asked how she felt – they had not said: did you finally give in? did you have an orgasm?

But in court, she thought, would they ask that in court? Faced with that question with a battery of eyes on her, what would she say?

Sitting up in rigid torment she hadn't known, but as the light began to fill the dawn sky she had calmed down enough to be sure her fears were just night fears. She was sure she hadn't – she remembered no sexual excitement, only black, sick terror. She had suffered the rape of her body, she had not accepted it. Yet now she felt she had been raped again – by her own mind. What twisted process had gone on in her own unconscious to prompt it to produce that dream?

She wished she dared ask someone: why? Why?

But she knew she couldn't, she would never dare to admit to anyone that she had ever had such a dream. It could only be seen as an admission of guilt, nobody would believe she hadn't enjoyed what was done to her, the dream would make it sound as if she had wanted the rape, but that was not true. And even the realisation that she dared not ask anyone, confess to anyone, made her feeling of guilt stronger, because surely she would not be afraid of what people might think if she was totally sure of her own innocence?

She might tell herself it was nonsense, she had been a victim, not a willing participant, but she knew it could be inverted, turned on its head so easily by modern psychology. She could just imagine what a defence psychologist would make of her dream – she would end up the guilty party, she would have incited it, invited it.

She felt she stood on shifting sand. Whichever way she moved her feet slid and slipped, she was afraid of disaster. She was no longer able to feel certain even of her own mind – it could play tricks on her, deceive and betray her.

It seemed impossible to believe that so short a time ago she had walked on the beach in the summer sun and laughed and felt strong and free.

What had happened so rapidly to her reborn sensations of inner strength? Where had they gone? She was back where she had been, trapped in guilt and self-doubt and fear.

'What are you brooding about now?' Larry asked her, glancing sideways. In the strong sunlight his tanned skin gleamed and his lashes made a dark, barred pattern below his eyes. Clare absently noted how attractive he was in profile, his features had a male strength which was reassuring. Tom had a powerful face, too, but lately she found his self-assertive aggression more than she could take. Although Larry was tough and decisive, he wasn't always attacking you. He was quite happy to let people go their own way so long as it worked out in the end. He gave you space, Clare thought, he left you free to move, treated you as an adult with a mind of your own. Tom didn't. He never had. Larry saw you as yourself, respected your integrity and personal freedom, probably because his mother had always treated him with respect even in his childhood. Tom's mother had taught him that women were objects; cushions for him to lean on, servants to bring him things, nurses to pamper him. They were not people existing in their own sphere, with lives of their own to lead. They existed for Tom's benefit, but Clare had had enough of giving Tom what he needed without ever getting anything back.

'I'm not brooding,' she said. 'Just thinking.'

172

'I shouldn't,' Larry told her, pulling up outside her flat. 'You're depressed at the moment, that's a bad time to do any thinking. You tend to see the world as a grey place when you're depressed.'

'Tell me about it,' Clare said drily and he laughed.

'Don't be in too much of a hurry to get back to normal, that just delays things. Sit it out, Clare. Let the depression ride and try to keep your mind off it.'

'You mean, come back to work?' Clare said in mild irony.

He looked at her, smiling. 'Not if you don't want to – feel free.'

I wish I could, Clare thought, I wish I could.

Larry drove off and Clare let herself into her flat. Pamela was lying full length on the couch drinking a glass of orange juice and staring at the television, where a trio of girls were bashing out a song which was brash and cheerful and almost totally tuneless.

The glass tilted in Pamela's hand as she felt Clare behind her. There was a tinkle of ice cubes. She put the glass down and jumped up, her face so bright Clare was almost taken aback.

'Clare! When did you get back?'

'This morning,' Clare said, feeling stupidly shy. It seemed years since she had seen Pamela, she hadn't expected such a warm welcome, it was unlike the Pamela she remembered, the self-sufficient, private girl she had lived with for the past two years.

'I've missed you,' said Pamela. 'The flat was like a morgue.'

'I'm sorry about the phone calls,' Clare said and wondered why she was apologising, as though she had been responsible for the man who had made them, but then she realised that that was how she felt. She felt responsible for him, almost as if she had conjured him into being, made him appear, drawn one of the monsters of the unconscious out into the light and given him a three-dimensional life which allowed him to impinge on others.

'Don't be silly, it wasn't your fault,' said Pamela. 'Are you hungry? Can I get you anything? I was going to fix myself a salad, I've got some cottage cheese.'

173

'I'm not very hungry.' Clare followed her into the kitchen and helped her slice tomatoes and cucumber, shred lettuce and wash it, talking as they worked. 'You should have told me you were still getting calls, I'd forgotten all about it.'

'Well, good, I didn't want to bother you, I'm glad you forgot it.' Pamela deftly removed the seeds from a pepper. 'He's a head case, you know. What do you bet they don't even put him in prison? They'll send him to have psychiatric treatment and tell him he's sick.'

Clare shuddered. 'He is.'

Pamela looked at her, biting her lip. 'Sorry, I shouldn't have talked about him. Don't get upset. God, I'm so tactless, I could bite my tongue out.'

Clare forced a smile. 'I asked about it. I can't keep pretending it didn't happen. Do you know what Tom said? He said he didn't blame me for what happened.'

Pamela hissed, going red. 'You're kidding? He really said . . . God, that guy needs kicking.' She looked anxiously at Clare. 'You didn't take any notice? I mean, look, Tom Prescott is a selfish, thick-headed swine, you . . .'

'I told him to take a running jump,' Clare said and Pamela laughed.

'That's more like it. You should have done that long ago.'

Over the salad, Pamela told her how the police had discovered some of their possessions in the man's flat. Clare felt sick. He had invaded her life, the thought of him touching her things was repellent, another violation of her. He was like the greedy tide, eating up the edges of the land inch by inch. She was partially digested already, not merely by the actual rape, but by having him in her mind, in her dreams. There were so many ways of possession – the least dangerous was the physical one. The mind was far more vulnerable than the body. It retained memories longer, it retained the imprint of event, like some plastic surface which receives the weight of whatever crashes into it and holds the impression of it, mimics and clones it. Unless she fought it, she might become him, his mirror image, his thing and possession. Her life had been in a state of turmoil already the night he broke into the flat. She had been in that impressionable state of mind which depression and weariness can produce. Ever since, she had been going through cycles of mood, of reaction; confused, bewildered, struggling to steady the balance of her mind as it see-sawed from one extreme to the other. She wanted badly to reach stable ground.

'What's Larry's mother like?' Pamela asked.

'I like her,' Clare said, which wasn't an answer to the question, but she didn't know what to say about Mrs Hillier. It would be like explaining to someone what a bird was like, you could describe the plumage, the colours, the size and shape – but would that tell the listener very much? Your eyes were unreliable witnesses. They could be misled and what they did report to the brain was often mis-interpreted.

'Is she like him?' asked Pamela.

'Yes and no,' Clare said and Pamela laughed.

'You're a mine of information, aren't you?'

'It's hard to describe her, she isn't like anyone I've ever met. Some people would call her eccentric. She's certainly different, it's hard to say how – she's more herself than anyone I've ever met. She says what she thinks when she decides to say anything at all and if she doesn't want to talk, she doesn't. Some days she didn't say a syllable to me.'

'She sounds ghastly,' Pamela said, frowning. 'Pretty self-ish, anyway. I mean, you were her guest and . . .' She broke off, wondering if it had been a good idea for Clare to go and stay with Larry Hillier's mother. It didn't sound as if the woman had been too pleased to have her there, she had hardly gone out of her way to make Clare feel welcome. Pamela looked at Clare closely, her face anxious. Clare really didn't look as rested and relaxed as Pamela had hoped, she was pale and drawn, she looked no better than she had before she left for Romney Marsh.

'She isn't selfish,' Clare said with certainty. 'It did me good to be with her, I learnt a lot from her.'

Pamela wasn't convinced but she decided not to argue

with Clare, from the look of her she might start to cry any minute. Changing the subject, she said: 'Your mother rang the other day to see if I'd heard from you. She said she hadn't heard a word since you went down to the Marsh. She seemed worried.'

'I'd better ring her,' Clare said reluctantly, and went over to the phone. Her mother answered it on the fourth ring, her voice tense, saying the number.

'It's Clare. How are you, Mother?'

'Clare! Are you still in Kent? How are you?' Beattie's voice was nervous, it sounded odd. 'I was anxious when I didn't hear from you.'

'I'm sorry, there wasn't a telephone. I'm back in London now and I'm fine.' Clare injected breezy confidence into her own voice.

'Did you have a good time?'

'It was peaceful, I didn't do much except swim and walk. How are you and Dad?'

'We're fine,' Beattie said, wishing she could think of some way of breaking through the barrier she felt between them. Did other women talk to their daughters in the same distant way she heard herself talking to Clare? Clare wasn't a child any more, she was a woman. They should be on the same level, able to talk honestly. It's my fault we can't she thought, it is all my fault. 'The weather's been very good down here, what was it like at Romney?'

'Sunny,' Clare said, aware of a peculiar anger inside herself. Who was this woman on the other end of the line, talking to her politely? What did she know about her mother, or Beattie know about her? Resentment choked her, she struggled with her feelings, afraid of them, refusing to face up to her own sense of betrayal, because it would hurt too much to think about things she had managed to wrap up in healing, self-induced amnesia and bury at the very back of memory. The griefs of childhood persist where others fade and fall away. Inside the young woman talking so calmly in a polite tone was a small child who had never been given love from her mother and had never known why, had carried a lifelong burden of guilt and rejection because of it. She had been so grateful for Tom's love, so eager to keep it, that she had been ready to let him walk all over her, she had been forced into humiliating shifts to make sure he stayed with her, just because as a child her mother had not loved her.

'Why don't you come down and stay for a few days?' Beattie asked without much hope. My own daughter and I don't know what to say to her, she thought; I'm ashamed, I've been so selfish all my life, I've thought of nothing but my own feelings, I never thought what I was doing to Clare. What have I done to her? I can't even ask her, I can only guess and maybe that's my punishment.

'I've got to start work again,' Clare said and heard her mother sigh.

'Clare, there's so much I want to say, we never talk, do we? Can't we try? I want to get to know you. Isn't that stupid, a stupid thing to say, but I don't know any other way of saying it. I want to help, you're my daughter, I know you're having a bad time and I want to help but I don't know what to say to you.' Beattie was stammering, her voice husky and nervous, she jammed all the words together in a blur because otherwise she might not manage to get them all out. If she paused or hesitated she would stop talking altogether.

Clare couldn't speak, she couldn't think of a way of answering. After a moment she said: 'I'll come down soon, as soon as I can, I'll let you know.' Clare knew her mother was trying to reach out to her, but she held back because she could not respond; she was frozen at some inner level which she could not reach. Her childhood had shaped her whole life, she saw that now. Life always seems to be in midstream to those involved in it, but from the bank an observer can see a final shape, the bends and twists of fate and character. Clare could see how much her own nature had been shaped by what happened to her as a child; a child which is not loved feels a complex knot of reactions, resentment, pain, guilt, yearning, grief. Only a fully aware adult can untie those knots and Clare knew she was going to have to, but not yet.

Beattie sighed again.

'I'll come soon,' Clare said quickly, emphatically, trying to get over to her mother that she meant it. 'We'll talk then, okay?'

'Look after yourself,' Beattie said. 'Keep in touch.'

As Beattie put the phone down, Derek Forrester came out of the sitting room, a newspaper in his hand, and looked at her sharply. 'Was that Clare?'

'Yes, she's back in London.'

'Why didn't you tell me she was on the phone? I haven't spoken to her for months. She's my daughter, too, you know, I've a right to talk to her. Why do you always try to keep her to yourself?'

'What are you talking about? I don't do anything of the kind.'

'You try to shut me out, you make it clear I don't belong here. I just sleep here and pay the bills, more fool me. I'd get out if I had any sense.' Derek had gone red in the face, his hands clenching on the newspaper.

'Why haven't you?' Beattie said quietly.

'You want me to go? Is that what you're saying? Don't beat around the bush, out with it. Why do you always shut your mouth like that, why don't you say what you're thinking? I'm sick of your frozen silences, your long faces.' He was shouting, quivering with rage. When he was angry his chin trembled, she thought, staring at him. It made him look like a child about to burst into tears.

'I'm worried about Clare. That break-in at her place had a terrible effect on her.' She tried to sound calm, she wanted to talk to him. Some days she never spoke to anyone but the milkman. The only times she and Derek ever talked, they seemed to shout at each other. In a way that was better than the years when they ignored each other altogether, at least they were no longer pretending not to see one another.

'I blame you,' Derek said. 'She'd never have left home at all if you hadn't frozen her out. You're not a woman, you're an icicle.'

Beattie wanted to cry. It was true, she couldn't deny it. They had all suffered because she hadn't been prepared to admit she was human, they were all human. She had gone on trying to punish Derek for his infidelity for years without ever actually letting him break away. She had condemned him to a lifetime of imprisonment with her but it had been she, herself, who had been in prison. Derek had escaped every day: to work, to his golf club, to other women. It had been Beattie who stayed inside four walls and suffered a living death. She should have divorced Derek and maybe married again herself – she might have had other children, she might have been a happy woman all these years, she would certainly have given Derek a chance to be happy. Now, looking back, she did not even care about what had happened the night Clare went into Donna's room and saw her father and her aunt making love. What did that matter now? For that one stupid incident she had wrecked all their lives – they had ceased to be a family that night. She and Clare had never been close, Nino had died and Donna had vanished. Beattie had laid all the blame on Donna and Derek. Now she sorted out their original act of infidelity and saw that her own later behaviour had been the worst crime.

Poor Derek, she thought – what a relentless punishment for so trivial a sin, and she didn't blame him for finding what comfort he could with other women ever since. He was human, he was just an ordinary man and she had punished him for his humanity, but, even worse, she had been punishing Clare from the moment of her birth for her mere existence. She looked at all her own actions ever since Clare was born and could find no forgiveness for herself.

'Do you think I don't blame myself?' she said. 'It's my fault, I wish I could forget that, but I can't. It's my fault I can't talk to my own daughter, just as it's my fault you have other women.'

He went red. 'What are you on about now?' He was blustering, uneasy, not sure what she was going to say.

'I don't blame you,' Beattie said and he looked angry.

'Aren't you bloody generous, then? Am I supposed to be

grateful? How you have the nerve to stand there and tell me you don't blame me in that patronising tone . . .'

'I'm not patronising you.'

'That's what it sounds like to me. I don't have to ask your permission to have another woman, you haven't been my wife for God knows how many years, you have no right to complain.'

'I'm not complaining. I want you to be happy,' she began and Derek's colour rose until he was crimson to his hair-line.

'You what? I don't believe my ears. What is all this?'

'If you want a divorce, I won't stand in your way,' Beattie said. It was what she should have said to him years ago but she hadn't been able to let him go then, she had wanted to keep him under her eyes and punish him, she realised that now and she hated herself.

Derek was staring at her, stupefaction in his face. 'Do you want a divorce? Is that it? Have you got someone else?'

'No, of course not,' she said, surprised in her turn. She had expected him to jump at her offer, he wasn't reacting the way she had expected. 'But I'll be fine, I'll manage on my own, don't let any worries about that stop you.'

'Oh, you can manage, can you?' he sneered. 'What would you do then? Get a job? You've never worked in your life, you wouldn't know how. Someone has always taken care of you; first your father and then me. All you know is how to run a house and you're too old to learn anything else. You'll be retirement age before long, don't you realise that? So will I be – a few more years and I'll be drawing a pension. It's too late for either of us to build a new life – if you'd said this to me twenty years ago I might have had a chance of finding someone else, but you didn't. You made me feel so guilty over Donna that I couldn't walk away from you then and the years have dragged by without me even noticing what was happening to me. Now I'm old, too old and it is too late. And now you stand there and say: do you want a divorce? Do you want to get out of my house, Derek, because I've decided I don't need you any more . . .'

He had worked himself into a fury, his face dark red, his

body shaking. Coming towards her, his hands thrust out as if he wanted to put them round her throat and strangle her, he shouted: 'You bitch, you damned selfish bitch, I'd like to kill you, do you hear? I'd like to kill you. You want me to be happy, do you? God, that's bloody funny, I haven't been happy in twenty years because of you. I couldn't leave you and I couldn't get near you. You bitch . . .'

He was crying by the time he had finished, his words wrenched out of him in thick, ugly sobs, his face distorted with emotion.

Beattie got up and put her arms round him. He stood there, trembling violently, and she rubbed one hand up and down his spine, murmuring as though he was a child. 'Ssh . . . don't . . . never mind . . . I'm sorry . . . ssh . . .'

'There isn't anyone else,' he said with his face against her. 'There was but it's over, she found someone else. I kept saying I'd leave you but I never could and in the end she found someone else.'

'I'm sorry, Derek,' Beattie said without any sense of irony. 'I'm sorry.'

'Where would I go? I couldn't . . . once I've retired I won't even have my job . . . I'm lonely enough now, God knows, but it would be worse.'

'Don't go,' Beattie said, her hand moving up and down in that gentle massage, feeling his body warmth with a sense of intense comfort. 'I don't want you to go, I'd miss you. I just wanted you to be happy if that was the way you wanted it, but I'd like you to stay.'

'We could try again,' he said without real hope, his voice weak and barely audible.

'Yes, we'll try again,' she said, strongly, and her hand went up to stroke his grey hair.

He was silent but his body leaned on hers, the trembling slowly died away, and his breathing slowed.

Clare woke up with a violent jolt and found herself sitting up in bed in the dark, shuddering from head to toe. The door burst open and Pamela crashed through into the room switching on the light.

'Are you all right? Whatever is it, Clare? You were screaming blue murder.'

Clare burst into tears. Pamela came to sit on the bed, put her arms round her, rocked her like a baby. Clare talked, not knowing what she was saying any more, the words spilled out jerkily in copious gushes. Once she had started she couldn't stop, she told Pamela everything, she felt like someone who pulls the bandage off a wound and lets all the pus and weeping foulness run out. She talked and talked, her face hidden against Pamela, and Pamela listened and held her, and went on with that gentle, rocking movement.

When she had run out of words, when she had drained her mind of the festering decay which had gathered in it, she gave a worn gulp. 'Sorry, I . . .'

'Don't be silly, that was better out than in,' Pamela said wryly. 'Why don't we make some tea? I could do with a cup, could you?'

Clare felt uncomfortable, she had said too much. She wished she hadn't talked her head off like that, she had told Pamela things she had never thought she would tell anyone, she felt raw and exposed, she wanted to hide from Pamela's eyes.

'Stop looking guilty,' Pamela said, holding Clare's dressing-gown out. 'Put this on, you're shivering. Do you think there's anything special about your secret thoughts? Don't you think we all have them? Are you surprised you dream about that bastard? You were terrified when it happened, you've been terrified ever since. You're trying to come to terms with it, your unconscious is processing those memories, trying to make them bearable.'

She went down the corridor into the kitchen and Clare followed, watched her putting on the kettle and getting out the cups.

'But why do I . . . give in?' Clare asked in a barely audible voice. 'Why, Pam?'

'Don't you think it could be sheer blue funk? Haven't you ever been scared of something – I mean, really petrified – and finally done it just to get it over with because if you didn't you'd go on and on thinking about it? A guy I knew was scared stiff of heights, he was convinced that if he looked over the edge of a cliff or out of a tenth storey window, he'd lose his balance and fall over. It obsessed him, he used to have nightmares about falling every night. In the end he went climbing in the Welsh mountains just to get over it and now he spends all his spare time climbing.'

'That's different,' Clare said. 'I mean – mountains are neutral, they don't threaten us. You can't compare the two things.'

'Why not? Fear is a neutral emotion – it's your fear that creates the dream, not the bastard who raped you. He can't do anything to your head, it's you who's doing it. It's the feelings you have during the dream that really matter, not what happens in it. Ask yourself how you feel when you're dreaming, not what you dream about.'

'It's the same thing,' Clare said, sitting down and putting her elbows on the table, her chin on her hands. Her legs were trembling. 'I keep dreaming it. I feel sick every time, I feel sick now, just thinking about it.'

The kettle boiled and Pamela went over to make the tea, warming the pot, adding the tea, pouring on the boiling water. Clare watched as intently as if she had never seen tea made before.

'I think you may be dreaming about it because you haven't talked about it,' Pamela said gently over her shoulder. 'You've got to get it out of your mind somehow, Clare.'

'I've done nothing but talk about it – the police . . .'

'Not about what happened,' Pamela said, cutting in, 'about what you feel. You've shut it all inside your head, so you can't forget it, you've got to let it out.'

Clare stared at the table as Pamela put a cup of tea in front of her. 'I couldn't talk about the dreams because I was ashamed. I didn't want it to happen, it was . . . why do I dream things like that?'

Pamela put an arm round her and hugged her. 'Stop blaming yourself and don't talk about being ashamed, you've got nothing to be ashamed about. I think you're dreaming like that just because you've been refusing to admit it ever happened, but your mind knows it did happen and it won't let you block it out. Don't feel ashamed – feel angry, hate the bastard, let your feelings rip, don't force them all down all the time.'

Clare laughed unsteadily, and Pamela said: 'That's better,' smiling at her. 'I'm going to make some toast, want some? To hell with my diet, we'll have a midnight feast. Did you read school stories when you were a kid? We had a craze for them, it was ridiculous, because they were pure fantasy.'

'I don't remember,' Clare said, watching her as she popped bread into the toaster and found a jar of marmalade.

'We did, all the time. They're a weird mixture, snobbish fantasy about being at a posh public school, and lesbian fantasy about mysterious French mistresses who are really spies in disguise – great traumatic scenes where the heroine in the cute little knee-high gymslip unmasks her with a sob in her throat because she has worshipped her from afar and now sees that her idol has feet of clay. Nowadays no publisher would dare put out such stuff. Freud ruined that branch of literature.'

Clare started to laugh. 'I used to read Enid Blyton, I think, those books of hers which read like junior Agatha Christie . . .'

'I know the ones you mean.' Pamela yawned. 'Even at school I liked my literature to have a strong sexual content of one kind or another.'

'How precocious.'

'I was,' Pamela agreed. 'Sex has always seemed to me to be a fascinating subject.' She grinned, then her eyes changed, lost their smile.

'What's wrong?' Clare asked.

'Nothing,' Pamela said. 'A cat walked over my grave, that's all.' She was silent for a moment, then said: 'Clare . . .'

'Yes?'

'I'm . . . I'm . . . oh, hell.'

'What is it?' Clare asked, surprised and amused by her irritated, disgusted expression.

'I think I'm in love,' Pamela muttered.

Clare couldn't help it. She laughed.

'It isn't funny!' Pamela looked as if Clare had hit her in the face.

Clare sobered. 'Sorry, it was just your face, as if you were telling me you had a terminal disease.'

'It feels like it. They tell you a hell of a lot about love, they never stop talking about it. You get it from pop music and romantic novels and women's magazines, you even get it from Shakespeare and the Bible, and films. They rhyme it, June, moon, soon, they sing it, put it on the backs of cornflake packets. They make it sound like the world's best offer, they never tell you that it hurts like hell and can make you wish you were dead.' Pamela stopped talking, her mouth open, horrified to realise what she was saying. Her words hung around the room like Christmas decorations, trembling and shining. Clare stared at her, incredulously.

'Who is it?'

Pamela's flush grew hectic. 'Oh, forget it.' She moved and Clare put out a hand to grab her arm.

'Hey, you listened to me, I made a fool of myself and you listened, why clam up on me now? You obviously need to talk.'

'Do I?' Pamela grimaced. 'I suppose I do. I wouldn't have said anything otherwise, would I? I'd have kept my big mouth shut.'

'It isn't Larry, is it?' Clare asked on a wild surmise, feeling an odd sinking inside her. She couldn't imagine Larry and Pamela in love – she could imagine they might fancy each other physically, but she couldn't picture them going crazy over each other somehow. Larry wasn't the type. But then she hadn't thought Pamela was the type to go crazy over anyone and she had been wrong.

'Larry? Hillier?' Pamela stared at her. 'Good God, no, you must be joking.' She hesitated. 'It's Joe, actually. Joe Harper.'

Clare was amazed. 'Joe Harper? The doctor from St Aidan's? You're in love with him?'

Very flushed, Pamela scraped butter thinly across a slice

185

of toast, pushed the marmalade over to Clare and handed her the toast. 'The middle of the night is a dangerous time for talking, you end up telling secrets you'd have sworn you'd go to the stake to keep. Forget I said anything.'

'I didn't know you saw much of Joe Harper, you've kept it very quiet.' Clare spread marmalade on the toast and bit into it, watching Pamela as she sat down and carefully put marmalade on her own, unbuttered toast.

'I don't see him, well, not often. And when I do, he's kind and indifferent, he treats me as if I was his sister. I hardly know the man.' She was half angry, half self-derisive. 'Oh, I'm crazy, I don't even believe in being in love, I must be out of my mind to think I'm in love with a man who treats me as if I had leprosy.'

'Does he know . . .' Clare stopped, biting her lip. That had been a stupid question to ask, and Pamela was looking as if she had hit her in the face.

'I hope not,' she said with furious emphasis. 'You don't think I've told him? I tried not to admit it to myself for ages, it seemed so stupid. His opinion of me is practically nil, I don't know why I can't stop thinking about him, but I can't.' She stopped and sighed, her mouth wry. 'But he probably has a shrewd idea – I kissed him the other night and he told me he didn't want to get involved with me, he was very kind but firm, like someone refusing you a loan. I felt two inches high.'

Clare felt very sorry for her, she didn't know what to say, because she couldn't imagine the two of them being happy together, they were so obviously worlds apart. Joe Harper was gentle and serious and a dedicated doctor, he would not fit into Pamela's frenetic life. Pamela couldn't have chosen anyone more disastrously wrong – why hadn't she fallen in love with someone whose life style fitted her own? But then, did anyone ever make a free choice about falling in love? Love did not wait to be invited, it just arrived.

Clare went back to work next day. Her talk with Pamela had convinced her it was the best idea. She was nervous about it. She spent a long time getting ready, she wanted to look normal, she wanted to look cool and confident. Larry had said he hadn't told anyone what had happened, all they knew was that she had been ill, she had had concussion after being knocked out by a burglar. He hadn't mentioned the rape. Clare couldn't help wondering if they would put two and two together when the case came up. She would have to be off work to give evidence. Suppose someone at the office read the story in the newspapers and guessed the truth?

The office was bright and modern. It took up half the third floor of a new office block. Clare had a room of her own, an office just big enough to fit her desk into, and a few rows of shelves with books on them, a couple of steel filing cabinets. Her secretary had a desk in the open office outside where all the typists and secretaries sat. Larry had an office twice as big as hers and the art editor had one next to his, but the largest office apart from Larry's was that of the accountant. He understood money so he had the biggest office.

Clare had to walk through the open-plan office when she arrived. The other girls were surprised and curious to see her. 'How are you? Better? How's the head? Terrible, having your flat broken into like that – did much get stolen?'

'Yes, no, yes,' Clare said whichever applied, and kept on smiling. Larry came through the main door and looked at her quickly.

'Oh, good, you're here,' he said, as though he had expected to see her, although she hadn't told him yesterday that she meant to start work.

'We'd better talk,' he said, striding towards his own office. Clare saw the other girls looking after him. Larry had his admirers among them, he was the sort of man some women find irresistible, he had a combination of charms which were so entirely masculine – ruthless determination to get his own way, domineering assurance and an ability to assume a little boy lost look when his overriding temper hadn't got him what he wanted. Clare grimaced at his disappearing back.

'I've got a pile of back stuff on my desk a mile high,' she protested. 'I ought to look at that first.'

'Come on in here,' he said in his most peremptory tone, and she gave a helpless, wry shrug.

187

'I'll see you later,' she told her secretary, who was slitting open mail and sorting it.

'Yes, okay,' Jeanie said, with cheerful complacency. 'I can cope,' she said. Clare had been away for so long that Jeanie was used to dealing with business on her own. Clare realised they might have a little problem there – Jeanie had the slightly smug look of someone who feels they're in charge. She would have to be disillusioned.

Larry was standing by the window in his office, his black hair given the blue-green sheen of a blackbird's wing by an aureole of golden light which fuzzed and blurred the edges of his razor-sharp profile. He was jingling the small change in his pocket, his shoulders back.

'Can't this wait, Larry?' Clare asked impatiently and he turned to stare at her.

'We've got a lot to discuss.'

'Until I've been through all the papers on my desk I shan't be able to discuss anything properly. You might give me time to adjust my mind to work again!'

'Why are you so belligerent this morning?'

'I'm not belligerent,' Clare said belligerently. 'I'm just in a hurry to get back to normal and I can't do that standing here chatting to you.'

'I'm delighted to hear you want to get back to work, but don't snarl at me.'

'Who's snarling?' she snarled. 'If anyone around here is doing any snarling, it's you.'

'I can see you got out of bed the wrong side this morning,' Larry informed her with an air of martyred patience which made her irritation rise like mercury in a thermometer. She had felt a tingle of nervous impatience ever since she got up. It had run through her whenever she was provoked by inanimate objects – the bus had lumbered slowly, like a landlocked whale grinding along; the bus conductor's ticket machine had jammed and he had spent some time poking inside it with his ball point pen, muttering; Clare's heel was faintly loose on her left shoe and a man had given her a wolf whistle as she was hurrying towards the office. Clare had flung him a glare, tempted to slap his face. She

188

was in no mood to put up with male advances this morning.

'What did you want to talk to me about?' she demanded of Larry and he walked across to sit down behind his desk, flinging one hand outwards in a commanding gesture.

'Sit down!'

Clare was tempted to walk out. The tone made every hair on her head bristle, her spine went rigid, like the back of an offended cat. She felt like spitting and hissing at him. For a minute she stood there, fighting with a desire to yell back, and Larry watched her, his expression making it clear he knew precisely what was going through her head.

'Don't turn feminine on me, Clare,' he said then.

'What's that supposed to mean?' she came back at once, infuriated.

'If I called Mike Fratton in here and told him to sit down he wouldn't turn on me like a demented hamster,' he said and Clare was torn between fury and laughter. While she was struggling with both she sat down and Larry grinned at her.

'That's better – can we have a moratorium on sexist issues? Can we agree you're a woman and I'm a man and so what and can we then get down to some work?'

Clare's laughter won. 'Yes,' she said, then: 'You're maddening, do you know that? I can't stand having you walking in and out of my head as if you lived there, will you please stop trying to read my mind?'

'I'm not trying,' he said. 'Your mind isn't hard to read – it lives on your face, you show everything at the moment. Once upon a time I didn't know what to make of you, you kept very buttoned up, but you've been going around showing everything for the past few weeks, totally zipless. If you don't want me to know what you're thinking, you'd better not be so obvious.'

'Thanks for the advice,' she said, appalled.

'I was expecting it, of course,' he said. 'Hostility to the male sex is often an aftermath of rape.'

She looked at the point above his head, her body tense with anger. 'You're an authority, are you?'

'Hardly,' he said. 'I'm going on what I've read about it. I can't remember ever knowing anyone who got raped . . .'

'Will you stop talking about it?' Clare felt flames shooting through the top of her head. 'You make it sound as though I was a traffic accident statistic . . .'

'In a way, you are, I suppose,' Larry said in a thoughtful voice, looking at her with an almost coaxing little smile, inviting her, she felt, to discuss the matter academically with him, to be grown up about it, to be calm and civilised about the brutal and uncivilised act which had been committed against her.

She began to get up, trembling with the force of her own emotions. If she stayed she might do something unforgivable – hit him, throw things, say blistering, savage words which she couldn't recall later.

'Sit down, for God's sake,' Larry said, leaning back in his chair. She looked at him with dislike. There he sat, God's gift to the world, aware of his power and grace, his precious masculinity which conferred on him an invisible halo, the sign of entry to a secret society so deeply entrenched that it could pretend it did not exist while at all levels of society it controlled the levers of power, while paying lip service to a pretence that the two sexes were equal. The equality was false while it was granted by men as a favour. Equals do not grant favours to each other. They exist side by side, on the same level.

'You're as much a victim of an accident as if you had been crossing a road when you were hit by a car,' Larry said.

'It was no accident!'

'You were in the wrong place at the wrong time,' Larry said. 'You were unlucky.'

'I can't believe I'm hearing this!' Clare said, almost speechless.

'Every man you meet isn't going to be a rapist any more than you're likely to get knocked down by a hit and run driver every time you try to cross a road. At the moment, you're confusing the general with the particular. You had a bad piece of luck. You met one man who was a sadistic bastard, that doesn't mean you have to shut yourself into a nunnery or go around attacking every other man you clap eyes on – you didn't choose to get raped . . .'

'I'm glad you realise that,' she hissed.

'But you chose Tom Prescott,' Larry said coolly. 'Out of all the men in the world, you picked one who was going to walk all over you with ruthless indifference to your feelings – and that was no accident. You're some sort of masochist, Clare, or you wouldn't have put up with what from where I sit looks like a prolonged and indecent act of sexual rape going on for years.'

Clare's mouth opened and stayed open. She stared at him and Larry gazed back, his eyebrows raised in silent challenge.

When she didn't, couldn't, think of anything to say in answer to that, he said: 'So can we drop all the hassle and touchy readiness to take offence and get to work like two sane adults? Because you're just wasting time and energy shooting at me – save both for more vital targets.' He stopped and looked at her. 'Okay?'

'Get stuffed,' Clare said without heat. 'You pompous self-satisfied baboon.'

Larry laughed. 'That's better.' He reached for a pile of folders. 'Right, now let's get down to brass tacks ... first, the Reid contract, I'll fill you in on how far the Graphics department have got with that.'

CHAPTER ELEVEN

Clare expected daily to hear from the police. Surely they must have a date for the trial? Each morning she opened her bedroom door, looked along the hall at the mat. She picked up the post as if it was an unexploded bomb. There was no news. Summer wore on hot and getting hotter, people were brown and irritable. They stopped saying: what wonderful weather, and started saying: when is it going to rain? It was far too hot to work. Everyone sat about, sighing. The sky sagged over the city, too blue, too bright, it made your eyes ache to look at it. Everyone wore sunglasses and when Clare and Pamela went swimming, the pool was so crowded you hardly had room to wiggle a fin.

Larry was unbearable, a whizzing spark which made her skin cringe. She ran after him and when he had flashed off again, furious at his inability to make people think as fast as he did, she stayed behind to calm and placate the spluttering, burnt out victims of his wrath.

'I don't know what I'd do without you,' he said.

'Sack them all if they didn't resign first,' Clare said. The hot weather was his element, he had a Mediterranean mind, his olive skin glowed with health and he was cheerfully energetic.

'I'm sick of sunshine,' Pamela said next morning. 'The first week of September and there isn't a sign of a break in this weather.'

'Don't complain, you'll want it back if it goes.' Clare was reading a letter from her mother. 'My parents are going on a cruise at the end of the month,' she said. 'To Egypt . . . I can't believe it. Egypt, of all places.'

'Why not? I'd like to go there myself,' Pamela said, then looked out of the window at the eternal blue sky and groaned. 'No, maybe not, too hot. Do you know, yesterday instead of having lunch I came back here and had a shower? I was so hot I was almost crazy.'

'Egypt,' Clare said, shaking her head as she slid the letter back into the envelope. She tried to picture her mother and father strolling around the temples at Luxor talking about embalming rites and sacred crocodiles and her mind boggled. 'They suggested I brought you down for a weekend, would you like to go?' She didn't make the invitation pressing, she couldn't believe Pamela would want to go. 'It's rather quiet there, it would be boring for you, I'm afraid.'

'I like Brighton,' Pamela said. 'I'd like that. When shall we go?'

'I thought I'd go down next weekend,' Clare said, too surprised to comment on Pamela's interest.

'Fine, that suits me.' Pamela got up reluctantly.'Oh, well, I'd better go – it's hell under those lights, even hotter than it is out of doors. One day I'll just melt and they'll find a little puddle where I was.'

That afternoon, Clare asked Larry if she could leave work early on the following Friday. 'I have to catch a train down to see my parents at Brighton.'

'There's that meeting with Colling at four o'clock,' he said, his frown impatient.

'Do I have to be there?'

'Yes,' he said with insistence.

'Larry, I need a break – this weather is killing.'

'Why don't I drive you down on Saturday morning?' he asked and then smiled. 'That's a good idea,' he congratulated himself before she could answer. 'Yes, I'll do that,' he decided, picking up his desk diary and studying it. 'I'll get Maureen to ring and book me a room in a good hotel. A weekend by the sea would be terrific.'

'Pamela's going with me,' Clare said, too taken aback to argue. Why on earth did he want to go to Brighton? Larry was given to impulsive decisions, he had a quick, sudden mind which enjoyed springing surprises on people. She suspected he enjoyed springing them on himself. It made life more interesting for him, he leapt out at life like a jack-in-the-box and made it jump, delighting in the shocks he caused.

'There's plenty of room in my car,' he said. He leaned back in his chair, his sinewy hands on the desk edge, his fingertips tapping out an impatient rhythm. 'Don't you like the idea? Afraid your parents will disapprove of me? Aren't I presentable enough?'

'Oh, don't be silly,' she said, but she knew he didn't really believe what he was saying, his accusations were all a tease, his eyes were gleeful.

'What did they think of Tom?' he asked. 'Approved of him, did they?'

'They barely knew him. I don't see much of them.'

'Why not?'

Clare looked at him with wry resignation. 'I didn't invite an inquisition. I just asked if I could go early on Friday.'

'I'm curious about your parents,' he said. 'I'd like to see what sort of background you come from, it might give me some clues about you.'

'Maybe I don't want you picking up clues about me, has that ever occurred to you?' She was prickling at his inquisitive, sharp gaze. He looked like an ant-eater, his nose quivering before he dissected her.

'That's what makes me curious,' he said. 'Why are you so damned reticent? What have you got to hide?'

'You really take the biscuit,' Clare said, laughing suddenly. He looked funny with that bright, probing expression in his face, it made her feel fond of him. She didn't feel so fond of him when he was burning up the ground in front of him as he strode from office to office, a human flame-thrower. She was the firefighter scurrying after him beating out the flames before they destroyed everything in sight.

He grinned at her. 'That's settled, then – I'll pick you and Pamela up on Saturday morning, I never get up before eight at the weekend so we'll say nine-thirty, shall we?'

'We won't get there before lunch at that rate,' Clare said but he brushed that aside.

'Of course we will.'

Pamela was surprised and curious when Clare told her. 'Larry's driving us down? Why?'

A Violation

They were having a cup of tea before going to bed. Pamela's habits had altered drastically, Clare had noticed. She rarely seemed to go to parties these days, she almost never had a date. They had fallen into the habit of watching TV or listening to music, talking in fits and starts. Pamela always talked about the same thing – Joe Harper. She had very little to say about him, she seemed to know very little about him, but she said it over and over again; the subject obsessed her. She came alive when she said his name, her eyes shone and her face was transfigured. Clare was worried about it. Joe never seemed to ring, Pamela never seemed to see him. It was an infatuation, that was clear. The trouble was, she didn't know how to warn Pamela what dangerous waters she had drifted into – Pamela must know, must have chosen to let herself drift there.

What puzzled her most was that Pamela of all people, Pamela who had always been so self-sufficient, so indifferent to the men she picked up or dropped, should get herself into this state over a young man Clare recalled as thin and quiet, so ordinary she had barely noticed him.

Pamela had sneered at romantic love, had proudly chosen to be her own woman, free, uninhibited, unfettered by old conventions or old fears. She didn't need a man to support her – she could support herself very nicely, thank you. She earned more than most men did, anyway. She didn't want children cluttering up her life. She wanted to be free to walk away whenever she chose, she despised the idea that one person could lift you to the stars or destroy your life – that was sheer garbage, she had always said. It had been the sort of bilge which kept women tied to the kitchen sink. Men hadn't wanted them out in the male world competing, taking jobs from men – so they sang them to lotus-eating sleep with love songs and convinced them that their true happiness lay in cooking men's meals and darning their socks.

Clare could hardly believe that now Pamela sat around yearning to do just that, daydreaming about making Joe's breakfast before he went off to work, wondering aloud what sort of children he would have, she could just imagine their hair, their eyes. It was pathetic, like hearing a free bird mewing to get inside a cage.

'Larry offered, God knows why,' she told her. 'He was curious about my parents, he said. Larry's mind works in a mysterious way its wonders to perform.'

Pamela gave her a secretive look. 'He likes you, doesn't he?'

Clare laughed. 'Don't get ideas – you don't know Larry. He is the least romantic guy I've met. Totally self-absorbed. When I met his mother I could see why – she's the same. They both go their own way ignoring everybody else.'

'He brought you those heaps of flowers, I've never seen so many flowers.'

'Larry has a terrific gift for gestures – that's why he's a great advertising man. It's a sort of sense of drama, he knows how to catch the eye, surprise, intrigue.'

Pamela stared at her, frowning. 'You've got very tough lately. I used to think you were too soft, but I certainly wouldn't call you soft any more.'

'Well, I'm glad to hear it,' Clare said, getting up to go to bed. 'I'm seeing a lot more clearly, that's all. I went around wearing rose-tinted glasses – now I've taken them off.'

'Don't get too hard,' Pamela said. 'There's no need to fly to the other extreme.'

'Am I? I don't think I am.' Clare felt that Pamela, wrapped up in her unreal, febrile passion for Joe, was trying to push her into a similar relationship. She was trying to whip up a love affair for Clare with Larry because she wanted Clare to be more sympathetic, more sharing. Love is a lonely affair when it is one-sided, Pamela wanted more than just an ear to pour her yearning feelings into, she wanted Clare to mirror her dreaming. Clare tightened against the attempt. The last thing she wanted was to feel. She had removed herself to a calm pinnacle above all that. She no longer dreamt about the rape, she refused to let herself think about it when she was awake. She had locked it into a past she never visited. Tom was locked away there too. He had rung several times when she first got back, but her distant voice had convinced him their affair was over.

He had stopped ringing and she had been able to forget him. She felt irritated with Pamela for trying to make something of Larry's offer. Clare hadn't had any such suspicions, she had been sure Larry was merely following his nose, investigating her out of idle curiosity.

That Saturday morning as they finished breakfast the letter box rattled. Pamela got up and went out, came back with several envelopes in her hand, tossed one to Clare and sat down to open her own letter.

Clare looked at the brown envelope fixedly. She knew before she opened it. Her fingers trembled as the knife slit the stiff paper.

'What is it?' Pamela said, looking up as if she had heard the thick intake of air.

'They've fixed the hearing at the magistrates court,' Clare said. She sounded remote and cool. Inside she was hollow, she had fallen away, her insides had dropped out, she was empty and sick.

'Can I see?' Pamela put out her hand.

Clare didn't move. Pamela took the letter from her cold fingers. Clare stared at the wall, shivering.

'They're usually very brief affairs,' Pamela said reassuringly. 'It isn't a full trial, just a preliminary. The defence don't waste their bullets at the magistrates court, they . . .' she stopped, grimacing, realising that that did not sound all that comforting.

'They wait for the crown court trial before they fire for the whites of your eyes,' Clare said bitterly, getting up. 'I know.'

'If he pleads guilty, you won't be called at all,' Pamela said to her back.

'He obviously isn't pleading guilty, is he?'

Clare went down the hall into her own bedroom and sat down on the bed, shoulders hunched as if in a high wind. She couldn't face it, the thought of standing in a witness box answering questions about things she only wanted to forget. She had just begun to feel she was really getting over what had happened. Now she was going to have to live with the threat of the magistrates court hanging over her. It would block out everything else, darkening the light.

Larry arrived and carried their cases out to the car. Clare was wearing a pale green skirt, pleated finely, with a lemon blouse with a neat round collar. She looked fresh and springlike but Larry looked into her eyes and frowned.

'What's wrong?'

He was too quick, he saw too much. Before Clare could tell him, Pamela did. 'She's had a letter, the magistrates court hearing has been fixed for next month.'

'He's pleading not guilty, then?' Larry's frown stayed where it was, black above his dark eyes, his forehead creased.

He didn't look at Pamela, he kept his eyes on Clare's pale face. She nodded.

'I suppose so.' She would have to give evidence, she couldn't get out of it. She prayed she would not be pressed for too many details. All those eyes . . . she couldn't bear the thought of them.

'It won't be so bad,' Larry said. 'He can't have any real defence. He burgled your flat, any story he's concocted will be as weak as water.'

'I can't see how he can plead not guilty,' Pamela said. 'Unless he claims he didn't do it, it was someone else.'

'That must be it,' Larry said. 'The defence won't be attacking you, Clare, they'll be attacking the prosecution's identification.'

The road was choked with cars, they had to crawl along in a fog of petrol fumes, and Larry swore under his breath. They had all the windows open, the sunroof of his car rolled back, but it was so hot that Clare felt her blouse sticking to her. Perspiration streamed down her body.

'I've never met your father,' Pamela said, fanning herself in the back seat. She had a paperback she was flicking through, the pages fluttered as she waved the book to and fro in front of her hot face.

For a second Clare nearly said: neither have I! Then she started to laugh at the thought and Larry looked round at her, startled. It was true, she didn't know her father. He was just a face, a shape, going and coming in the house – but behind the outwardly recognisable form was a man she had never known.

'Don't get hysterical,' Larry warned her.

'It's the heat,' Pamela said quickly, too quickly.

Clare stifled her helpless choking laughter. 'My bottom's sticking to the seat,' she said, shifting herself and feeling her skin unpeel painfully.

Pamela put a hand to her hair, lifting it from her nape. A bead of sweat crawled down her temple.

'How much further?'

'We should be there in half an hour,' Larry said, looking at his watch.

'Lunch time,' Clare said. 'I told you . . .'

'All right,' Larry said irritably.

Later she said: 'My father doesn't know about the rape – you won't mention it to him, will you?'

'Of course not,' Larry said, his eyes sharp. She knew that look. He was working out why she didn't want her father to know – not hard to do but Clare did not want Larry's clever, probing searching mind going to work on her. He thought too much about things which didn't concern him. He was a man who did not take note of warnings against intrusion. They merely incited him.

When they got to Brighton she stared at the sea, a very different sea from the empty, milky blue expanse at which she had gazed while she was in the marsh. This was a flashing, technicolour sea; far too blue, vulgar, ostentatious; crowded with swimmers whose heads bobbed like dark balls. The beach was crammed; sunbathers lay on towels, broiling; stretched out on deckchairs or paddled at the water's edge. Children ran and screamed or dug with gaudy plastic spades. Clare thought of her own childhood, how the shouts, the sound of the waves, brought it back to her – an attack on her senses which had nostalgia behind it.

'I'd love a swim,' Pamela said.

'You'll have to direct me,' Larry told Clare.

She dragged herself back from her childhood, and told him which way to drive. As the car halted, Beattie came to the front door. She had the look of someone who has been waiting, watching. She waved and Clare waved back. She felt her mother staring at Larry.

'Will you come in and have lunch?' she asked him, hoping he would say no, he ought to book in at his hotel.

'Love to,' he said, climbing out of the car.

Beattie kissed Clare's cheek, her gesture gruff and clumsy, rather shy. She was unsure whether it would be rebuffed, but Clare smiled.

'You look very brown – isn't this weather amazing? I don't remember a summer like it.'

Pamela smiled at Mrs Forrester who said happily: 'Hallo again, Pamela, nice to see you, I'm glad you could come.' She looked at Larry, standing behind Clare, his shoulder almost touching hers, his black head striking sparks off the sun.

'This is Larry Hillier, my boss,' Clare said and they shook hands and exchanged polite smiles.

Clare felt how unreal it all was, she wished she had come alone, she wasn't going to be able to talk to her mother, she had thought she did not want to, she had not wanted to be alone with her and now suddenly she did. How contrary, she thought wryly.

'How nice of you to drive them down,' Beattie said to Larry. 'You'll stay to lunch, won't you?' She had salad and cold meat for them, surely there would be more than enough for five? She could quickly boil some more eggs and maybe find a can of sardines in the cupboard, she was sure there was one.

'Thank you,' Larry said, looking past her.

Derek Forrester had appeared, clutching a newspaper. He waved it in jocular, heavy greeting. 'Ah, you've arrived, good, good. How are you, Clare? Better?'

'Much,' she said. He pretended to kiss her averted cheek, she saw the crooked red lines of veins on his nose, on his cheeks beneath his tanned skin. His hair was all grey, as if time had snowed on him since she last saw him, he had shrunk, withered, his body moved as if his limbs had no sap in them, were dry and sticklike. She thought he's my father, and felt nothing, not even dislike, mere null acceptance of the fact. She did not wonder about him, she felt no curiosity about him. The absence of feeling was calm like the sea in the morning when no breath of wind breathed across the surface of the water. She remembered the night she had woken up from nightmare and gone into that room to see his naked body on the bed moving against the other pale, bare limbs. He had looked over his shoulder and she had seen a face, but not the face of the father she had known, a strange face, contorted, frightening, in a rictus of physical release, making sounds which died away as he saw her. Now she looked at him and the images died, the memories closed up and were gone. Far away and long ago there had been a man and a woman in a room and a child screaming, but this old, tired grey man was nothing to do with any of it.

He shook hands with Larry, beamed at Pamela, a flicker of himself in his surprised eyes.

'Too hot to eat indoors, we thought we'd have lunch in the garden, we have a little patio out there, under a rose trellis.' He put a hand under Pamela's arm and steered her through the house, talking. 'So you're a model – what sort of model? Photographic?'

'Before we go outside, they might like to go upstairs,' Beattie said to him. 'You must be hot after that drive, Pamela, would you like to wash?'

Clare took Pamela upstairs. She showed her the little bedroom in which she had always slept at home. Pamela picked up a school photo of Clare in uniform, her face fuller, rounder, innocent. 'You've changed.'

'I should hope so,' Clare said. 'I was fifteen then.' She thought of herself at fifteen with a sort of surprise that she had ever been so young. She couldn't remember being fifteen, her school years had passed almost without incident. She had begun to live when she escaped from home, from the empty negativity of a life without love. Equipped with a rounding, developing body she had sought out feeling, experimented with sex as if it was a habit-forming drug. It had never been the caresses, the preliminaries she needed – it had been the moment when her body was wrung with pain, her mouth tortured by a cry of hope. Orgasm, the little death, when the brain stops working, the lungs stop breathing, the heart stops beating and eternity is reached. How painful the trek back to mundane existence, the reality of another body lifting, drawn out of you, the rush of wetness between the open thighs, the heat of the skin, the terrible sadness, the desire to cry, because that instant of pure joy, pure extinction, was over and the man beside you meant nothing, needed nothing from you.

She had felt no sexual impulse since the rape. The idea of lying with a man on top of her made her ill. She did not want to be touched like that, ever again. She thought of love with distaste; the passivity of the female, the thrust of the male, nauseated her. Never again, she thought, never.

The table was a rickety white wicker one Clare remembered from her childhood, it rarely came out of the shed where it was stored. If anyone leaned on it, it rocked, the milk jug spilt a dampness into the cloth when Larry put a hand on the table top. The trellis overhead creaked, the roses tumbled raggedly down through the diamond lattice-work, the petals lacy with the depredations of greenfly. A swarm of insects danced just below the thickly set green leaves – they did not make a sound, just hovered there, like tiny black humming birds, drinking air not pollen. Larry talked, the shadow of the roses on his face.

Clare watched him and listened and thought about the coming trial. Her bones tightened every time the picture came back. Her jaws ached. All along the side of her face she felt a stabbing pain.

She helped her mother with the washing up and Beattie asked: 'Why don't you come to Egypt with us? We could still book you on the cruise, we'd pay, dear, why don't you come?'

'Thanks, I'd have loved to, but I'm too busy, I can't have any more time off work, and then there's the trial . . .'

She had told Beattie about it. Beattie sighed. 'Are you sure you wouldn't like me to come to London to . . .'

'No,' Clare said firmly. She put down the tea towel. Her mother was standing with her hands in the washing up water, her head hanging down. Clare felt a stab of remorse. She put an arm round her mother and hugged her.

'But thanks for offering.'

'Don't keep shutting me out, Clare,' her mother said,

putting a wet hand on her arm. 'Locking things up inside you doesn't work, I ought to know. I locked things up for years, I iced up inside and wasted the best years of my life. Don't you do that. I know you must be feeling terrible now, I know what you're going through, but keeping it to yourself won't help. After Nino . . .' She broke off and Clare looked at her attentively, really listening now, although until that moment she had been trying not to hear what her mother was saying. Beattie's eyes were shiny, as if she was crying, but there were no tears in them.

'Do you still think about him?' Clare asked, feeling oddly guilty because she had almost forgotten the baby. He had been there for so short a time and it had been so long ago, he had barely impinged upon her life.

'Often. At first it hurt so much I wished I had died too, but then I got used to the fact. I started thinking about him as if he was alive, he'll always be alive for me, the way he was, he'll never be anything but my baby.' Beattie laughed. 'Sounds silly, doesn't it? I've never imagined him getting older, though. I just remember how it felt to hold him, how he laughed. When he died, though, it was more than I could bear, I felt my whole life had been smashed to pieces . . .'

'Yes,' Clare said, startled, because that was how she had felt ever since the night she was attacked.

'It was worse than when I saw your father with Donna.'

Clare flushed, amazed to hear her mother mention that so casually. She had never spoken about it before, Clare didn't know how to react.

Beattie seemed unaware that she had taken Clare by surprise. She began to dry her hands, her face wry. 'Coming so soon afterwards, Nino's death was an even bigger blow. I didn't have the strength to get over it, I think it made me feel nothing would ever matter again. I did come out of it, eventually, but by then something inside me was broken. I'd learnt that to care about anyone left you open to getting hurt, so I wouldn't let myself care.' She looked at Clare pleadingly. 'Don't let that happen to you, it could, if you aren't careful. You only get one life, don't waste it the way I did.'

'It's too soon,' Clare said, struggling with words which might explain how raw and sensitive she was at the moment. 'I've got to have time to get over it.'

'I know, of course you have. It was a terrible thing, you've been so brave . . .'

'You don't expect it,' Clare said. 'Out of the blue.'

'I know, that's just how it was with Nino, too sudden to be borne, a shock that rips you apart.'

Clare winced, the words were too vivid, too close to what had happened, and her mother looked horrified.

'I'm sorry, I . . .'

'It doesn't matter,' Clare said and saw her father and Pamela walking in the garden. Hurriedly she said: 'I hope it won't be too hot in Egypt, won't you have to have injections before you go? That won't be much fun but you don't want to catch anything nasty.'

Beattie accepted the change of subject, sighing. 'Your father's enjoying himself making lists of all that sort of thing, he loves to organise things.'

'You seem to be getting on much better,' Clare ventured and Beattie smiled, nodding.

'We are, we're trying. I was too hard on him, nobody has any right to be so unforgiving and what does it matter after all these years? Life's too short.'

Clare looked at her and suddenly kissed her, hugged her briefly. 'Don't forget to send me a postcard, will you?'

Later she walked with Larry in the garden while her parents sat and talked to Pamela under the rose trellis, their voices lazy.

'I like your mother,' Larry said, pulling a leaf from a rockery plant and absently rubbing it against her hot cheek. It was ice-cold, thick and rubbery and pale green, it sent a delicious shiver through her. 'I've never seen this plant before, what's it called?'

'You'll have to ask my father. I don't know.'

On the garden shed a bird sat chinking, ducking a head beneath a wing to preen, tail fanned.

'What are you thinking?' Larry asked and she looked at him with irritation.

'Nothing.' She was thinking that when she was raped she had been wounded. She had been bleeding ever since, but her body, her mind, were busy healing themselves, binding the tear in the flesh of her life over and over with fragile, fine threads which would close up and eventually disguise what had happened. When she was small they had had a cat which was run over. There had been a gash in its legs. The vet had bandaged it, but the cat had torn off the bandages and sat there licking the bleeding flesh for hours. Patiently, with dignity, it had healed itself, with untiring attention to the task. Clare kept going back to the pain she felt, she kept approaching it from different angles, thinking in new ways, but what she was doing all the time was healing herself. She did not want to be watched while she was engaged at the work, she wanted somewhere private and quiet where she could settle down to cope with her own renewal. Her job supplied a camouflage – behind her hectic activity, she was constantly licking her wound, like a secretive cat; with ears back, tail coiled, intent and self-absorbed, and she didn't want Larry watching her while she did it.

'Sometimes you make me feel like getting legless,' Larry said and she was startled.

'What's up with you?'

'Me?' he asked, scowling. 'Why are you so spiky? Talking to you is like trying to work out how to touch a thistle.'

She laughed. 'The answer to that is: don't.'

'You're right on target,' he said with violence and walked away. She stared after him, brow wrinkled. What was wrong with him?

Seeing her parents talking together in a placid, easy way she found it too surprising to talk about, she could hardly ask her mother what had brought about the change. She almost believed she had imagined the bitter tension which had once racked the house. They had both changed – they had aged, suddenly, the alteration showed in their calmness, as though they had accepted something – perhaps age itself? They were looking forward to their cruise; they had books on Egypt and showed her large coloured photographs of temples and green palms and gold-leaf covered antiquities; Nubian faces and the heads of queens with lapis lazuli eyes of a blue like the colour of spring hyacinths. She listened as they exclaimed to each other, 'Look at that, I wonder if we'll be able to see that pyramid . . .' and envied and pitied them, like someone tossing on a turbulent sea who both longs to be safe on dry land and knows that the end of the voyage must be a sadness.

CHAPTER TWELVE

Clare had expected the weather to break with a thunderstorm which would shatter the shell of throbbing heat clamped down over the city, but the change came without warning during a night early in September. She went to bed sweating profusely, and woke in the dawn feeling cold, and hearing rain beating down on the pavements.

'That's the end of summer,' Larry said when she met him running into the office building. He was wearing a fawn burberry; his black hair slicked down against his head, his lashes clinging together, his brown skin wet, and looked sleek and dangerous in that city environment, his stark bone structure emphasised by the way his hair clung to his head. Clare looked at him in surprise, noting the difference, and he gave her a sharp stare.

'Wake up! You look as if you're sleep-walking.'

'Sorry, do I?' She shook her umbrella and closed it. 'Aren't you going to the studio to watch that biscuit ad being shot today?'

'Oh, hell,' he said, disgusted, 'I forgot, I haven't time, not today. I'm seeing Smith for lunch and I've got meetings all day. Could you . . .'

'No,' Clare said firmly, not letting him finish. 'I'm up to my ears as it is, you'll have to ask someone else.'

They walked into the lift and Larry looked at her speculatively. 'There isn't anyone else, couldn't you fit in a quick visit? I want someone to check Grantham isn't overplaying it; you know his tendency to turn a sixty second ad into a new version of *Wuthering Heights*.'

'I'm not made of elastic,' Clare said irritably. 'I can't do everything.'

'Almost,' Larry said with coaxing flattery and one of his sudden, brilliant smiles. 'Superwoman, no less.'

'Cut the flattery,' Clare told him, but couldn't help smiling back. 'I'll try to make time,' she agreed as the lift stopped and the doors opened.

'Thanks, you've saved my life,' he said as she walked out.

'So, tell me about it,' Clare said without looking back. That was her job, why was she complaining? She was Larry's backstop, his right-hand woman, that was what he paid her for, and she was finding it much easier to cope with her job since she stopped trying to operate on two levels at once; the professional and the personal.

If she was tired when she got home now, she had a bath and went to bed, or watched TV mindlessly without needing to make conversation. Often Pamela was in the same limp state, the two of them slumped out in their chairs and ready to go to bed early if there was nothing on TV. She no longer had the stress of coping with a man's demands at the same time as coping with her work. Tom had presented her with his own image of her; of how a woman should behave, had made it clear that if she did not live up to that standard she was a failure, she was unfeminine. She no longer had to worry about failing as a woman – she had stopped trying. For the moment she was concentrating on being Larry's assistant, and she had merged the two roles. She was Clare Forrester and the only standard she was trying to meet was her own, she was learning to live with herself.

She had begun to think about the future, to glimpse ideas she had never considered before, she was being educated by what had happened to her, by starting to think from a new angle. She had never had any real ambition; at the back of her mind she had always felt that one day she would marry and stop working. It hadn't been a conscious decision, it had been too deeply ingrained for that. It had been a subtly imprinted brain-washing begun before she was aware of herself as a separate person, in her pram, while she was toddling, during her earliest years. The thousand and one tiny images which built up to a woman had flashed daily before her; words like warm, soft, gentle, yielding, giving, tender, the feminine words which dictated how she must behave if she was to prove herself a woman; impressions from other women in action, cleaning, cooking, mothering, nursing; the places where they were, kitchens and homes and hospitals and in minor roles in offices and shops. A woman's place is in the home, a woman needs a man... The subliminal moulding had begun from the moment she opened her eyes for the first time, and she had never stopped to ask herself how and why and for whose benefit she was being fitted into that mould.

Now she saw that her life was her own to live, she could do anything she chose to do; if her role was limited, it was only by herself, her own preconceived ideas, her own acceptance of the way she was seen by others. Tom had only been able to cast her in the traditional feminine role because she allowed it; even in bed it had always been Tom who took the initiative, she had never been anything but submissive, that was how he liked it. Looking back, she couldn't remember ever trying to coax him into making love when he made it clear he didn't feel in the mood, but Tom had always brushed aside her occasional weariness or disinterest, it didn't matter how she felt, it was only how he felt that mattered.

It was like a honeymoon, coming to terms with this stranger who was herself and yet whom she had never really known. She was shedding old, embedded ideas like snake-skin every day, unchallenged she had accepted so many things which she now held up to the bright light of a new vision and questioned. She even questioned her position in the firm. Larry was using her in that all too familiar role – a feminine one, of course; mopper-up to his war effort, nurse to his victims, seductress to his clients, a maid of all work who could be whistled up to take loose ends in tow, but who was not involved in the decision making.

'I'm going to do something about that,' she said to Pamela that evening as they relaxed in front of the TV after eating their meal.

'Best of luck, sweetie,' Pamela said, grinning at her. 'Can I be a fly on the wall that day? Invite an audience. It should be the show of the year.'

'This time Larry's going to listen,' Clare said, meaning it.

'Take your clothes off first,' Pamela said. 'It's the only way to get their whole attention.'

'Not any more, not for me,' Clare thought aloud, and Pamela stared at her assessingly.

'You're different these days – oh, I don't just mean the jokey stuff about taking off your clothes, I mean you seem to have more energy.' And that was odd, Pamela thought, you would have expected Clare to be rather quiet and withdrawn, as she had been for the first weeks after she was raped. Where had all this aggressive energy come from? And where was it going? Into her job? Or into a stand-up fight with every man she met? Sometimes it looked that way, Clare bristled if a man so much as looked at her lately.

'I don't know if I have more energy, it's just that I have more to spare for my work, I'm not burning the candle at both ends any more.'

'Gets a bit boring at times, though,' Pamela said, sighing and looking at her watch. 'Don't you miss having a man around?'

'I don't miss Tom,' Clare said, meaning it. 'Do you?' She looked at Pamela sharply and Pamela started to laugh.

'Miss Tom? My God, no, are you kidding?'

'Not Tom, a man, any man. You don't go out much lately, either.' Was Pamela still yearning for Joe Harper? Clare wondered. Clare couldn't understand it – he was nothing that spectacular, you couldn't call him good-looking or magnetic, he was just a nice, pleasant guy, and when Clare remembered some of the really sexy guys Pamela had once dated, she was totally at sea. They said love was blind, but this was ridiculous.

'No, I don't, do I? I've been working pretty hard, my-self.' Pamela was defensive, rather flushed, she didn't meet Clare's eyes. She rarely mentioned Joe Harper these days. Clare had no idea if she still felt the same, but Pamela had changed, there was no denying that, whether she was in love or not.

Thinking about love, Clare grimaced. She had thought she was in love with Tom, but she hadn't been, she saw that now. Love was an illusion, but it operated with the eager cooperation of its victims. People fooled themselves, they wanted to be hoodwinked; they were drug addicts who cannot face life without the kindly clouding of the romantic dream. For most people the world was a dark and lonely place in which they wandered like lost children. Love was the fitful gleaming of a glow worm in the night, it beckoned, it led, it comforted.

Not me, not any more, I'll never fool myself again, love doesn't exist, she thought. All there is, is sex – Larry is right, so was Pamela once. Why had she altered her mind? Did it scare her when I was . . . She broke off, swallowing, balking at the word, then forced herself to think it. Raped, I was raped, and yes, this change in Pamela began that night. The brutal violation of their lives, of their home, had altered both of them, but in very different ways. Pamela had never been a woman who sat around yearning for one man – she had shrugged and walked off to find someone else, she had been strong and independent and adult. Now she rarely went out, she had no lover, she came straight home from work and was very quiet.

Was she turned off sex because of what had happened? Was that it? Clare frowned, staring at the television without seeing the programme Pamela was watching.

I couldn't blame her if she has been – I wouldn't want a man to touch me, either. I couldn't stand it. She felt her teeth tightening, grinding together, at the very idea. Couldn't stand it, she thought, her jaws aching with tension.

Was that what Pamela saw in Joe Harper? Was he a safe object for her to fix her emotions on? He was indifferent to her, a quiet thoughtful young man without much sex drive, he wouldn't threaten her or demand anything from her. Loving him could be a cover for the real change in Pamela, the fear of men she wasn't prepared to admit.

'You ought to go out more,' she said and Pamela looked at her with a start.

'What?'

'You stay at home too much.'

'What is all this? What are you talking about? Look, I'm watching this film, if you aren't.' Pamela was irritable, she did not want to talk about it.

A few days later Clare had to go to the magistrates court to give evidence. She had been refusing to let herself dwell on it, thinking about it wouldn't help, she had to go through with it. She wished she had the courage to refuse to go, but if she didn't give evidence he would get away with it. She was torn between sick terror at the thought of giving evidence under a battery of curious, knowing eyes and a bitter determination to make sure he paid for what he had done to her.

When she arrived at the court she felt conspicuous, she felt everyone was staring at her, but the thing that was worrying her most was that soon she would see him, soon the faceless, sadistic monster from her unconscious would have a face, would be a human being to her, a man with eyes and hair and a nose like any other. That idea made her stomach churn. While she had no idea what he looked like, she could force him out of her mind, but once she had actually looked at his face – how could she ever forget it?

Nobody seemed to look at her, though, they were all too busy hurrying into the building. Lawyers in black robes flapped past her, policemen stood about, eyeing everybody suspiciously. She asked the way at the reception desk and was sent off to find a stone-floored lobby where people sat and stood, whispering to each other in apparently urgent consultation.

A policeman with a sparely modelled face eyed Clare as she arrived, she flushed, then realised he was admiring her figure, his gaze wandering down to her legs and up again. He gave her a grin, half-winked.

She glared at him, her colour high, and he looked startled and shifted his feet, glancing away.

There was a clock ticking on the wall. The place had a strange smell: sour and dusty. Someone sitting next to her had been eating garlic. The woman on the other side of him moved with a resentful glare and nobody came to take her place. An old man in a dirty raincoat kept humming. The policeman told him to stop. For a few moments he was quiet, then began again, under his breath. You couldn't make out what he was saying, he sounded like a kettle coming towards boiling point. One of the other women was knitting a delicate white garment. She was visibly pregnant, her swelling stomach stretched her purple skirt, the seams were splitting. Clare stared at the orange smock she wore and wondered if she was colour blind. She was the only one there who was smiling. She seemed to be happy, her happiness seemed out of place, alien.

It was hours before Clare was called. People came and went. They sat and waited and at last their names were called and they got up with a sigh of relief and irritation. Clare almost went to sleep. Her anxiety and nervous dread had given way to boredom. She tried to read the magazine she had brought but her eye couldn't take in any of the words. She looked at the pictures like a child. It was all so unreal, a shiny pretty world so far removed from this place that she closed the magazine and dropped it into the waste bin fixed to the wall. The policeman looked at her quickly. He looked at the folded magazine as if suspecting it was a message or a bomb. Clare half expected him to come over and investigate. She gave him a cold stare. He shuffled his feet and looked at the ceiling.

When she did hear her own name she jumped in alarm. For a second or two she didn't move, then she got up and walked into the courtroom. Her knees were trembling, she was chill and scared.

'This way, Miss,' the usher whispered, showing her through a little wooden door. 'Up the steps.'

The wooden stairs creaked under her feet. She looked dazedly across the court. It was smaller than she had expected, sunnier. The windows sent shafts of dust-laden light across the panelled room. She felt people looking at her.

'Would you state your name, please?'

'Clare Forrester,' she whispered.

'Would you speak up, please, Miss Forrester, we can't hear you.'

She looked at the man who had spoken. He was sitting with several other people, facing her. They were the magistrates, she thought. They looked so ordinary. One of them was a woman in a grey pin-striped suit with a frilly white blouse. She was smiling at Clare, encouragingly, like a schoolteacher.

Clare swallowed and cleared her throat. Her voice sounded firmer, clearer, when she spoke again. She took the card she was given, on which the oath was printed. As she read, clutching the black testament in her other hand, her voice strengthened. She looked up as the usher removed both card and book and found herself looking at the man seated a little way away from her. He was staring at her. She met his eyes briefly, then a sharp sensation went through her. She looked away, going rigid. It was him.

No wonder she had not recognised him, no wonder she had felt no warning signals – he was so ordinary she had never even considered it might be him, although she had walked past him twice. He was younger than she had expected, skinnier; about twenty-two, she thought, maybe younger, a boy with a pasty face, sharp, stupid eyes and darkish hair cropped very short. She had barely noticed him in the line-up.

'Miss Forrester, would you tell us . . .'

She dragged her attention back to what the prosecution counsel was saying, but she felt the accused man watching her. She couldn't look at him again, she never wanted to set eyes on him. But he sat there looking at her, as if he was curious about her. She wasn't looking his way yet she was sure he was smiling, his thin lips had worn a sly, secretive smile during the brief second while she stared at him. There had been confidential meaning in his face – as if they shared a secret which the others here did not know.

His presence anaesthetised her, made it possible to answer the carefully worded questions she was being asked – she was too busy hating him to be embarrassed any more.

When the prosecution counsel sat down, Clare waited for the part of the proceedings she had dreaded most – the questions from the defence. The magistrates looked at him enquiringly as he rose to his feet. He only had one question to ask, however.

'Miss Forrester, do you recognise anyone in this room?'

Clare stared, bewildered. 'R . . . recognise?'

'Do you think you can identify anyone here as the man who attacked you?'

Clare faltered, on the point of looking towards the silent figure in the dock.

Then she shook her head. 'I didn't see his face – how could I?'

'You did not see his face, you have no means of identifying the man who broke into your flat and attacked you?' the defence counsel said, looking not at her but at the magistrates. 'No further questions,' he said as he sat down.

Clare left the room in a dull state of relief. It was over – for the moment. She had got through yet another ordeal, and it had not been as painful as she had expected. Her chief emotion after it was anger. She thought of the young man who had sat there with no visible sign of regret or shame – he had violated her home and herself without motive, he seemed indifferent to what anyone thought of him or what he had done. If anything, she had the feeling he was enjoying himself. It had been Clare who had stood in that courtroom feeling shame and guilt.

As she hailed a taxi to take her home, a blue mini crawled along the kerb and the driver leaned over to give her a grin and say: 'Want a lift, darling?'

'Get lost,' Clare said and walked away to where a taxi was slowing. She climbed into it and slammed the door.

She had not waited for the magistrates to reach a decision, but next day she rang Inspector Lucas to ask what was going to happen.

'They've sent him for trial,' the Inspector told her. 'If he continues to plead not guilty, you'll be called to give evidence at the Crown Court. If he changes his plea to guilty, which is highly unlikely, your evidence won't be required. We'll be in touch when the case comes up. It may take months before it's heard.'

'The defence only asked me one question,' Clare pointed out.

'They're obviously going for the identification angle – all they need to do is prove we've got the wrong man. Our case is all circumstantial – a good defence counsel could get him off, I'm afraid. We're sure we've got the right man, and the evidence is quite strong, but you never know. There's many a slip . . .'

'I thought he admitted it, you said he'd made a statement.'

Inspector Lucas sighed. 'He did – his solicitor made short work of that. Police pressure, harassment . . .'

'But he had some of the things he stole from our flat!'

'He bought them from a friend, a guy he met in a pub – so thin you can see through it, but he hasn't got any previous and he's managed to produce a girlfriend as an alibi. She's lying in her teeth, but there you are. That's the job, I'm afraid.' Inspector Lucas was in a hurry, she was busy. She apologised. 'I'm up to my ears with paperwork,' she said. 'We'll be in touch.'

The week that followed was hectic; she rarely had time to do anything but work, go home and go to bed. She was always tired, but it was easier to cope if she kept her head down and worked away without looking around. It was like wearing blinkers which obscured what was happening around her, it was the only way she could deal with life at the moment.

On the Friday evening she and Larry took some clients out to dinner and afterwards they all went back to Larry's flat to drink and talk. It was midnight before the clients left and Clare lay back on Larry's couch with her eyes closed while he was showing the clients the way out to the car park behind his block of flats. She ought to be going, herself, but she was too tired to move. She felt like a piece of chewed string.

'You look comfortable there,' Larry said, sitting down beside her, and she forced her eyes open to half smile at him. He was closer than she had expected, she found herself looking into his eyes, their dark pupils gleaming, hypnotising her.

'That colour suits you,' he said and ran a stroking hand down the seagreen silk which clung softly to her thigh.

Clare felt a pulse flutter in her throat, panic surged inside her. Larry was far too close and she recognised the way he was looking at her, the little smile curving his mouth. She knew he was going to kiss her and for a second she was on the point of pushing him away, getting up, then she thought of herself and Pamela sitting silent in the flat each night. The drift towards isolation which had trapped her was dangerous, sooner or later she had to start relating to men again, she didn't want to turn off men altogether, did she? She knew Larry, he didn't frighten her, he wouldn't hurt her. How would it feel to be kissed by a man again?

She looked at Larry's mouth curiously. How many times she had seen his face and never really looked at it as she looked now, understanding with a shock that the lines of it were all male; tough, clear, filled with driving energy. Involuntarily she moved back from that masculinity and as she did so, Larry leaned over and kissed her. She stiffened, rigid against the back of the couch. His mouth was cool and undemanding, touching her lips without force. Clare kept her eyes open, she could see the pores in his tanned skin, the black lashes below his eyes, then Larry's hand came up and framed her face, tilted her head a little, and his mouth gently parted her lips and deepened the kiss, she felt his tongue touch the inside of her lower lip, his hand sliding up her body.

It wasn't unpleasant, it didn't frighten her, it was warm and comforting, a tactile sensuality which soothed. She let her eyes close and began to kiss him back, an arm curling round his neck. Larry's hand moved caressingly on her breast, his other hand was stroking her neck, her hair, he began to kiss her fiercely, heat in the way his mouth moulded hers. Deep inside her body she felt the growing throb of desire, she was weak, yielding in sensuous excitement, forgetting everything but the breathless movements of their bodies. Larry's hands were everywhere, his lips were on her throat, she had her head thrown back, her eyes shut, a low husky moan escaping her parted lips. He had pulled down her zip, her dress was sliding away, his head burrowing between her breasts, his hands on her thighs. Too fast, too fast, Clare thought in sudden panic, what was she doing? She couldn't, she hadn't intended to go this far, he wasn't giving her time to think, how had they got to this stage so quickly?

She opened her eyes, Larry was pushing her down on the couch, she saw his face, darkly flushed, the bones beneath the brown skin tight and tense, his eyes glimmering briefly through his lashes, the pupils distended in sexual excitement.

'No, no, Larry, no,' she said and his mouth came down against her lips, jammed the words inside her, his hands were touching her breasts, her hips, her thighs, one sliding between her legs, intimately caressing her. She went as stiff as a board, Larry's mouth lifted and she let out a hoarse scream, then she was hitting him, struggling, her face white and chill with sweat, her mind dissolving in waves of sick horror.

'For Christ's sake,' Larry said, and he sat up and held her, his hands on her shoulders while she writhed and made involuntary retching noises in her throat, gulping on burning acid. 'Clare, don't, for God's sake, stop it.'

She looked at him with hatred and he flinched. 'Don't . . . don't touch me . . . don't ever touch me again.'

He let go of her and got up. She lay shuddering and trembling on the couch and Larry went out of the room. Clare fought to regain control, she did up her zip, straightened her dress, ran a shaky hand over her hair. Larry came back.

'I'll drive you home.' He sounded calm and distant, his face was pale now, his eyes didn't meet hers.

In the car she tried to think of something to say, she ought to apologise for reacting like that, she had been responding, encouraging him, she ought to say something, but he must understand, he must know how she felt, surely? She couldn't force anything out, the words wouldn't come, she just wanted to forget it had happened. It had been a disaster, she had thought she was actually going to be sick, for a second she almost had been and that would have been even worse, how humiliating if she had been.

When the car stopped Larry didn't look at her, he sat staring ahead with his hands resting on the wheel. Clare hesitated, glancing at him. 'Goodnight.'

He didn't answer. She opened the door and got out and before she had walked more than two steps the car rocketed away in a burst of speed.

CHAPTER THIRTEEN

She was relieved that a weekend followed, it would give Larry time to get over what had happened. When she went into work on the Monday, though, he was in a mood of scalding irritability which kept her nerves on edge, and had her on a very short fuse. She found herself arguing with him every time she saw him and wasn't sure if the fault was his or her own. Larry would try the patience of a saint at the best of times, but suddenly Clare was in no temper to put up with his brand of tyranny.

A wet autumn followed, changed to a grey, misty winter; the leaves blew off the trees in October gales and for a few days they had fine, dry, cold weather before winter closed in. Larry kept her working hard. He was on the other side of the Atlantic for days at a time, and Clare had to carry both jobs while he was away. She saturated herself in work, it stopped her thinking, but it made her temper difficult and unpredictable.

'Careful, you're turning into a female version of Larry,' Ian said as she snapped at him over his latest set of graphics, and he wasn't joking, his scowl was sulky.

'Never mind the jokes, do these again,' Clare said. 'They're as flat as Salisbury Plain, there's no life in them at all. What's the matter with you? You just aren't trying any more.'

Ian went purple, his eyes bulging, the veins in his neck swelling in rage. 'I'm not taking that crap from a bloody woman, what do you know about artwork? You couldn't draw a straight line. I'll take criticism from Larry, but not from you, so go to hell.'

'What's my sex got to do with it?' Clare was almost as flushed as he was now, she was so angry she was shaking. 'While Larry's away, I'm running this office, and you'll take orders from me or . . .'

'Or what?' Ian sneered, cutting in.

'Or get out,' Clare shouted, throwing caution to the winds.

'Stuff you, you want my resignation? Okay, baby, you've got it, and you can explain to Larry when he gets back why you're minus one art designer.'

Clare stared after him as he stamped away, feeling sick. What on earth would Larry say? He had warned her, after all, that Ian was in a difficult mood since his wife left him. Ian was obviously anti-women at the moment – it was unfortunate that Clare was feeling equally anti-men, the clash had been inevitable, but she wished she hadn't let her temper rip like that. Ian was a brilliant man when he wasn't in an off-mood, his work was erratic but often outstanding, and Larry was not going to be happy about losing him.

Larry returned three days later and Clare nervously confessed that Ian had handed in his notice. Larry leaned back in his chair, staring at her unreadably, his face immovable.

'I'll talk to him,' was all he said.

Clare waited for him to comment on her lack of tact, but he didn't apparently have anything to add. He was different lately, she thought, leaving his office. He kept her very slightly at a distance and when she did see him he was either terse and irritable or cool and offhand. Maybe his ego had been wounded when she rejected him that night in his flat – male egos are delicate things, easily bruised, and Larry's ego was bigger than most. He wouldn't have taken her brush-off very well.

Ian left a month later, having got another job without difficulty. Whatever Larry had said to him had made no difference, obviously. Clare felt very guilty about it.

A new graphics designer joined them. Larry had head-hunted him from a rival firm because he had a brilliantly inventive mind and was capable of work of an originality which was worth far more than the very high salary Larry had had to pay to get him.

A well-built, curly-headed young man with a slightly snub nose and a curling grin, Terry Benson lost no time in making it clear he liked Clare. Within a few weeks of arrival, he was a constant fixture in her path and she got rather tired of turning him down. She had tried everything from cool disdain to sharp frankness.

'Don't you understand the word no?' she asked one morning. 'Look it up in the dictionary. It is a negative answer meaning a refusal. No. When I say no I mean no, I'm not being oblique, I'm not playing hard to get, it isn't a disguised yes. It is a no. No – no. Now, do you think you can remember that?'

He gave her his happy grin. 'What about next weekend?' he asked, leaning over her desk to smile into her eyes.

'God give me patience!' Clare seethed, exasperated.

'Amen to that,' he agreed. 'Saturday is my favourite day, we could have lunch somewhere and then in the evening we could see a film or maybe you'd like to see a show?'

'I'd like,' Clare said with exaggerated patience, 'to see the back of your head as you go out of my office.'

'Shall I pick you up at your flat on Saturday?' he asked and then fled in a shower of reference books. When he had gone, Clare got up and began to pick them up.

The door opened again. She turned, a dictionary in one hand, on the point of hurling it, when she realised it was Larry, not Terry, who stood there. His dark brows rose and almost vanished into his hair as he took in the book-littered floor.

'What the hell have you been up to?'

'Nothing,' Clare said, going pink.

He bent and helped her pick up the books. 'Thanks,' she said, tidying them into a pile, on the margin of her paper-piled desk.

Larry propped himself against the wall, arms folded. 'I saw Terry come shooting out of here a minute ago. Had you had a row with him?'

'In a sense,' she admitted.

'In what sense, precisely?'

'He's too persistent,' Clare said.

'I like my staff to have staying power,' Larry said.

'This had nothing to do with the job.'

He scrutinised her, eyes narrowing. 'I see.'

'What did you want to see me about?' she asked, lifting her chin with a defiant look about her mouth.

'I wanted to remind you that tomorrow we're having lunch with Sir Isaac Liov.' Larry straightened in a graceful movement she found herself watching absently until she hurriedly looked away. Even if she had not been very much off men at the moment, she would be a fool to let herself become too aware of Larry Hillier. He was a dangerous playmate, and Clare had no taste for danger, particularly at the moment.

'I had it in my diary,' she said drily.

'Well, good,' he mocked before he went out, leaving her wondering why he had come into her office in the first place. Had his curiosity been aroused when there was a crash behind her door and then Terry came flying out?

At lunch the next day, Sir Isaac concentrated most of his attention on her. A small, sharp balding man with knife-like eyes he had been a client of the firm for the past year and Clare had largely been in charge of his campaign, which was extensive both in the press and on television and commercial radio stations up and down the country. He questioned her closely and Clare had to keep all her wits about her to give him answers which satisfied him.

Over the coffee, he turned to Larry and said with sac-charine good humour: 'You should cherish this girl, Hillier. She's clever, I could do with her running my P.R.O. department – the clown I've got in there at the moment couldn't organise a church bazaar.'

'I'm glad you're happy with what we're doing for your firm,' Larry said evasively. 'Brandy, Sir Isaac?'

Back at the office, Larry said to her tersely: 'Watch him! I suspect he's head-hunting – he's right about their P.R.O. guy. The man's an idiot. Don't let Liov get you into a corner and proposition you. When you turn him down, he could turn nasty and we might lose the contract.'

'Maybe I wouldn't turn him down,' Clare said. 'It might be good experience to run a P.R.O. department in a firm that big. The salary would be terrific, I should think.'

Larry glared at her, bristling. 'You aren't telling me that if he makes you an offer you'll listen?'

'Why not?'

'Why not?' he repeated, the colour rising into his hard-boned face. His eyes glinted with aggression and she met that stare with cool defiance.

'I'd be a fool not to listen. I don't say I'll accept, if he does make me an offer, but why shouldn't I hear what he has to say? I don't want to run around after you for the rest of my life acting as a bandaid to your victims. I want to have my own department, have more responsibility, a better salary. What makes you think I'm not as ambitious as anyone else?'

'I've trained you,' Larry said, apparently barely able to speak out of sheer fury. 'I made you what you are today.'

Clare laughed and he spluttered.

'What's so goddamned funny?'

'You are,' Clare said. 'You're talking a lot of rot and you know it. You didn't make me anything – I made myself, with the help of heredity and state education.' She gave him a deliberately patronising little smile. 'I never thought I'd hear you talking such moonshine, Larry. You didn't expect me to take it seriously?'

'I ought to fire you,' he said, looking confused and furious.

'That's your privilege,' she said sweetly.

'You're turning into a very pushy lady,' Larry told her.

'Thank you,' Clare said, smiling.

'Where's your sense of loyalty?' he accused.

'Larry, don't try to blackmail me with emotive words,' she advised. 'We're in the same business, remember? I know how to manipulate the feelings, too.'

He eyed her, his brows heavy. 'You think you're so clever!'

'If it's clever to refuse to let you apply two standards,' she began and he interrupted.

'What do you mean? Two standards? Two standards about what?'

'You think because I'm a woman I'm not executive material – you want me in a subordinate position.'

'Don't be absurd! Don't start slinging feminist jargon at me!'

'So you have nothing against promoting women to the higher level of the firm?'

He observed her shrewdly, suspiciously. 'If they're able to do the job I've no objections on the grounds of sex. All I care about is getting the work done.'

'I'm glad to hear it.'

He grimaced. 'Okay, out with it – what do you want?'

'I'm not ready to discuss this at the drop of a hat,' Clare said. 'You won't take it seriously.'

'Right,' he said. 'We'll have lunch one day next week and kick your ambitions around.'

'I don't like the way you put that.'

He looked at her with sudden amusement. 'Too bad, I'm not rephrasing. And don't get too cute, Clare. You're not totally indispensable, remember.'

Clare returned the smile. 'Nobody is,' she said and Larry laughed.

'Meaning me?'

'I wouldn't dream of suggesting such a thing. We all know the firm wouldn't run without you.'

'Hmm,' he said. 'You'll want my job next, I suppose.'

Clare smiled. 'Why not?'

'Why not?' he repeated, regarding her from under his lashes, his face rueful, as though she was a strange landscape he viewed with curiosity and with doubt.

'I do it while you're away,' Clare said calmly. 'All it entails is a decisive mind; the ability to fuel creativity and control the various departments when they start squabbling and trying to have things their own way at each other's expense. Knowing when to shout: shut up, the lot of you! is one vital gift.'

'Oh, is it?' Larry said. 'I'll be watching you,' he added. 'I must have gone blind not to have noticed you sitting there hatching plots behind my back.'

'Don't be melodramatic,' Clare said.

'Like a big black spider,' he said mournfully, 'waiting for a poor helpless little fly.'

'As a description of you that is way off course,' Clare told him. 'In fact, I'd reverse it – you're the spider, not me.'

He gave her a gleaming look, dark eyes wicked. 'Be careful I don't pounce, then.'

Clare felt a shiver run down her back. 'I will,' she said, 'I will.'

Larry did not give in easily. They argued for a week before they came to an agreement. Clare emerged with a substantial rise and a new title. She was now Assistant Manager. There was to be a sign on her door announcing the fact. She was given a seat on the board as well – she wouldn't get a vote in any financial matters but she would be able to influence the running of the firm and she would be advising the board from the staff point of view. She realised that as far as the board was concerned, her position would depend entirely on how seriously she pressed her advice on them. It would be very easy for her seat on the board to be a hollow victory, in name only, but Clare firmly intended to keep pushing her own ideas at them. Larry ran the board, of course, but the other members were all men. She was the first woman who had ever sat on it. She was pleased with herself, a fact Larry noticed without Clare needing to be obvious about it.

'I hope you're satisfied now,' he said. 'You've got what you wanted, even though it took some blackmail and arm-twisting.'

'I'm satisfied,' she said then added: 'For the moment.'

On the verge of impending explosion, Larry ran a hand through his dark hair, grimacing.

Clare looked at him with laughter. 'Angry?'

He moved abruptly and she drew back in sudden alarm, like a cat from a tongue of flame, leaping back in self-defence, her skin heating.

Larry looked at her, his brows jerking together. 'Don't do that!'

'What?' she asked defensively, but she knew exactly what he meant.

'Jump when I come near you – what do you think I'm going to do?' He cut the words off, drawing a deep breath as her eyes flickered nervously. He knew what she thought he might do and his mouth compressed. 'Clare, isn't it time you rejoined the human race? It's months now since . . .'

'I don't want to talk about it,' she said, interrupting.

'That's obvious, and it's obvious why. You haven't got the guts to look it in the face, you're blaming all men for what one twisted bastard did to you, isn't that a bloody stupid way to carry on? I don't like being treated like a potential rapist, nor do I like feeling unclean, the way I did last time – I thought you were going to throw up all over me for a minute, it took the ground from under my feet. One minute I thought we were making sweet music together, the next you were screaming blue murder and beating me off as if I had leprosy. I know you've had a bad time, I realised I had to be patient...'

'What are you talking about?' Clare broke in, very flushed. 'Be patient? What do you mean?'

He looked at her, his mouth wry. 'Oh, come on, you know I fancy you, I haven't made any secret of it.'

Her nerves leapt. 'Oh,' was all she could manage and Larry laughed shortly.

'You look staggered!'

'I am.'

'You mean you didn't know?'

Clare looked away, very hot. 'No.'

'Then I'm not as obvious as I thought I was.' He sounded dry, half self-derisive, as though reluctant to take even himself seriously.

Hadn't she known, though? Hadn't it dawned on her long ago? Now that she allowed herself to think about it honestly, the secret knowledge which had been pressing at the back of her mind was released and she remembered looks, smiles, gestures which had had an impact, but which she had been trying hard to ignore. She had been aware of Larry even before the rape, half-conscious of the way he looked at her, and far too aware of him in her turn, although she had refused to dwell on that. He was very attractive, very male, she hadn't known whether he sent out those signals to every woman he met; and, anyway, he had had other women around ever since he got back from the States when his father died. He had hardly been celibate and lonely all these months, whatever he felt for her couldn't be very serious.

226

He was watching her face, one brow lifted. 'What are you thinking?' He was smiling, a lighthearted mockery in his eyes. 'Clare...' He put out a hand again and touched her cheek caressingly.

She jerked her head back and the smile vanished from his eyes. He frowned, his mouth straightening.

'I'm sorry,' Clare said incoherently. 'I can't, I don't want... I'm sorry, Larry, it wouldn't work, it's too soon.'

He didn't move, watching her.

'I just can't bear to be touched,' she said.

After a minute, Larry said: 'No need to look so worried, it can keep, I'll wait,' and then he smiled again with lazy charm and was gone.

It was only after he had vanished that Clare thought he had his lion-tamer's expression on then. She knew that assessing, wary glance, Larry's mind was far too shrewd, he had been weighing up his chances with her and had decided to play it cool. The thought amused her all day, she felt like lashing her tail and baring her teeth at him every time she saw him, that would shake him.

Her parents rang that evening to ask her to spend Christmas with them. Clare was surprised by their lively talk of what they were doing. Their lives had obviously opened up. Her mother was doing an evening class in art and her father talked a lot about a portrait in crayon which Beattie had done of him.

'It's good, Clare, really good,' he said and he sounded proud, he sounded excited.

'Oh, take no notice,' her mother said, chuckling. 'I'm a rank beginner but it is fun, I really look forward to the class each week. It's nice to have a hobby.'

'Do you do nudes?' Clare teased, laughing, and was taken aback when her mother said: 'Of course we will, maybe next year – at the moment I'm doing still life. I did a very wobbly milk bottle this week – glass is so difficult to draw.'

'It must be,' Clare said, trying to picture her mother drawing nude young men – or did they wear loin cloths? She had no idea, but it made a funny picture, a slightly

227

embarrassing one. The trouble with people is that they never stand still, she thought, they change in ways you haven't anticipated and couldn't expect.

When she put down the phone, Pamela looked up from the magazine she had been reading. 'Parents well?'

'Fine, they both sent their love – you made a big hit with my father, he's never met a model before. You really bowled him over.'

Pamela smiled. 'He's a sweetie.'

'What are you doing for Christmas?' Clare asked. 'I'm going down to stay with them, you're welcome to come, they'd love to have you, they made a point of inviting you.'

'That's kind of them,' Pamela said slowly, looking back at her magazine and fingering the pages. 'Thanks, I'd like that.'

'You never go home, do you?' Clare had learnt to tread carefully when she talked to Pamela about her background, Pamela wasn't very forthcoming on the subject.

'Not if I can help it.' Pamela looked up, frowning.

'You've lost weight,' Clare said. 'You ought to eat more, your face is hollow, you're working too hard, not going out enough.'

'Boring you, am I?' Pamela asked disagreeably.

'Of course not, it's just . . .'

'I notice you go out a lot,' Pamela said with heavy sarcasm. 'We're quite a pair of party-goers, aren't we?' She flung her magazine down and stood up. 'Oh, hell, I'm so bored I could scream, you're right, I'm going to make some cocoa and go to bed. I'm tired.'

Clare stared after her, feeling worried. Pamela never mentioned Joe Harper these days, but Clare sometimes got the feeling she thought about him a good deal. She certainly thought about something, or someone, her face was often sunk in lines of depression and apathy and it was beginning to show in her eyes, her skin, her figure. Her looks were her stock in trade, Pamela couldn't afford to lose those.

During the following week Pamela went out several times. Models were showered with invitations to parties.

You could be a party girl every night of the year if you chose, although it wasn't wise to have too many late nights or it began to show and, if you were working hard all day, you often did not have the energy to go out in the evening.

She told herself each time she went to a party that this time she would not be going home alone, she was not sleeping alone, eating her heart out over a man who had never given her a second thought. But each time she could not bring herself to accept any of the casual invitations to go on elsewhere, she could not let herself drift into a brief encounter with an indifferent stranger or even resume one of her light relationships with acquaintances. The idea of going back to her old way of life nauseated her. She felt no desire when someone pressed a thigh against her or looked into her eyes and started to flirt. She was merely irritated.

The next weekend she was walking along the Kings Road with a rush basket full of salad when she bumped straight into Joe. Unnerved, she gave a whimper of helpless fury as tomatoes rolled across the pavement and a grapefruit landed on a nearby pram, making the occupant scream in shock and bringing an irate mother running from a shop.

'Sorry, sorry,' she said to Joe and to the mother.

'Well, really!' the mother said, handing her the grapefruit with a frozen stare. 'He was fast asleep.'

Joe deftly scooped up those tomatoes which hadn't escaped into the road and been squashed by cars. 'I'm afraid these aren't in very good shape,' he said, dropping them into her basket.

'I should have been looking where I was going,' Pamela said, avoiding the eye of the mother who was rocking her infant back to sleep. On the lacy white pillow, its little squinting eyes glared damply at her before it closed its lids.

'Let me buy you some more tomatoes,' Joe said, putting a hand under her arm and steering her away with the wrathful stare of the offended mother following them.

'No, it really doesn't matter,' she protested.

'Some coffee, then,' Joe said, smiling at her.

She felt her intestines loop until they knotted. 'Thanks,' she said breathlessly. If she had imagined she might see him

229

she wouldn't have come out in old yellow cord jeans and a
t-shirt, she was a mess. Her hair was limp and tired, her face
had almost no make-up on it. Just my luck, she thought,
following him into a café.

'How goes it?' he asked as they sat down. 'Busy?'

'So-so,' Pamela said. 'You?'

'Hectic, as usual,' he agreed. 'I'm having a party next
week, by the way, if you'd care to come along . . .'

'A party? I'd love to,' she said, her mouth going dry.
'Any special reason? For the party, I mean, is it your
birthday or something?'

'It's a farewell party,' Joe said and Pamela sat there
smiling with the stiff forced cheerfulness of someone who
just got stabbed and does not want anyone to notice.

'Really?' That one word cost her more than anything had
ever done before. Her lips were numb as she forced it out.

Joe looked up as the waitress came over to them.
'Coffee, please, Miss,' he said.

'Hamburger? Doughnut? Slice of cake?' the girl asked,
chewing gum.

'No, thank you, just two black coffees,' Joe said and the
waitress removed herself with a sniff.

Joe looked back at Pamela, grinning. His skin was as pale
as ever, his black hair neatly brushed. She looked at him
and the ache of misery inside her was so bad she wanted to
double up with her hands over her middle, curl up in a ball
and die. Why, after years of staying well clear of all human
emotions, had she had to fall in love with someone who
barely seemed to see her? All these years she had been
sitting on a calm little plateau above everything, now she
had tumbled over the edge and was falling helplessly towards the unfathomable depths of a feeling she found
terrifying.

In the last five minutes she had been through enough
emotion to last a lifetime. From the first blinding joy of
seeing him, to embarrassment over dropping her possessions all over the place, to delight when he offered to buy
her coffee, to a greater excitement when he invited her to
his party and then this – this black misery of hearing that he

230

was having a farewell party. It was as if all the feelings of her whole life had been saved up and were now being squandered on him.

'Yes,' he said cheerfully. 'I'm leaving my flat, the hospital – I've got a new job. I'm rather chuffed with myself, actually. I didn't think I stood a chance, this is a big step up.'

'How wonderful,' Pamela said. She swallowed. 'Where are you going?'

'Oh, not far,' he said. 'The other side of London, St Ann's at Bilton, do you know it? A big Victorian monstrosity, the building, but it has been carefully modernised lately. They shed the maternity unit and the other departments have more room, they've spent a lot of money on some flash new equipment, you should see the operating theatres, my present place has nothing to touch them. Talk about all mod. cons. I can't wait to get to work.'

'I thought you were a physician,' Pamela said.

The waitress brought their coffees, slammed them down and sent black coffee all over the table top.

'Thanks a lot,' Joe said as she walked off.

'I'll mop it up,' Pamela said, using one of the paper napkins. A boy in a leather jacket put a coin into the juke box occupying one corner and the strident beat of one of the top ten burst on their eardrums. Pamela hated it, hated everything. It was sordid and squalid and noisy. She wanted to be alone with Joe. She wanted to walk with him along a beach in the sunrise and watch him laughing, his black hair blown around by the wind. She stared at the coffee-stained paper napkin as she crumpled it and pictured the scene, a sigh trying to escape. Stifling it, she said again: 'I thought you were a physician.'

'I am,' he said. 'But all the departments interlock, you know.' He looked around the café, looked out of the window at the choked London traffic. 'Only one more week, and then goodbye to all this. I shan't be sorry, Bilton's right on the edge of the countryside, I'll be able to get out for walks on my off days.'

'That should be fun,' Pamela said, her eyes on her coffee.

231

She drank some, then looked at her watch. 'Good heavens, look at the time – I must be off, I've got a busy day ahead. It was nice to see you again, have a good time in your new job, I'm sure you'll be very successful.'

As she stood up, he rose, too, and smiled at her. 'Look after yourself, give my love to Clare.'

'I will,' she said. ''Bye.'

She couldn't wait to get away before the pain showed, before the tears burning behind her eyes slipped out and betrayed her. She didn't know pain could be so bad. She had no idea how she got back to the flat and she was glad Clare was out when she arrived back, she didn't want anyone to see her like this. The minute she was safely in her bedroom she let her control slip and stumbled on to the bed, sobbing.

She cried for a long time, abandoning herself to a grief which seemed limitless, and it was only as the tears subsided that she realised she had been crying for far more than the loss of Joe. She had been crying in a way she had never cried before. She had cried for everything she had never cried about before, all the feelings she had suppressed and forced down came bursting up to the surface and overwhelmed her with the force of that black grief, like crude oil spouting into the sky, after centuries of being compressed below the earth.

She had not realised until then how strongly she felt about cutting herself off from her family, how angry she was with her father, how she resented him, how deeply she felt about her mother and how bitterly she blamed her for the dull greyness of that childhood from which she had escaped. She lay shuddering, and exhausted, on the bed and thought about her life in a sort of horror. She was lonely, there was no one who cared about her, nobody she cared about and it had been like that for a long, long time. That was what she had been running from when she let herself go crazy over Joe. He had insulted her, but he had seemed to actually see her, he hadn't just been looking at her body and wanting it, as most men did, she hadn't been an object to him. She had been choking with unused, unwanted feeling, and the first man who seemed to be different to the rest had released it all, it had all poured out in his direction, but how vainly, how uselessly. He hadn't wanted her or her love, and now he was going and she would sink back into the empty life which was all she knew.

Staring at the ceiling, she ached, her hands on her stomach, curling into a foetal position and not moving while the room darkened with falling dusk.

CHAPTER FOURTEEN

The Saturday before Christmas, Clare was in Oxford Street doing some last-minute shopping when she bumped into Tom outside Selfridges. He was staring blankly into the festive window at some manic dwarfs and a simpering Snow White. Clare would have walked past him if he hadn't suddenly turned right into her path.

'Sorry,' he muttered, then did a double-take. 'Clare! Hallo.'

'Hallo, Tom,' she said, noticing that he was wearing a very expensive-looking new overcoat, camelhair, smoothly tailored and fitting him perfectly. 'You look very prosperous, how are you?'

'I just got some promotion; higher salary, a bigger office – doing very nicely, thanks.' He was looking pleased with himself, his grin was triumphant, and he stood there in the frosty morning sunlight talking about his new job for several minutes before pausing and asking as an afterthought: 'How are you?'

'Fine,' Clare said. Her eye wandered to a little girl who was staring wide-eyed at Snow White, her mouth slightly parted on an excited breath, and Clare began to smile at that expression. She looked up at Tom, still smiling delightedly. He was waiting for her to say more, so she said: 'I'm just fine now, Tom, thanks.' Then she looked at her watch. 'But I must fly, I've got to get a present for my father, I haven't been able to decide what to get him. See you.' She smiled again and hurried off into the crowds flocking into the department store.

Clare met Pamela for lunch and afterwards they did some more shopping together. By the time they got back to the flat they were laden down with parcels, and Clare was exhausted. Pamela rushed off to have a shower and change, she was going out with a cameraman she had met while making her last TV commercial. 'We're going to a party somewhere in deepest Norfolk,' she said, groaning. 'God knows when or if we'll get back – why did I say yes? I need my head examined.'

She was saying yes to every invitation lately, Clare thought, sinking into a chair while she waited for the kettle to boil. Pamela had picked up her old life almost where she left off, but there was some indefinable difference in her; she was like a faulty light-bulb at times, her sparkle came and went and in between she looked tired and grey, her eyes had a sadness in them.

The cameraman arrived half an hour later. Clare let him in and Pamela whirled out of her room in a wild silk dress slit at the sides to show her long, smooth thighs. The colour should have shrieked at her hair, but she had sufficient panache to carry off that clear scarlet.

'You look sensational,' the young man said, awed.

'Thanks, you're looking good yourself.' Pamela gave him a dazzling smile; not quite real, thought Clare, watching. It didn't reach her eyes. 'Have you met Clare? My flatmate? Clare, this is Jerry.'

'Hallo,' they said to each other. Jerry was in his late twenties; thin, tall, with a lively, intelligent face. Clare decided she liked him, more than she usually liked Pamela's escorts. 'Have a drink before you go,' she said, and he shook his head.

'The roads are icy, I want to get there in one piece, thanks all the same.'

'He's the careful type,' Pamela said, looking at her wryly, nose wrinkling.

They left a moment later, Pamela wrapped in a fluffy white fun fur and drifting in a cloud of expensive perfume. How long will that last? Clare wondered as she shut the door on them. Jerry wasn't the sort of playmate Pamela normally took up with, but from the way he had been staring at her, he was totally sold on her, and Clare frowned as she wandered down to the bathroom. Poor Jerry.

Her body was aching with tiredness, she had been on her feet all day, pushing through crowds of shoppers. She ran a bath, poured in some scented bath oil and a moment later was soaking contentedly, her head pillowed on her arms, listening to a tape of Spanish guitar music she had bought at a bargain price. Her mind floated, anchored to nothing; she thought about the presents she had got for her parents, it was so hard to know what to buy them. She was looking forward to Christmas, which must be a first, because she had never enjoyed her visits down there before. Her parents were different now, they talked to her, to each other, they were threatening to show her the cine film they had made in Egypt, which she had already seen twice. Next year, they said, they were going on a Mediterranean cruise, they were planning it already.

She stayed in the bath until the water was almost cold, then reluctantly climbed out and dried herself lightly, slipped on a towelling robe and blow-dried her hair in front of the mirror.

Bare-legged, she went to make herself some supper; scrambled egg and mushrooms, coffee, toast. She had just beaten the eggs when the doorbell went. Clare frowned. Who on earth was that at this hour? Then she remembered that Larry had said something about calling round. He was going down to Romney Marsh for Christmas with his mother, this Sunday, and had said he had a present for Clare, which he would drop off sometime before he left.

She opened the door and stared in surprise. 'Tom!'

'We didn't get a chance to talk this morning, so I thought I'd call in on the off-chance,' he said, looking at her towelling robe. 'Going somewhere?'

'No, I was planning on an early night, actually.' How was she going to get rid of him? she thought frantically, barring his way.

He smiled, satisfied. 'It's a long time, I want to hear all your news.' He inserted himself neatly into the little hallway, put an arm round her and closed the door for her. Clare looked at him wrathfully, very flushed.

'Tom, I'm very tired,' she began and he smiled, producing from behind his back a bottle of champagne.

'This will wake you up.' He kept his arm round her and she tried to sidestep, too late, because Tom kissed her quickly on the mouth before she could evade him. 'You look very sexy,' he said, looking at the low v-neck of the robe where her breasts showed, pink from the bath. His mouth was cool, his skin glowing from the icy air outside, he looked healthy and aggressively male and Clare felt like kicking him. He hadn't even thought of her for months, no doubt, but seeing her out of the blue that morning had put her into his mind, and here he was, in no apparent doubt about his welcome. It was unbelievable.

'I was just going to dress,' Clare said, backing.

'Don't bother on my account.' He laughed at her, waving his champagne. 'Get the glasses and I'll open this while it's still cold.'

'No, really, Tom, I . . .'

He walked into the kitchen. 'I know where they are. Scrambled egg or omelette?' She followed and found him staring down at the table on which stood her supper preparations; the mushrooms peeled and sliced, the bowl of beaten egg. 'Enough for two?' he asked, shedding his overcoat and dropping it over a chair.

'I'm going to get dressed,' Clare informed him firmly. She could see it wasn't going to be easy to evict him, he was in an assertive mood, he had always had a skin as thick as an elephant's. She wasn't standing around half-naked while Tom looked at her the way he was looking at her now, there was a distinctly nostalgic look in his eye, he was remembering moments she only wanted to forget.

'Must you?'

She didn't answer, hurrying out of the room. She bolted her door before she found some jeans and a sweater and began to dress. As she pulled the sweater over her head the doorbell rang again. Clare dragged the sweater down, ran a hand over her dishevelled hair, and opened her bedroom door, just in time to hear Tom saying: 'Clare's getting dressed, she won't be a minute, come in if you like.'

Clare stood in the hall, flushed, staring down towards the two men. Larry was in a grey suede jacket with a fur collar, he stood facing her, his features tight and cold. Slowly, Clare walked down to join them.

'I won't stop,' he said, dropping each word separately like tinkling ice. 'I brought this.' He shoved it into her hands as she reached the front door; a large square parcel wrapped in gold foil and tied with a crimson ribbon, a real red rose thrust through the carefully tied bow.

'Thank you,' Clare stammered, completely off balance, and got a look which went right through her and sent a jab of pain along its path. Larry had never looked at her like that before. She was shaken by the hardness of his eyes, by the straight, contemptuous line of his mouth.

'Happy Christmas,' he said, as if the words were a deadly insult, and turned and was gone.

Tom closed the door. 'I can't stand that guy,' he said. 'The champagne's open – come and have a glass.'

Clare looked dazedly at him. He had taken off his jacket and his tie, his collar was open, he looked at home, relaxed. What had Larry thought? As if she didn't know!

'I don't want any champagne,' she said in a stifled, shaking voice. 'I just want you to go, get out, Tom.'

'What on earth . . .' He stared, incredulous, his mouth open.

'I said, get out! What do I have to do to get the message home to you? It's over, I don't want to see you, go away – take your champagne with you and find somebody else to drink it with.'

'I've opened it now!' Tom was looking affronted, indignant. 'What brought this on? What did I do?' He looked at the front door, then at her, then sneered. 'Oh, I get it – Hillier? Been making it with him, have you? I . . .'

'Get out!' Clare ran into the kitchen, grabbed the champagne and thrust it at him. 'Go on.' She opened the front door, put a hand in his back and shoved.

'My coat,' he said and stamped into the kitchen. She heard him putting his jacket on, then shrugging into his overcoat. He came back, his tie in his hand, tne bottle of champagne gripped in his fist. Clare held the door open, avoiding his eyes.

Tom halted, she heard him draw breath to speak, then he let it out again noisily and walked out. Clare let the door bang behind him. She went into the kitchen and sat down at the table, biting her lower lip, still clutching the parcel Larry had brought with him. Had he tied the bow himself? She looked at the rose; long-stemmed, perfectly formed, half-opened, it was a deep dark crimson, a damask rose with petals like velvet. Its perfume was subtle, she bent her head to sniff at it, and found herself crying suddenly. Larry had looked at her with such icy contempt, it hurt.

She got up abruptly and ran into the sitting room, dialled his flat. The phone rang and rang, but nobody answered. Clare reluctantly replaced the receiver. She would try again later, she had to speak to him, explain, she couldn't let him go on thinking she was back with Tom.

She made her supper, ate half of it without real appetite, then went and rang Larry again, but he still didn't answer. She was frantic to speak to him, she couldn't rest until she had explained Tom's presence in her flat, her own state of disarray. She tried all evening without getting through. Perhaps he had decided to go on down to Romney Marsh today? In the end she gave up. She would have to wait until after Christmas. Maybe by then Larry would have cooled down enough to listen.

Two days later she and Pamela arrived at the Forrester home in a flurry of snow, the large soft flakes melting as they fell and making the pavements slippery. A smell of hot mince pies met them as Beattie opened the front door, the cold wind set the Christmas decorations in the hall tinkling and sparkling; a great silver star from which hung mistletoe, loops of coloured foil rings strung back and forth from the ceiling. Beattie laughed as she saw their cold, damp faces.

'Come on in, you look as if you're freezing, what sort of journey did you have? Give me your coats. There's a fire in the sitting room, go and get warm, I've just got the kettle on.'

'I hope this snow won't lie.' Clare threw herself down in a chair, sighing.

'Not cold enough,' Pamela said, squatting down in front of the fire and holding out her hands to the leaping blaze. 'Nice to have a white Christmas, though.'

'So long as we don't have to go out in it.'

Pamela looked over her shoulder. 'You okay?'

'Fine, why?'

'You look a bit down in the mouth.'

Clare smiled wryly. She hadn't told Pamela about Tom's visit and Larry's leap to conclusions but the incident had been on her mind ever since. She didn't know why it should bother her so much that Larry had got the wrong end of the stick, but it did.

Derek Forrester came in, wheeling a trolley on which was laid tea. He kissed them both and chatted about the weather while Beattie poured the tea and he handed the cups. They all sat around the fire, watching the blue and green sparks from the logs spitting sideways every few minutes, and their talk was lazy, unhurried. The cosy isolation of Christmas fell on them, the knowledge that for the next few days they weren't going anywhere, doing anything, the world had stopped for a short time, the streets would be empty, the shops closed.

Clare helped Beattie get supper a couple of hours later. They were having steak followed by fruit or cheese, Beattie was saving her energies for Christmas Day's mammoth cooking effort. Clare admired the turkey and her mother said: 'It's far too big, of course, but your father bought it,' and they both laughed, their glances conspiratorial. Clare felt a shock of surprise, realising how easily she was talking to her mother now. At times she almost felt Beattie was a friend, rather than her mother, they had somehow moved on to an equal footing without Clare noticing.

'How's that nice Mr Hillier?' Beattie asked and Clare heard herself sigh.

'He's staying with his mother for Christmas.'

Beattie looked at her, head to one side like a curious sparrow. 'Oh.' The question was careful, it didn't press itself, but it was there, Beattie had picked up the uneasy note in Clare's voice.

Clare still couldn't talk about her feelings, though. The instinct to lock her thoughts away was too strong. You don't discard the habit of a lifetime that easily.

'This steak's ready,' she said. 'Where are those tomatoes?'

On Boxing Day they all went for a walk along the promenade in the teeth of an icy wind, well wrapped up, but determined to use up some of the calories they'd taken on during Christmas Day's turkey, roast potatoes, Christmas pudding and mince pies.

Derek and Beattie stopped to watch some children chucking stones into the waves and Pamela and Clare strolled on, talking. 'Jerry seems nice,' Clare said and Pamela shrugged.

'He's okay.'

Was she reverting to her old pattern? wondered Clare and said impulsively: 'Too nice to get hurt, I think he really likes you, Pam.'

Pamela gave her a wry smile. 'Don't preach, I'm playing it by ear, okay?'

'I wasn't preaching, just... oh, well, it's your life.'

'Yes, it is, isn't it?' Pamela was slightly sarcastic but she linked her arm in Clare's and nudged her with her elbow. 'Don't fret, I like Jerry – so far; I've only just met him, for all I know he'll turn out to be Dracula incarnate. You never know with people.'

'Do you ever see Joe Harper?' Clare heard herself ask it and the next second could have bitten her tongue out as she felt Pamela's arm stiffen against her.

'He moved away,' was all Pamela said, then she pointed out to sea: 'Look, what's that big ship, I wonder? Where's it going on Boxing Day?'

They paused and stared out to where the pearl grey mist veiled the horizon and through it saw a great dark bulk moving very slowly. Clare wished she was on it, going somewhere, travelling towards something, then she looked back towards the quiet streets and was content to be where she was on safe land. Another couple of days and they would be back in London and she could talk to Larry, the memory of his angry face haunted her, she couldn't rest until she had put things straight. On Christmas Day she had opened his present and everyone had exclaimed in admiration at the white silk and lace negligee set she found in the box.

'It must have cost an arm and a leg,' Pamela had said, and Clare had felt irritated, it wasn't the cost of it that counted, it was the sheer dreamy beauty of it. She had loved it on sight, she wished Larry was there so she could tell him. The generosity of the giving was typical of him, as had been those flowers he had brought her in hospital, Larry was larger than life, you couldn't call him a wallpaper person. She hated to feel that he despised her, that he was harbouring a belief that she had resumed her old affair with Tom.

As soon as she and Pamela were back in London, Clare rang Larry, but he still wasn't answering his phone, perhaps he was staying on in Romney for a while? She would have to wait until he showed up in the office.

Things were still very quiet for the first two days after she started work again, but on the Wednesday morning Larry strode into her office and deposited a pile of paper in front of her. Clare looked up, a smile ready, flushing at the sight of him.

'Sort through this, will you? See what you make of it, let me have a memo before tomorrow lunchtime.' He turned on his heel before she could speak and went out, letting the door slam behind him, and Clare stared in blank silence. She wanted to cry, how could he talk to her in that voice? Brusque, harsh, cold – it hadn't sounded like Larry at all, it had been like a slap in the face.

She sat, irresolute, for a few minutes, then went into his office. He was talking on the phone. She sat down on the edge of his desk and felt his eyes slide towards her but he went on speaking crisply, succinctly, ignoring her. When he replaced the phone, he turned in his swivel chair, his hands planted on the desk.

'Well?'

It was not an encouraging question, but Clare pretended not to notice. 'Thank you for the beautiful negligee set – I loved it and it fits me perfectly.'

Larry let her finish, then picked up his phone and dialled, nodding without looking at her. 'Good.' The word was delivered in a terse way, his lips barely moved.

Desperately, Clare said: 'Larry, I want to explain...
about Tom...'

'Nothing to explain,' he said, then, into the phone:
'Hallo? Craig? Hillier here, have a good Christmas?'

Clare hesitated for a moment, then went out, closing the
door quietly. Perhaps she would get a chance to talk to him
later, his mood might improve over the next day or two.

It didn't. Whenever she saw him, she felt she had walked
into a belt of arctic weather, if she spoke he looked at her
from a great distance, his eyes icy, and when he spoke to
her he seemed to measure out his words to use the mini-
mum necessary. Clare couldn't get near him, and gradually
she got angry in her turn. What gave him the right to pass
judgement on her? Jumping to conclusions on flimsy evidence, stalking off in that way and carrying on like this
now? Who did he think he was? It was so unfair, he
wouldn't even give her a chance to explain, he was behaving in a high-handed, autocratic way which made her
want to hit him. Even if she had started seeing Tom again,
was that any business of his? He might not like Tom, but he
had no right to treat her like public enemy number one just
because he thought she was dating him.

If there had been anything serious between them, she
could understand it, but apart from that one pass, Larry
had always been just a friend. He had no right to behave
like a jealous lover, particularly at the office. People were
beginning to notice, she knew there was whispering going
on, she heard people talking in low voices before she went
into offices and at the sight of her the talk would stop dead
and then start again too quickly in a very unconvincing way.

One evening during the first week of January, Clare was
on her way home feeling distinctly irritable when Larry
sprinted into the lift just before the doors closed. As their
eyes met she saw his face tighten, his brows jerk together.
He nodded but didn't say anything. The lift went down, her
stomach plummeting even faster. She felt angrily breathless. Larry stood a foot away, his coat open, his briefcase
under one arm, staring at the steel door of the lift. Clare
could see a shadowy reflection of him on the steel; his face

indistinct but instantly recognisable to her, the strong features and dark hair blurred in image. She flickered a quick sideways look at his profile and at that instant he glanced at her, their eyes tangled and she felt her heart constrict inside her as she looked quickly away again. She could hear Larry breathing, quick, shallow sounds as though he had been running, and her own breathing sounded painfully loud.

The lift stopped, the door opened and Larry walked out at top speed like a bullet from a gun, he couldn't wait to get away from her. Clare followed slowly, aching.

It was only on the tube that it dawned on her; she was in danger of falling in love with Larry, she was thinking about him far too often, he was never out of her thoughts, it was driving her to distraction that he wouldn't speak to her.

In the past when she and Larry disagreed over anything she had always given way to him without much argument. It had kept the surface of their working day smooth, but it had worn her out, left her with a feeling of tension, frustrated impatience, resentment and low self-esteem. Over the last few months she had been acting differently, she had fought for her own point of view when it came to a clash, and Larry had seemed to accept it, he had been ready to listen, to admit her right to a point of view. Lately his attitude had been different. If she began to argue in conference, he brushed her aside without looking at her, he was sarcastic, dismissive, he seemed to want to hurt her, and if that was his aim, he was succeeding.

She could take Larry when he was explosive, when he was domineering or buzzing with adrenalin; she couldn't bear it when he was ice from head to foot, he was suddenly a stranger and it was only now that Clare realised how deep her attraction to him really was, how strongly she felt about him.

She sat at home in the empty flat, staring at the phone – should she ring him? Pamela was out again, with Jerry, maybe, she hadn't told Clare where she was going or with whom. The silence in the flat pressed down on Clare's head, she felt very lonely. She should have gone out tonight, a couple of girls from the office had been going to see a film and had asked her to go, but she had refused. Her social life was still very flat, she knew she ought to make more effort to get out, but most days she didn't have the energy.

Would Larry be at home? Or was he out, too, with one of the pretty girls he used to date? Clare got up and went over to the phone, dialled his number. He picked it up. 'Yes?' His voice was brusque. Clare hesitated, then couldn't say anything, she put the phone down without speaking. For several minutes she walked to and fro like an animal in a cage, torn between a raging desire to make him listen and a reluctance to expose herself to another icy shower of indifference from him.

Making up her mind, she grabbed her coat and went out. She caught the bus at the end of the road and sat in her seat feeling very silly. What if Larry had gone out when she arrived? What if he refused to listen? Or, if he did listen, refused to believe her? Or even worse, said: 'Why should I be interested?' Was she on a wild goose chase? How humiliating if Larry shut the door in her face or laughed at her!

She was assuming that he was interested, that the root of his present hostility was jealousy, but what if she was wrong?

Clare had grown up in a society where girls didn't chase men, it was the other way around, but that was what she was doing now. She was going to Larry, since he wouldn't come to her, and she felt uneasy about it. A year ago, she wouldn't have dreamt of chasing a man, she would have sat and pined and waited for him to come to her, and if he hadn't come she would have accepted it. She had changed more than she realised, or perhaps she was just following her mother's example.

She and her mother had talked alone on Christmas Eve, while they made the stuffing for the turkey, and fished a new batch of mince pies out of the oven. Pamela and Derek Forrester had been busy in the sitting room, tying small gifts on the tree, and trying to make the lights work properly. They were a new set, recently bought, and the connections were loose. The radio was blaring out Christmas carols, the sound of them came mutedly to Clare and Beattie in the kitchen.

Clare's parents had relaxed towards themselves as much as towards each other. They had given up all the angry, tangled emotions which had kept them apart, they were asking for nothing from each other now but a gentle tolerance, a sharing of what they finally admitted they were: flawed human beings.

'You both look so happy,' Clare had said and her mother had smiled.

'We are. My one regret is all the years I wasted. I wanted him to be perfect, I suppose, I refused to forgive him because he wasn't, which was stupid, because I wasn't perfect, either, I had no right to expect him to be . . . don't make that mistake, Clare. Either forgive someone or just forget them. Don't go on year after year punishing them, the way I did, or you'll end up getting the worst of both worlds. We only have one life, it's pointless to waste it.'

Clare had listened then, but it hadn't meant much to her, except that she was glad her parents were happy.

Beattie had sighed contentedly. 'This has been a very good year on the whole.'

'Its been a terrible year for me,' Clare said, sprinkling sugar over the hot mince pies. 'The worst in my life.'

Her mother looked at her hesitantly. 'It may look that way now but in a year or two you may see it differently. Sometimes you have to go through what looks like a bad patch to get to something better than you had before. Don't you think we learn from what we suffer? We're like plants – we need some rain before we can grow. Maybe this is a growing year for you. You won't know until much later, you never do. People don't grow while you watch them, any more than kettles boil right in front of your eyes. Whether it's yourself or someone else, the growing is always done out of sight. You only know it's happened later.'

'Maybe,' Clare said. 'But what happened to me was so

unfair. Why me? Why like that? If I'd caused what happened I suppose I wouldn't feel so angry, but it was so motiveless. I was just in the wrong place at the wrong time. It was just my bad luck.'

'Accidents always seem unfair,' her mother agreed. 'If you drop a cup because you're trying to carry too much, you know it's your own fault, but if you're walking along the street when someone drops a brick on your head you're entitled to feel aggrieved.'

'Well, I do,' Clare said, laughing without humour. Her mother made it sound like a Marx Brothers film but she couldn't find it funny.

'It isn't what happens to you, darling, that counts. It's how you cope with it.'

Clare looked at Beattie and made a wry face. 'And I'm not coping very well, you mean?'

'I think you are, I think you're still getting over it, but you will. Give yourself time, be a little easier on yourself. Stop looking around for someone to blame for what happened. It seems to me you're carrying a whole lorryload of resentment about it and looking for a door to unload at.'

'Oh, I know who to blame!' Clare said, her face stiff. 'And the sooner he's behind bars the better. Do you know, they've let him out on bail? Would you believe it? I couldn't credit my ears when Inspector Lucas warned me. She said if he tried to ring again I was to get in touch with her at once. Now, what sort of world is it when a dangerous lunatic like that is left to wander the streets as he likes? That's one reason I talked Pam into coming here for Christmas – I didn't want her left alone in the flat. I decided not to tell her because it would worry her, she had to put up with his calls before.'

'You ought to warn her,' Beattie said, looking anxious. 'Why ever did they give him bail?'

'Don't ask me! The Inspector said he had no criminal record and wasn't tried yet so, as it might be months before the case comes up, they had released him on bail. Apparently, his uncle put the money up and has promised to keep an eye on him. He's having psychiatric help, the Inspector said!'

'That's an easy get out,' Beattie said. 'Call him in need of medical help and let him off.'

'If he gets off when we get to Crown Court, I'll be angry enough to spit teeth,' Clare said. 'I wouldn't have called myself vengeful, but when I think . . .' She broke off, she did not want to think about what he had done to her. The months which had passed had dulled her memory of the events of that night to some extent. Whenever she came close to thinking about them she hurriedly sheered away. The hearing in the magistrates court had re-opened it all, but how ugly and sordid and squalid it had sounded in that sunny room. She had somehow expected more drama, more tension. All she had felt was distaste as she went through her statement with the muted sound of the court typist taking her words down, the spectators gaping like tired fish in rows, the magistrates looking politely phlegmatic and the prosecuting counsel in his dusty morning coat prompting her now and then with flat questions which made her answers sound normal and expected.

She had not been able to relate that court hearing with the terror and shock of the night she was raped.

It had made her angrier, made her feel grubby and shabby and sick, but it had at the same time continued the healing process because it brought her feelings within the realm of ordinary life. She had known that the court officers, the policemen, the very walls, had heard it all before. It did not surprise or appal them. They listened politely. They took notes. They consigned her to their statistics. How many girls got raped each year in London now? How many flats were burgled? The statistics were published in neutral numbers. So many rapes, so many muggings, so many burglaries. Behind the figures the human emotions churned like dammed up floods behind a concrete wall. That did not concern the court. It sat and listened and weighed the evidence. It had nothing to do with the consequences, the price paid by victims, the myriad little results of those statistics.

'Just don't let it warp you,' Beattie had said, watching her. 'I know it isn't easy, but try to put it all behind you.

When something like that happens, what happens afterwards is often far more dangerous. When I found your father with my sister, I should either have turned him out of the house there and then or somehow found the humanity to forgive him in time. I let it warp me and that was the worst thing I could have done.'

'Do you think I've let this warp me?' Clare hadn't been sure, at that moment, she couldn't remember how she had been before that night when she woke up in the grip of a living nightmare. It seemed so long ago, some other girl had gone to sleep that night, and Clare could barely remember that girl.

'I hope not,' Beattie had said.

Clare got off the bus at the stop nearest to Larry's flat and began to walk, her head full of what her mother had said. If she let things drift, if she waited for Larry to get over his present mood, it might be too late, she didn't want to live with regret, the way her mother had.

Nerving herself, she rang the bell. Larry opened the door a moment later, casual in a dark blue sweater and jeans. He looked at her in silence, his brow rising.

'Hallo, can I come in?' Clare said, pretending to be coolly sure of herself.

'What are you doing here?' Larry didn't move out of the way and his eyes had a dangerous sharpness in them.

'I want to talk to you.'

'What about? Can't it wait until tomorrow?' He held the door, as if to slam it.

She ducked under his arm, seeing that otherwise he might close the door in her face, and Larry banged the door and turned on his heel to look at her irritably.

'What the hell do you think you're doing?'

'You're alone, aren't you?' Clare was suddenly nervous, afraid he might have a girl there, her eyes skating towards the open sitting room door from which came a low sound of music.

'Yes, what do you want?' Larry put his hands on his hips, bristling aggressively, and at least that was familiar, she found it reassuring to see his scowl.

249

She walked into the sitting room and he followed. Clare turned and faced him, clutching the collar of her winter coat. Before she lost her nerve she plunged into a tumult of words. 'I'm not dating Tom again, that was the first time I'd seen him for months, he just arrived on the doorstep without warning. I was just getting out of the bath when he rang the bell, I didn't know what to do, he pushed his way in, so I went to get dressed while I thought out how to get rid of him. I threw him out as soon as you'd gone, I would have done anyway, I didn't want to see him.' She stopped speaking, breathless, and Larry stared at her without moving. She couldn't tell from his face whether he believed her or not, his eyes were steady, his mouth level. After a minute, Clare began again, less certainly, her voice husky. 'I tried to tell you after Christmas, but you wouldn't let me.' She paused, waiting, then said angrily: 'You're a bad-tempered swine, what right do you . . .'

Larry took two paces and clasped her face between his hands. He bent and kissed her fiercely and Clare felt her heart turn over inside her like a landed fish, her lungs seemed to cave in, airless. Her arms went up round his neck, she clung to him, moving closer until their bodies touched, her mouth parted, yielding and vulnerable, to the invasion of his gentle tongue. She wound her fingers in his hair, touched his nape and felt the pulse of his blood beating under the skin. Larry fumbled with the belt of her coat, undid it, unbuttoned the coat and slid his hands inside, closing his fingers possessively around her breasts. Clare moaned at the touch, and he lifted his head, detaching his mouth from hers slowly.

She was reluctant to open her eyes, the light seemed dazzling. Larry was watching her, his skin hotly flushed and his eyes very bright.

'You stupid bitch, do you know what you put me through when I saw Prescott that night? I almost smashed his face in. He grinned at me, very pleased with himself, and it seemed obvious that he'd just been to bed with you, that was what he meant me to think. I was so jealous I don't know how I stopped myself from hitting him.'

'I don't even like him any more! Why didn't you let me tell you?'

'I wasn't thinking,' he said drily. 'I was feeling, which is always a mistake. That's why women get themselves into such a mess, too much feeling, not enough thinking.'

'Don't turn chauvinist on me, not you,' Clare said and he smiled at her, amused, so that she leaned on him, her arms round him, hearing his heart beating close to her ear.

'I'm crazy about you,' Larry said into her hair, his lips moving and stirring the strands. 'I think I have been for a long time, but it wasn't until after you were raped that I really admitted how I felt. I was out of my mind when I heard, I had to get there to see you as soon as possible, to make sure you weren't too badly hurt.' He held her tightly, his hands moving and gripping her back. 'Clare, my love, Clare,' he muttered, his face buried against her hair so that she felt the hardness of his bone structure pressing fiercely against her own. 'I began to hope you liked me too when you came back from Romney, but it hasn't been straight-forward, has it? I didn't dare move too fast in case I scared you off, I knew you'd be off men for a long time, I had to go easy with you. I'd take two steps towards you and then have to take one step back again.'

She laughed unsteadily. 'A bit like Snakes and Ladders,' she agreed. 'You no sooner think you're getting some-where than you run into a snake and find yourself sliding back to where you started.'

'And then you feel like tipping over the board and re-fusing to play any more,' Larry murmured, laughing softly as he kissed her ear.

'We don't get much of an option, do we? Unless we opt out of the game altogether, we have to play by the rules we didn't make and can't alter, or even understand half the time.'

'I've noticed you trying to bend a few lately,' Larry said with mocking humour. 'I'm going to have to treat you with caution from now on, or I'll find you sitting in my chair one morning.'

'Think so?' Clare laughed and he tipped her chin up to look down into her face.

'But not yet,' he said, amused. 'Unless you're sitting on my knee at the time.' He stepped back and pulled her coat off, slung it over a chair. 'Which is a very good idea, come to think of it,' he said, sinking on to the couch and taking her with him. Clare curled up on his lap, her head on his shoulder, warm and relaxed with his arms round her. She felt his hand tunnelling under her sweater and looked up at him.

'You've been a nasty, suspicious, sulky brute,' she said.

His hand curved round her breast and he kissed her nose. 'Sorry, Miss.'

'It isn't funny, I'm not laughing, I've been miserable.'

'Have you, Clare?' He looked into her eyes, his face grave. 'So have I.'

'You deserved to be miserable, I didn't. It was all over nothing, jealousy is so stupid, don't ever do that again, if you ever suspect anything like that, ask me, don't just rush off in a fit of the sulks.'

'If it had been anyone but Prescott,' he said, making a wry face. 'I could never understand what you saw in him, but you were with him for a couple of years, I knew it had to be serious and I thought you had gone back to him once you began to get over being raped. Women do these crazy, irrational things...'

'And men don't? How about you, if we're talking about being crazy and irrational? You could have let me talk about it but you wouldn't listen.'

'I didn't want to hear,' Larry said. 'I couldn't have borne it – I thought you were going to tell me you still loved Prescott and I simply couldn't have sat there and listened without giving myself away. I've never felt like this about anyone before, I didn't know what to do about it.' He tightened his arms round her and she lifted her face, going weak, as if her limbs had suddenly turned to water. Larry kissed her passionately, she felt the need burning in his mouth and her own emotion flared to meet it. They kissed until she was suffocating, then Larry released her slightly and looked at her, his eyes feverish.

'I love you, I've never been in love like this since I was in my teens and fell for a happily married woman with three children who thought I was a dear sweet boy, so she told me, curse her.' He was talking in a flip voice, smiling, but his eyes were very serious. 'Clare?' he asked, husky suddenly.

'I'm not sure, I think so, that's why I came, because I cared so much, I was so miserable because you wouldn't talk to me, but I don't know, Larry, is this real? Nothing has been very real for ages, I don't know myself or anything else any more . . .'

Larry stared at her, his face full of shifting, uncertain feeling, then he stood up, lifting her in his arms. 'Let's find out,' he said, the words blurred by the jerkiness of his voice.

Clare stiffened, but he took no notice. He walked across the room, carrying her held close to his body, and put her on the bed in his bedroom.

'I don't . . . not yet, Larry, it's too soon . . . I don't know if I could . . .' She was very nervous, Larry was a volatile chemical which could blow up in your face without warning. If she refused him now, he might fly into a temper, and yet she didn't know if she was ready for any new experiments with love, how would she react to having a man touch her, lie on her, enter her? She hadn't been to bed with anyone since that night, she felt shaky and cold at the idea.

Larry was naked, he had stripped off his clothes so fast they littered the floor. He knelt on the bed and she looked away, her face burning.

'No,' she said as he touched her, his hands gently raising her sweater. 'Please, don't force the issue, Larry, let's take it slowly, be patient.'

'I've been patient, relax, I'm not going to force anything, I'm not even going to take you if you say no, I just want to see you, touch you, show you that it could be good for us.' He had her sweater off, his hands were deftly undoing her brassiere. Clare shivered, yet was burning hot. She looked at Larry's pale brown skin, the lean, muscular body so close to her own, and she swallowed, her mouth dry, her ears ringing with the beat of her blood.

'Clare, you're beautiful,' he whispered, kissing her breasts, and her teeth chattered in cold and shock. She shut her eyes because terror was dragging her down into darkness, Larry's hands were touching her, taking off the rest of her clothes, and she panicked, arching in rejection, moaning: 'No, no, I can't. Don't, no, don't.'

'I won't, I promise, don't be frightened, I won't,' he said, stroking her hair. He cradled her naked in his arms, her shivering body held warmly on his own, her head on his chest, her legs sliding between his.

Gradually Clare relaxed, her body gaining warmth from his, the quilt over both of them and the darkness of the room comforting. Larry's hand travelled down her spine, his fingers tracing the deep indentation in her back, the tiny hairs on the skin brushed by his fingertips. His other hand stroked her hair as if she was a child, he kissed her cheek, then her ear, and she raised her mouth, her head heavy on her neck, limp and sleepy. Larry kissed her lingeringly, his tongue flicking between her lips. She felt his hand on her thigh in a slow, sensual brushing, then it moved upwards and she shuddered uncertainly at the intimacy of the caresses he was giving her. He felt her body stiffen and kissed her again, his other hand on her rounded breast, his fingertip on her hard nipple.

'Touch me,' he whispered. 'Don't be scared, just touch me and don't think.'

Clare put out her hand, it shook as it touched his bare flesh, then the tactile contact broke through her fear and her other hand moved, too, then she was on her back and Larry was kissing her urgently, touching her, their bodies moving in fevered uneasiness together. He gently parted her thighs and Clare said huskily: 'Yes, yes,' a second before he entered her. She said it again as they met in erotic necessity, their bodies clamped together, their skin moist, clinging. 'Yes, Larry, yes, I love you, I love you.'

If she had feared that she would never again be able to enjoy sex with a man, she knew then that she was wrong. The open, clamouring, throbbing moistness of her body took him willingly, she cried out in a crescendo of satisfaction, her lips apart, her jaws clenched in the tension of desire, and a few seconds later Larry gave a harsh cry of release, both arms round her, under her riding body, his head buried against her breasts.

His body arched, taut, then he lay against her in limp exhaustion, their skin burning. Clare put a hand out to touch his hair, felt him kiss her body.

'Okay?' he asked, laughter in his voice a moment later.

Clare ruffled his hair lightly. 'Offering to do it again if I'm not satisfied?' she mocked and he turned his head to peer up at her.

'What, now? What do you think I am, Superman?'

'I'll tell you what I think you are when I'm on my feet and have a weapon handy,' she teased.

'That's my lady,' he said, then said: 'You are, aren't you? Mine, I mean, and a lady.' He was putting it jokily. Larry, like herself, had grown up independent, inhibited, slightly withdrawn, and she knew that for people like them the emotions so tightly controlled could, if they were released, cause havoc. The more those feelings were forced down, frustrated, hidden; the more they grew, until the power they held was like an earthquake which when it erupted could rip the earth apart and send shock waves in all directions. Clare felt a tremor of nervous agitation.

'Larry, don't . . .' She stopped because how could she say to him: don't feel too much, don't crowd me yet, don't want too much from me. I'm frightened of the way I feel, the way I think you feel, let's take it slowly for now.

He looked at her, then sat up in the bed. 'Look, no hands,' he said, holding out his hands; bare, empty, vulnerable. 'I'll play it the way you want to play it, darling, there's no need to feel pressured.'

He understood. She looked into his eyes and they smiled at each other, then Larry lay down again and held her and they went to sleep, safe in each other's arms.

Fontana Paperbacks

Fontana is a leading paperback publisher of fiction and non-fiction, with authors ranging from Alistair MacLean, Agatha Christie and Desmond Bagley to Solzhenitsyn and Pasternak, from Gerald Durrell and Joy Adamson to the famous Modern Masters series.

In addition to a wide-ranging collection of internationally popular writers of fiction, Fontana also has an outstanding reputation for history, natural history, military history, psychology, psychiatry, politics, economics, religion and the social sciences.

All Fontana books are available at your bookshop or newsagent; or can be ordered direct. Just fill in the form and list the titles you want.

FONTANA BOOKS, Cash Sales Department, G.P.O. Box 29, Douglas, Isle of Man, British Isles. Please send purchase price, plus 8p per book. Customers outside the U.K. send purchase price, plus 10p per book. Cheque, postal or money order. No currency.

NAME (Block letters) _____

ADDRESS _____

_____

_____